The House with The Georgian Door

The House with The Georgian Door

✠

by

Anna Marie Jehorek

To Sarah
Keep dancing
and smiling
Sláinte!
Anna Marie 2020

Dedication

For Mom, I miss you.

Note

This story is fictional, but I do use the names of some real and not-so-real places. The real places in the story are written about fictitiously because it's fiction. The names and characters are completely fictional, any similarity to real people living or dead is coincidental.

In case you're not familiar with some of the Irish expressions or terms, I'm including a list of definitions which may come in handy as you read.

- Bitta Fluff – an attractive woman
- Jumper – a sweater
- Cuppa – a cup of tea
- Boot – the trunk of a car
- Sun is splitting the rocks – the sun is shining so the Irish head to the beach
- Babby – a baby
- Hurling stick – Hurling is one of Ireland's native Gaelic games and it's played with a stick
- Hal Roache – a prominent Irish comedian who holds the Guinness record for the longest-running engagement of a comedian at the same venue. 26 years at the Jury's hotel in Dublin. Trivia - I met him on my first trip to Ireland.
- Ah goway – Let's be reasonable
- Blade – girl
- Hen Party – a bachelorette party
- Loo – bathroom
- Skoda – a Czech brand automobile
- Wellie – a nickname for boots known as Wellingtons
- Torch – a flashlight
- High Nelly – an Irish vintage bicycle

- Black Donkey Brewery – a craft brewery in Co. Roscommon
- Galway Hooker – an Irish craft beer brewed in Galway
- Brilliant and grand – words used to mean excellent or outstanding
- Paddy Flaherty – nickname for Irish whiskey brand called Paddy
- Barnbrack – an Irish quick bread made with raisins and sultanas
- Donkey's Years – a long time/ages
- Garda or Gardaí– Irish police
- Not on yer Nelly – not going to happen
- Bush telephone – gossip mill
- Beaker – a mug for drinking
- Plaster – adhesive bandage (Band-Aid)
- Stop the lights – astonished – wait what did you say?!!
- Craic – having a good time or a laugh
- Banjaxed – broken, ruined, can also mean tired
- Moaning Michael – a complainer who usually sighs and moans about everything

Pronunciation –Cara Maith – pronounced Car (as in automobile)- A- Maith

I have spread my dreams beneath your feet;
Tread softly because you tread on my dreams.
— W.B. Yeats

Chapter 1

The tip of my pen dances across the clean page of the journal. Yes, a journal. This will not be a diary of rehashed emotions. In my mind that's a foolish waste of time. But I do need a daily record of my new business, the Cara Maith B&B here in Boyle. Today I'll chronicle details of sanding the front door. It's a Georgian door, and I'll paint it a happy color. Yellow? Bright red? Kelly green? I'll have to think about this decision for a day or two since the color of the front door will set the tone for the first emotions guests will feel about this grand home.

I place the pen in the crease of the book and reach for my coffee cup sitting on the nightstand. Taking a sip, I gaze around the bedroom, surveying what work still needs to be done to make it more cheerful. Looking at the window, I smile in quiet satisfaction with the newly purchased curtains. I'd found them online and was nervous about the accuracy of my window measurements, but when they arrived two days ago, I hung them immediately and they fit perfectly.

I allow myself a small grin of fulfillment. I'm delighted with the progress I've made in only a few short months. Though my timing isn't the best, I plan to open the Cara Maith Bed and Breakfast in late September. Cara Maith is Irish for *Good Friend*. I could use a good friend in my life right now, and hopefully I'll find one here in Boyle. I moved away so long ago, it's truly a fresh start and a new day, but there are still shadows and memories of the girl and the life I left behind.

I put the cap back on the pen, take another sip of coffee, and look at the clock. 6:26 a.m. Dylan is probably out for a jog about now, as if I still care about Dylan Cooney's whereabouts. Letting out a long sigh, I stop and take another sip, interrupting my thoughts before allowing them to circle around to how I've come to this new phase of life at thirty-seven.

Placing the coffee cup back on the nightstand, I swing my legs over the side of the bed and stand. For the past five years, when I wasn't busy working at the publishing house in London, I was thinking of Dylan. Today, I'm waking up alone, in an Irish village, turning to a new page in my life story. A story I haven't exactly been proud of in recent years, but my hopes are high, and I'm determined. This time, things will be different.

I was always too career-minded in my 20s and early 30s to make time for a man, now, ironically, I'm forced to forsake the man of my dreams in an act of self-preservation. Yes, I'm flawed, but I'm smart, thoughtful, and generous. It's time to start behaving like the woman I used to be and want to be, not the woman I've become – the *other* woman.

✤

September 10th - Woke up early to the chatter of a bird outside my window. I realize now it was a blessing, as this is the morning of the dry run and I could have easily overslept. So much to do in order to prepare for the test guests who will be spending the night at Cara Maith.

"Imelda, hold the door open for me." Mrs. Flood's voice booms from the courtyard outside the kitchen as she enters the house with an arm load of fresh flowers. "Thanks, dear, aren't they lovely?" She sweeps past Imelda in search of a spot to lay down her harvest.

"Yes, Gran. They're lovely." Imelda closes the door and follows her grandmother back into the kitchen where moments earlier she was organizing the pantry. "Where will you put them?"

The older woman puts the flowers on the kitchen table and brushes her hands on the front of her apron, "Why, all over the house. There's nothing more welcoming and cheerful than fresh flowers." Imelda nods in agreement, flips her long blonde hair over her shoulder, and returns to her organizing.

I stop my ironing for a moment to admire the flowers. "Oh, Mrs. Flood, they're gorgeous. We have

3

several crystal vases in the china cabinet. Why don't you see if you can find a few that are suitable?"

There's a twinkle in the housekeeper's eyes as she breezes out of the room and calls back to me, "I know just the ones!"

In the months since I purchased the Cara Maith, Mrs. Flood has been a lifesaver. She and my mother were friends years ago, so when I approached her and asked if she wanted to help, she couldn't have been more excited. She is now the official housekeeper and if all goes to plan, she and Imelda, will be cleaning rooms and preparing morning meals allowing me to focus on the business and marketing end of this enterprise.

However, today it's all hands-on deck in preparation for our first guests. I return to pressing table linens and my mind wanders, reflecting on how I came to be the proprietor of the Cara Maith Bed and Breakfast in my old hometown.

When I left Boyle, I was still a teen. Going to university wasn't just a career path, it was also my escape route. My mother had worked so hard to make it possible for me to have a better life, and I was determined to succeed. From the time I was eight years old, it had been just the two of us. My older brother, Jack, Jr., had moved to London and seldom came home after Dad died. I feel a small catch in the back of my throat whenever I think of

Dad. Not because I'm sad he died young, but because his suffering ended and only caused more suffering for my poor mother. There was never a doubt in my mind, his death brought on my mother's early death.

"Mick Reynolds is at the door for ye, Nora." Mrs. Flood shouts from the foyer, breaking me away from sad memories.

"I'll be right there." Placing the iron upright, I tuck a stray strand of hair behind my ear and proceed down the hall to find the tall farmer standing in the foyer wearing muddy Wellies. He sees me inspecting his boots and swiftly steps back onto the mat in front of the door.

He clears his throat before speaking. "Sorry, about the muddy boots. I'll just take a second of your time – I know it's a busy day for you."

Mick Reynolds fills the foyer with his physical presence, but his deep, soft-spoken voice is almost a purr in contrast. I look up to meet his intent brown eyes and inquire, "How can I help you, Mick?"

Mick and I were in school together as kids, though he was a year ahead of me. His father farmed for a living and even though Mick had good marks and could have gone on to university, he stayed in Boyle to carry on the family tradition. His farm is directly behind the Cara Maith. Mick's father retired a few years ago and he's taken over the farming operations and expanded the family business considerably.

"I hope it won't be an inconvenience, but the sheep will be moved to your front field today. I wanted to let you know in case you had any problem with that happening *today*." Mick slips his hands into his pants pockets as he drops the last word of his sentence.

"No, that won't be a problem. Actually, it will add atmosphere to the whole farmhouse B&B experience." I smile up at him and continue, "That was the arrangement, right? I lease my fields to you for your sheep, and I get *atmosphere*." He smiles back at me, takes one hand from his pocket and brushes back his wavy brown hair before replying, "Right, so. Then we're good on that, and again, I'm sorry about the mud." He places his hand on the doorknob to leave, but turns back and says, "Now, if you find you need any help or anything at all, don't ye hesitate to call."

"Thanks, Mick. I appreciate the offer, but we should be just fine." I turn to see Mrs. Flood standing beside me and nod, adding emphasis.

"Well, then, ladies, I wish you good day."

I close the door behind Mick. Mrs. Flood's mouth twists in an expression of disapproval.

"What? Did I do something wrong?" I brush past her to retrieve a broom to clean the clumps of mud from the floor.

Mrs. Flood follows me. "He was only offering to assist yourself should you need anything. That's all. You needn't be so abrupt."

"Sorry, Mrs. Flood. Turning down help has become somewhat of a reflex for me. You know, like when someone asks how you are, and you say *fine* even though your whole world might be crashing down around you? It's more of a habit than an accurate response."

"In the future, just say 'thank you.' It's really quite simple." She smiles, pats me on the arm, and scampers off to arrange flowers.

Jeanne and Jim Buckley are the first to arrive along with their kids, Des and Mary. Jeanne and I were friends in school and kept in touch over the years. She lived just up the road from us and there was many a night her mom, Mrs. Costello, would invite me for a meal or to spend the night if my mom was working late. I'm grateful to have one friend still here I can count on.

I answer the door and Jeanne slips into character. "Hello, yes. We're the Buckley family and we've made a reservation through the B&B Board of Ireland." She can't complete her words before breaking into giggles. "This is so exciting!"

"Calm down, now, Jeanne." Jim says rolling his eyes as he enters the house. Des and Mary trail behind wearing knapsacks on their backs. Jim sees my quizzical look and adds, "Jeanne thought they could pretend to be backpackers from the Continent over here on holiday."

"Ah, well, we are in character, aren't we?" I give Mary and Des each a quick peck on the cheek. At nine and eleven, they're already almost as tall as their mother. No doubt they're going to take after Jim in the height department, but Mary is the image of her mother at the same age. Curly red hair and espresso brown eyes fringed with ginger lashes. Des, on the other hand, is a mixture of the two. His hair is more brownish with flecks of red and his eyes are hazel. Both children are blessed with ample freckles across their noses. Jeanne likes to tell them that's where they were kissed by the angels.

Mrs. Flood walks down the hall and joins us. "May I show you to your rooms or would you prefer a cup of tea first?"

Jeanne looks up to Jim before responding, "I think we'd like to get settled in our rooms and then have our tea, if that's okay with you?"

"Ah, grand. Follow me, please." Mrs. Flood gives a conspiratorial wink to Des and Mary before leading the family up the stairs.

As they're ascending, Jeanne shouts down to me, "Back in three shakes of a lamb's tail, Love!"

I'm halfway to the kitchen when the doorbell rings once again. I pivot and go back to answer. I put on my most gracious smile and open the large door. My eyes behold a heavy-set, gray-haired, bespectacled woman of about sixty or more years old. She looks vaguely familiar, but I can't place where I know her from or even *if* I know her.

My surprised expression prompts the woman to say, "You were obviously expecting somebody else. Allow me to introduce myself. I'm Nancy Roach. I own the Fairview Bed and Breakfast in town. I thought I'd come by and introduce myself and welcome you to the business."

I'm surprised at the unexpected guest but collect myself and invite her to step inside. Once she's in, she proceeds, "Oh, my. You've really brought the old place back, haven't you?" She leans to peek inside the dining room to her left, then turns back to me. "It's just this house had really gone into quite a state of disrepair after sitting empty all those years." She shakes her head and makes a tsk, tsk sound with her mouth before continuing. "Yes, this was indeed a grand old home. I suppose you know the history of the old place and the priests who once lived here, don't you?"

"I do indeed, I grew up in Boyle," I say in hopes of wrapping up her visit before my other beta-guests arrive. But she jumps in, "I know, dear. You went to school with my daughter, Ava. You do remember her, don't you? She went on to school at Trinity and lives in Westport now."

Ava Roach is a name I haven't heard since the day I left Boyle, but before I can reply, Mrs. Roach continues, "She's Ava Lenehan now, but my, she's done well for herself in Westport..."

She trails off, so I jump in, "Well, tonight we're doing a bit of a dry-run before we open next week, and I've got folks arriving, so I'll thank you for stopping, but I must tend to the guests who are here."

Mrs. Roach gives a tiny glare of disbelief, but Des and Mary come bounding down the stairs, so I finish, "As you can see. Well, thanks a million for calling."

I have my hand on the door as she's stepping outside when Mick appears with his large, droopy-eyed Saint Bernard, Debby. This time, he's nicely dressed and doesn't have on his muddy Wellies. Instead, he's carrying a small overnight satchel slung over his shoulder and wearing a tweed cap.

He tips his cap, "Evening, ladies."

Mrs. Roach gives him a once-over and sardonically says, "Good evening, Mick. I take it you're one of the... *guests*."

I'm catching her tone and my curiosity is piqued now, as Mick dryly retorts, "Indeed, I am. Couldn't be more flattered to be invited for a trial run in this magnificent establishment."

I'm not sure what's gone on with these two in the intervening years since my departure, but my instincts tell me her motives for visiting may not be all sunshine and friendship from one B&B owner to another.

Mick passes us and enters the house, so I call back to Mrs. Roach, "Goodnight. It was lovely meeting you. Again." I shut the door before she has a chance to answer and turn to Mick. "I'm glad you could come tonight, but I haven't got a bed for Debby. Is that okay?"

Mick looks back at the door, "Oh, Debby will just go back home, or she'll sleep outside your door. She likes to follow me. She's a good watch dog, but harmless nonetheless."

"Ah, good to know. Hey, what was that all about with Mrs. Roach?"

11

"Oh, that. I went on a few dates with her daughter years ago and she's still bitter. I broke up with Ava and I guess she took offense." He looks down at his shoes then smiles back at me. "No mud this time."

I look down and grin. "Thank you. Now, can I show you to your room for the evening or would you prefer a cup of tea in the drawing room with the other guests?"

Mick looks to the front room where Mary and Des are awaiting their parents. "I think I'll put my things upstairs and then come to tea."

Mrs. Flood is descending the stairs as Mick finishes his reply. "Oh, good. You came, Mick." See, Nora, I told you he'd be happy to help. Let me get the key to your room and I'll direct you upstairs." Mrs. Flood scoots by me and walks behind the desk where the keys are stored.

"I'll let you take Mr. Reynolds to his room then and I'll start the tea." I turn towards the kitchen as I hear Mrs. Flood giving Mick details about the room, the bathroom and what time breakfast will be served in the morning. As her voice fades down the upstairs hallway, I feel pride welling up inside. I think this really *will* be successful.

From the time I was young, I had to get myself up and going early in order to get to school on time. Mom worked for a solicitor in town and was always the first one in the office. She'd make the coffee, sort through the day's caseload, and tally up the previous day's billable hours before the rest showed up for work. I got in the habit of waking early to make her a cup of tea, a soft-boiled-egg, and toast before she had to leave. I came to relish the pre-dawn time with my mother; it was *our* time. It was peaceful and when I was a teenager it was a time for Mom to touch base with me to make sure, despite all she had on her plate, I was on the right path.

The kitchen's still dark when I flip the light switch to find Mrs. Flood turning the key to the door and entering. She sees me and gasps, "Oy, Jaysus, you scared the life out of me!" She takes a dramatic breath and puts her hand to her heart before smiling and putting her handbag down on the counter.

"Sorry, Mrs. Flood. I just came into the room. So, are you ready to make breakfast?"

"I am indeed, but why do we have to start so early when it's just friends staying here?" She turns to take her apron from the hook on the wall and as she pops it over her head and ties it around her waist, she mutters, "Six o'clock is an uncivilized hour."

She heads to the sink to wash her hands. "I know it's early, Mrs. Flood, but when real guests are staying here, there will be days when guests will need to eat an early breakfast. Might as well practice for such occasions, now."

She turns the faucet off and wipes her hands on a towel. "I guess, but do Mary and Des know they have to wake up this early?"

I pat Mrs. Flood on the shoulder. "Oh, they're the late crew. We're rehearsing that scenario too." I pick up a basket that's sitting on a stool next to the door and take my jumper off the hook. "I'm off to gather some eggs. Back in a few." I pull the door behind me, take one step, and tumble forward. Whatever it is I've tripped over begins moving as I manage to catch myself with my hands before planting my face in the dirt. The basket lands several feet in front of me. The object that tripped me is now sitting up and licking my face. As I try to brush the dirt from my hands and push my hair out of my eyes, I hear a soft chuckle coming from in front of me.

"Here, let me help you up." I know the voice, but I'm still sweeping strands of hair out of my eyes as the hand appears and pulls me up.

"Thanks, Mick."

"Sorry, I'm afraid Debby was lounging too close to the door." He inspects my hands as he brushes the dirt off

14

them. "You didn't break skin. Just a good handwashing will do the trick. No blood drawn."

"Thank goodness. That's the last thing I need. We open in a few days. I'd hate to greet my first guests with my hands bandaged. Or worse, would you want a meal prepared by someone with oozing open sores?"

His face contorts into a horrified expression. "Feck, no."

I laugh. "I love your candor, Mick. What are you doing out here? You're my first shift for breakfast which is in thirty minutes in the dining room."

"Not to worry, I'll be on time. I came out to look at your *Hippy Chicks*."

I tilt my head. "Are you checking out my work? Do you doubt my hen house building abilities? I'll have you know I did a great deal of research and even had some input from the folks at Farm Fowl. My birds are open for business and have been cranking out eggs for weeks, thank you very much."

He lifts his hands in a defensive posture. "I was going to compliment you. You've done a fantastic job." A loud cluck emits from the hen house behind us resulting in several soft replies from the others. "I did indeed notice how happy the hens look. Will ye be hugging them and thanking them for their hard work as you snatch the eggs from under em?"

There's a twinkle in his eye that betrays the serious look on his face. Rather than continue discussing my free-range hens, or as he refers to them, my 'Hippy Chicks', I admonish him, "Go back inside and please tell Debby, if she's going to hang out here, she needs to give me a three-foot buffer-zone around the doorway. She and I were both lucky. This could have turned out much worse."

Mick tips his head, gives a mock salute, and walks back inside. I proceed to the hen house and collect a basket full of eggs – Cara Maith B&B's first official breakfast.

Mick's the early shift for breakfast at half-six. Jeanne and Jim are down at half-seven followed by Mary and Des at half-eight. They all rave about the delicious breakfast – Mick has the full-Irish, Jim has poached eggs with rashers and tomato, Jeanne has yoghurt and porridge with brown bread, and the kids eat *Chocky Rockies* cereal and fruit.

I pepper them with questions: *How was the bed? How was the shower? Did you have enough towels? Do you like the brandy and glasses in the room? Was there anything missing?*

I happen to mention to Jeanne that Nancy Roach stopped by last night. Jeanne snorts with laughter. "She's not wishing you well, she's spying. She's terrified of the competition. Mark my words, she's a sour old lady and she's been dying to come see what you've done here. I heard she was livid when she found out someone was turning the old place into a B&B. She could have spit nails when she found out *you* were the buyer. She hated your father with a passion." Jeanne takes a big slug of coffee and finishes, "Nah, she's jealous, and I don't know what happened between her and your Da before your mother married him, but she's never had a good word for the Fallons."

After they all finish eating, pack their things and leave, Mrs. Flood, Imelda and I sit down to evaluate how it went and strategize for the grand opening Saturday.

Chapter 2

September 13ᵗʰ – Today is the big day! I'm a bundle of nerves. Boyle Tourism Board, local press, Shannonside Radio, RealBoyle website, The B&B Association – all attending the ribbon cutting. Only two boarders with reservations tonight, but one is from a travel magazine, so Cara Maith B&B must impress!

After hours of polishing the brass doorknob, sweeping the walk, planting annuals in the window boxes, and washing the windows, I finally feel like the entrance looks ready for visitors. I had stopped by Pure Flowers on Bridge Street and ordered a large floral wreath to put on the door for the opening and purchased a giant white ribbon to drape across the threshold for the ribbon cutting.

I stand back and admire the pretty wreath of flowers and the white ribbon that make the bright red Georgian door pop. The sun's reflecting off the fanlight above the door. I spent thirty minutes perched on a ladder with newspaper and glass cleaner making it sparkle. As I silently admire my work, Mick approaches and stands next to me.

"Well done, you. I have to say, Nora, the old place is looking brilliant."

I'm startled by his sudden appearance. "You're like the wind, Mick. I didn't hear you coming. What's that?" I look down at the giant shears in his right hand.

"Oh, I have these for working with the sheep, but they're so big I thought they'd be perfect for a ribbon-cutting." He lifts them to show me. "They're clean. I polished 'em up really good for you."

I'm touched by the gesture, so I take them from him. "Thanks, Mick. They're huge, but perfect! I was going to use a pair of sewing scissors, but these will look so much better in pictures."

I begin maneuvering the shears in a mock cutting motion. "Should I have the president of the Chamber of Commerce cut the ribbon or should I do it myself? Or wait, maybe someone from the B&B Association?"

"That's something you'll have to decide. Though, the shears are large enough, they could all put a hand on 'em and cut at the same time." Mick nods towards the shears then puts his hand on his chin in thought.

"That's a great idea! Even if they don't all cut the ribbon, it's a great idea for a picture." I smile up at him and add, "Sorry. After years of working in publishing, it's hard for me to *not* think of the public relations angle of things."

"Ah, that's why you're the successful lady you are." He smiles and pats my hand still holding the giant shears. "Well, now that's done, I'm off." He turns and walks back towards the field of sheep. As he opens the gate he looks back. "Three o'clock?"

I wave and say, "Three o'clock. You're coming, right?"

He turns and waves as he walks off. "Aye."

I watch Mick as Debby joins him in the field and the pair walk down to where the sheep are grazing by the old stone altar. The amazing old structure dates to the early 18th-century when Queen Anne had forbidden the Mass in Ireland, forcing priests into hiding. The rock structure is where Catholics would meet for Mass, often in disguise and at great personal risk to all in attendance. Mick steers a few of the flock to the left of the altar, and Debby sends them hopping farther into the field.

Mick Reynolds is an enigma. Smart, quiet, a bit of a loner, never married, though I remember Jeanne telling me of a serious relationship he had some years ago. He's ruggedly handsome, strong, and has a wickedly dry sense of humor. He's puzzling alright.

I'm jostled out of my thoughts when I see the florist's truck coming up the drive. I do a cursory look around the front of the house. Did I forget any flowers? No. Mrs. Flood used most of the ones from the back garden to make arrangements for the rooms, and I have the wreath for the door already.

I stand in front of the door and watch as the driver walks to the back of the van, opens the door and pulls out a large spray of flowers. "I'll need a signature, please."

He hands me a pen and clipboard.

"Are these for me?"

He takes the clipboard back and says, "You the owner? Nora Fallon?"

"Yes. I'm Nora Fallon."

"Well, these are yours. Cheers!"

He hands the flowers to me and climbs back in the van to depart. I stand staring at the beautiful arrangement of pink and white roses, snap dragons, and Stargazer lilies – all favorites. There's a card, but I'm still holding the shears, so my hands are full. I struggle to shift the shears into the other hand and open the door holding the arrangement in the crook of my arm. Once inside, I carry them into the dining room and sit them on the buffet sideboard.

I open the card and read, *Congratulations and best wishes on your big day. Love, Dylan*. I put the card in my back pocket and walk out of the dining room. It's been months since I heard from Dylan. I was doing so well. He must have seen the adverts I ran in the London papers.

Angry with myself for having publicized the grand opening, I put my hand on the stair rail. With one foot on the bottom step, I take a deep breath, then begin to climb.

Nope, I won't think of Dylan, now. I've got a ribbon-cutting and grand opening to think of today.

I'm moving forward.

Chapter 3

October 31st – Halloween Party at the B&B. Tonight there will be a costume party and bonfire. Mrs. Flood busy making Colcannon for dinner and Barnbrack Cake for dessert with the help of Imelda. Invitations sent to the St. Joseph's youth for a costume contest and games. After being open one month, will close for the season after this big party. Will spend next few months preparing for re-opening on Valentine's Day and a full season.

I spot Imelda taking the Hoover upstairs, so I ask, "Has the couple from Paris checked out?"

Imelda puts the vacuum down and turns to me. "Aye, they just drove off. I'm going to clean the room, so I can get back and help Gran in the kitchen."

"Grand. I'm going out in the garden to see if I've got any pumpkins suitable for our party tonight." I exit the house and walk the path that leads to the garden. The last of the vegetables are coming in, a few heads of cabbage and kale, some late turnips and a couple of pumpkins. Mrs. Flood has turned most of the rhubarb into jam and put the jars in the pantry beside the black currant jams she made from berries we picked in the summer.

Gardening doesn't come naturally to me, but I had the benefit of working with a writer on a gardening book back in London. Reading and editing and helping to re-write and revise made me a bit of an armchair expert by the time it was published. I couldn't wait to try it out, but living in London, the most I could do was plant a few herbs in a window garden. Now, I've got my own plot of land, sheep manure, and cow manure – I just need time and dedication to make my garden grow.

I find three pumpkins in the back of the garden that are ideal for carving. I bring the wagon from the potting shed, put the pumpkins in, and take them up to the house. I've told Jeanne to bring Mary and Des by to carve them for me and promised the pair some hot apple cider and cookies in payment.

When I get back to the house with the pumpkins, Jeanne is already there with the kids. They're waiting with carving tools and newspaper spread across the kitchen table. "Auntie Nora, look! We're ready to make jack o' lanterns for the party." Mary beams as she gestures to the tools on the table in front of her.

"I'm going to make a scary one, and I want the biggest pumpkin," Des declares over Mary's protests.

"The pumpkins are just outside the door in the wagon. You two work it out. There are three. Maybe you can each do one of your own and then collaborate on the third."

"That sounds like a fabulous idea," Jeanne says as she takes my arm and pulls me aside, "You two work in here, Auntie Nora and I are going out to inspect the bonfire Imelda's boyfriend has planned for tonight."

"Are you trying to get me out of the house for any particular reason, Jeanne?" I say as she pulls me out the kitchen door.

She waits till we're halfway to the field where Robby has piled wood and kindling for the bonfire. "Are we far enough away for you to tell me what this is all about?" I pry Jeanne's hand from my arm.

"Okay, okay. The reason I dragged you out here is, I want you to be the first to know. I think I'm pregnant." Jeanne clenches her teeth and gives me a look of terror.

I stop in my tracks as a momentary flash of Jeanne pushing a pram down Patrick Street pops into mind.

"Say something. Nora, I'm counting on you to say something brilliant, because I don't know what to say."

I'm surprised but gather my thoughts and consider what I'd want to hear if I found myself pregnant this close to forty. That almost happened with Dylan. I take a deep breath and say, "Is Jim the father?"

Smacking my arm, Jeanne laughs. "You Bitch."

I start laughing too. "Sorry, it's just one of those moments and I couldn't resist. In all seriousness, how do you feel about it?"

"You know, at first I was panicked. Mary's nine - that's a big age difference, but then I remembered you and Jack Jr. are ten years apart. So, it's not that crazy, right?"

Trying my best to be helpful I add, "My grandmother Fallon was forty-one when she had my father, God rest her soul, and Grandma Brennan, God rest her soul, was nearly forty-four when she had Ma. Though she did mistake my mother for the menopause. All those years of being childless, I'm surprised the shock of it didn't kill her." I stop and think before continuing, "I don't know if we're the best family to gauge it by, but it's not that huge of an age difference. Besides, it's very *Hollywood* and you're a young thirty-seven. You'll have plenty of help. Mary and Des are great kids; I know they'll dote on the little one."

"See, Nora. I knew you'd make me feel better." Jeanne lets out a long sigh.

"Have you told Jim?"

"Not yet. That's kind of what I wanted to talk to you about." She gives me a sheepish glance. "Would you mind if I leave Mary and Des with you tonight? I know you've got a lot going on, but there will be all kinds of kids here and I just thought, if Jim and I could have tonight alone, I can break the news to him without little ears around. In case he isn't thrilled, or it doesn't go well, it would be nice to not have them listening in or overhearing a conversation."

There's apprehension in her eyes. "Of course, they can stay with me. And as for Jim, you have nothing to worry about. If I know Jim, he'll be thrilled. Besides, it makes him look good. After all these years of marriage, he's still pleasing his lady."

Jeanne laughs and adds, "Honestly, I don't know how it happened, we're both so exhausted at the end of the day, but you're right."

"When is the bundle-of-joy due?" I'm curious, but also a little selfish, since she handles the office work and books reservations during the week while the kids are in school. I'm wondering when I'll lose my office help.

"Looks like he or she will be arriving in mid-June."

"Ah, June babies are always such happy children. That's what me Ma used to say to Jack Jr. He was a June baby."

Turning serious Jeanne says, "You know how proud she'd be of you. Your Ma."

I nod in recognition. "She'd be proud of some things." I give Jeanne a knowing look.

"Oh, come on. You've moved on from Dylan. Look at all you've achieved. You worked your way up in the publishing world, made yourself a fortune investing and saving, and now look at you. Owner and proprietor of the old parochial house. The Cara Maith Bed and Breakfast isn't just a B&B. It's you, come home to show the world that shy girl with the difficult upbringing has made something of herself. That's huge."

I wrap my arm around my oldest and dearest friend. "You're right, but I thought you dragged me out here to make *you* feel better. How did you turn this into a *Nora* moment?"

Jeanne winks. "Come on, I've left my children alone with carving knives. If I'm going to be doing this all over again, I'll need to remember how to be responsible."

"Now, Sophie, don't stand too close to the fire, dear." Nancy Roach's voice echoes above all the other parents and grandparents bellowing to her granddaughter. I stand close by and supervise as Father

Mark corrals the youngsters to begin telling the story of All Hallows Eve.

"She's a right old cow, isn't she?" I hear the purring deep voice I've come to know approaching behind me.

"Mick. To whom do you refer?" I joke.

"That Mullingar heifer – beef down to the ankle." He nods toward Mrs. Roach.

"I hadn't noticed," I comment dryly.

Mick hands me a black ceramic beaker. "Have some cider."

Taking the cool mug from him I ask, "What were the odds her precious granddaughter would be in the St. Joseph's youth group that's here at Cara Maith, tonight?" I shake my head before taking a sip of cider. Once I swallow, I recognize this isn't the apple cider Mrs. Flood's been doling out to the kids and the priest.

I look back at Mick. "I'm surprised."

He gives a conspiratorial grin. "You shouldn't be, the town's crawling with Roaches."

I laugh until a small snort comes out. "You know what I mean."

"Ah, I couldn't find the good stuff, so you'll have to settle for this." He takes a sip from his own beaker.

We stand and listen as Father Mark begins the tale of ancient Druids and how they'd honor the dead the following day which we now call All Saints Day. As he regales them with the traditions and how they started, I see Nancy Roach walking towards us. Mick spots her as well and is about to leave me when I grab the sleeve of his jacket. "Oh, no you don't. Don't you dare leave me with her."

"Hello, Nora. My, don't you have a festive affair for the children tonight? I guess you need to keep the B&B in the public eye as best you can with so few bookings."

I know that was meant to be a dig at the fact we've only had a half-dozen bookings since opening last month, but I pretend not to catch her stinging remark. "Oh, no. Not at all. I just love Halloween. This was Mick's idea. He suggested I do a big end-of-season party for the kids. He remembered how I loved Halloween when we were in school, isn't that right, Mick?"

Mick keeps his gaze forward, fixed on the bonfire, takes a sip of cider, and says, "Yes, indeed. This one was a right fanatic when Halloween rolled around back in our youth. Besides, Jeanne was telling me the other day, they're already booked up for opening night in February and have several holidays booked next summer."

I'm thankful for Mick embellishing the facts, but now feel pressured to pack the place when we reopen on

Valentine's Day. Mrs. Roach gives a small harrumph and says, "How lovely for you." Her voice betrays her true emotions and Mick chuckles softly under his breath.

Father Mark completes his lecture on All Hallows Eve and retrieves his fiddle. Mick leans in and whispers, "Ah, we're in for a treat, now."

I turn to him and say, "I had no idea Father Mark's musical."

"He's not," Mick grumbles, then turns and walks off.

Keenly aware of her presence beside me and the fact I've just lost Mick, I'm grasping for something – anything- to take me away from my present company. "You know, Nora." *Oh gosh, here it comes, I feel her ready to prick me with nettles as she starts to speak.* "I've heard from a few other B&B owners that your room rates are a little too dear for these parts."

Thankfully, it's too dark for her to see me rolling my eyes when I respond, "Oh, really, is that so? And these *'other B&B owners'* have felt compelled to speak with you rather than contacting me? Goodness, I'd think they'd worry people would think they're gossiping or worse, jealous of another business." I take a sip of cider and swallow, "Now, if you'll excuse me, I've got guests staying at the B&B this evening I should tend to. I'm so glad you could come with your granddaughter. Be sure she gets a party favor before leaving."

I pivot and walk back towards the house where I find Imelda and Robby standing by the chicken coop. Robby sees me coming and calls out, "Awesome party, Ms. Fallon. You going inside?"

"Yes, would you mind making sure the fire is completely out after Father Mark and the kids leave? I've got to tend to a few things inside." I really want to get another beaker of cider, but I got away from Nancy Roach.

"Sure thing, not to worry. We'll mind things out here," Imelda calls to me as I walk inside.

I take my jumper off and place it on the hook by the door as Mrs. Flood steps out of the pantry. "Ah, Dear, everything is put away. Are the kids gone?"

I gesture over my shoulder with my head. "Not yet, but they'll be leaving shortly. Father Mark is playing the fiddle which indicates it won't be long until they've had enough."

"Oh, dear. He's at that again. He took it up last year when he won the fiddle in a raffle. God bless him, but he's no musical talent at all."

"I noticed. Anyway, Imelda and Robby are out there and said they'd tend to the group's departure. Thanks again for all of your help."

"Oh, I'm more than happy to help. I'd say it looks like the youngsters have had a marvelous time and will tell their folks all about this wonderful inn." She smiles and picks up her purse from the counter. "Get some rest. I've made the beds for Mary and Des tonight and I'll send Imelda by tomorrow to clean their rooms. You need the time off, so rest. Sleep late, if you can. Why, with all the renovations and preparing to open this old house, it's been an exhausting several months for you."

I smile at her. "You go home and rest too. You've been right there with me the entire time."

She's almost out the door when she reaches into her pocket. "Oh, I almost forgot, this was in the post box." She slips a small letter out of her pocket and adds, "It's got a London post mark. Perhaps a letter from Jack, Jr.?" she says hopefully.

"Who knows? Last I heard, he's in America… I've learned over time that he'll fade in and out of my life and not to get too excited…" I trail off as I look at the handwriting on the envelope.

Mrs. Flood ignores my comment. "That's Jack Jr. for sure. Goodnight, Nora."

"Goodnight, Mrs. Flood." The door closes behind her and I take a knife from the drawer and use it to open the letter. It's written on plain white stationery and the handwriting is all too familiar. It's from Dylan.

Dylan Cooney. I left him in London, but this is twice he's reached across the Irish Sea to me. I stand for a moment reflecting on the past five years. Dylan had my heart on a string. Each time he tugged that string, I was powerless to his charms - not to mention my own desires.

I recall his gentleness and how I miss his touch. My neck is ticklish, but somehow, when he kissed it tenderly, I'd melt. His embrace was all I needed to feel alive in my soul. For all the years I'd fought hard to never need another person, he managed to unlock the door that kept me inside, that kept me from being my full self.

My eyes well up and my resolve wavers. If I read his note, he'll convince me to come back or to meet him. I'm weak where he's concerned, and he knows it. If I read what he's written, I'll begin making the litany of excuses again. *It's all he can give you. If just a piece of Dylan is all you can have, that's something, isn't it? He can't walk away; he'd lose everything he ever worked for.* I hear the justifying thoughts returning in my head and it makes me angry. Angry with myself.

I tuck the note back into the envelope, gather my wits, wipe my eyes, and walk out the door. I pass Robby and Imelda who are bidding farewell to the last of the Halloween revelers, so I say, "I'll take care of the fire." I march down the garden path and out to the field to the remaining flames of the bonfire. I look at Dylan's handwriting and run my index finger over the cursive loops spelling out my name. Lifting my gaze, I examine the stars dotting the black sky. The distant diamonds are battling with the full moon as if trying to out-shine the brilliant orb of night. I shut my eyes and toss the letter into the fire.

Standing still for a moment with my eyes closed I think about what may have been in the letter. Perhaps it's just a good wish or a gesture of friendship. Maybe he wants to see me again. Or, what if he's finally left Kimberly? What if he's telling me he's done with the loveless, sexless marriage and is free to be with me? Or explaining why he doesn't call, text or send an email?

"You did the right thing, ya know."

Startled, I snap around to find Mick. "You did the right thing. I don't know what was in that letter you tossed in the fire, but it's been my experience in such matters, it's usually for the best." His tone is melodic, low, and soothing.

"You're probably right."

We stand silent as the last of the letter is engulfed in the flames. Mick's holding a shovel. He looks at it and says, "I came down to put out the fire. I hope I didn't intrude."

"No. You didn't intrude. I was just putting something to rest. Something from the past, from London." Mick doesn't speak so I continue, "something that wasn't a healthy situation for me… I'm moving forward with my life." I nod to emphasize my declaration, but maybe more to convince myself.

"I'd noticed that. You're single-minded when it comes to that. Moving forward, I mean."

"Is it that obvious?"

He tips his head. "What do you think? Jaysus, you're determined."

I feel the corners of my mouth curling into a smile as Mick steps to the fire and begins burying the embers with shovels of dirt. "Just don't let it eat you up inside. Whatever, or if I know you, *whomever,* isn't worth losing your joy over."

I think about what Mick's said. "Is this wisdom from experience speaking?"

He's expressionless, filling the spade with dirt and tossing it into the dying blaze. He tosses a final shovel full on the coals before stomping on them, patting out the last smoldering flame. He hands me the shovel and walks by. "Let's go have another cider."

I watch Mick walk toward the house, then I look at the shovel. Wrapping both hands around the wooden handle, I jab it into the ground, gather some soil and toss it on the remnants of the bonfire and the ashes of Dylan's letter. I leave *it* behind.

Chapter 4

November 2nd – I will take an entire week off, even though I find that difficult. Today is lashing with rain so it won't be hard to stay indoors and get caught up on bills, paperwork, and maybe finding some time to read a book.

I place the teapot in the center of the tray, the small jug of milk on the right corner, the plate with the scone on the left corner, and take measured, deliberate steps down the hall into the library. I gingerly place the tray on the end table beside the massive leather recliner next to the fireplace. If ever there were a day made for sitting by the fire reading a book, it's today. Rain pelting against the windows, wind howling like a banshee, gray skies, and a nip in the air – I don't think I'll even get out of my sweatpants today.

All the months of hard work seem to have caught up with me. I've got absolutely no energy nor desire to do anything today. And it feels great. I tip the pot and pour myself a cuppa, pick up the book I've been wanting to read since last fall, *The Lady and The Laird*, and lean back in the chair. As I take a slow sip from the steaming cup, I gaze around my favorite room in the entire house.

The four walls are covered with floor to ceiling bookshelves, which I've managed to nearly fill with volumes I've read, edited or promoted over the years - most are signed by the authors. There's still a little shelf space and I intend to fill it with books I'll choose to read simply because I want to and not because I must.

I place the teacup back in the saucer and pick up the pen on the table. Some habits are hard to break. From the time I began as a copy editor at Barret & Cuthbert Publishing, I've held a pen in my hand. Always underlining, marking text or making notes in the margin – it's what I do. I roll the pen between my fingers studying the sterling silver marker and the *Tiffany blue* enamel cap. It's the most special and expensive pen I've ever owned so I'm careful when using it and tuck it away in its box when I'm done. It was a birthday present from Dylan – *Tiffany & Co.*

He gave it to me the year we first started dating. I hadn't been aware he'd even noticed my propensity for keeping a pen in my hand until he gave it to me. "I want you to think of me whenever you hold it in your hand." His words still echo in my mind. He *did* or *does* love me, I *think*.

I shut my eyes to better envision him the day we met. I was given the assignment of helping this former Member of Parliament and renowned financier write a book about success and financial freedom. Heaven knows, I had no interest in either subject, but then he entered my office and our eyes locked. The attraction was immediate though I fought it – he was a married former Member of Parliament, older, and all-around important guy. There was no way this bookish girl from Boyle could consider someone like him even in her league, not that I had a league. I'd pretty much shunned all dating, but a married man – never.

I think back to one Saturday while we were working on his book. I'd gone shopping and was in Harrods when my mobile buzzed in my pocket. It was a text from Dylan, *can you meet for coffee? I have some ideas for the book.* My hands were full of shopping bags and it was Saturday, for crying out loud. As I fumbled to try and type my reply, I heard from behind, "Let me hold your bags." I turned to see Dylan smiling at me. His air of confidence and good looks made my insides melt and my stomach flutter. His smile said everything a woman ever wanted to hear a man say. I just knew I was in trouble.

Dylan took one of the shopping bags, placed his free hand on the small of my back and guided me to the coffee shop. We sat for two hours talking about the book, but it was the unspoken dialogue, the subtext he spoke with his eyes that captured me. We were, after all, in a public place with a very legitimate reason for being together, but I knew he wasn't there because of the book. He wrote a final idea on a napkin as he stood to leave.

"Here's another thought I have, perhaps we can discuss it further next week at your office." He projected his voice as he stood and slid the napkin across the table.

I picked it up and glanced at it, then looked up at him. His brown eyes twinkled and with a wry grin he lowered his voice and said, "I'll be in touch." I watched as he walked away, then looked back at the napkin in my hand, *probably crossing a line, but I'd like to see you.*

After years of focusing on doing the right thing and advancing my career, with one handwritten note, on a napkin no less, this principled girl was willing to cross that line with him. Yes, he had been at Harrods shopping for a birthday present for his wife, but then he saw me, and he chose me. For a while, anyway.

I jump out of my thoughts when the phone on the desk rings. I pop up from the chair and answer, "Cara Maith Bed and Breakfast, may I help you?"

"So, it's official. This B&B is for real?"

"Hello, Martin." I know the voice on the other end. Martin Wilson and I worked together for years. He climbed the ladder the same way I did. We both started working in Barrett & Cuthbert bookstores while we were at university – me in Dublin, him in London – before making the move to copy editors in their publishing division at B&C headquarters.

"Well, aren't you a ray of sunshine to talk to today? How are things in *Oy-re-land*?"

"Are you making fun of my accent, again, Martin?"

"When have I *not* made fun of your accent?" He laughs so loudly I must pull the receiver from my ear until he stops.

"You wouldn't be calling if you didn't need something, so let's hear it."

"Aye, my dear, *Oy-rish Lass*, you're sounding a wee bit cynical, but as a matter of fact, I do need something."

I sit down behind the desk and wait for it.

Martin continues, "I've got a book and I know you said you'd be available from time to time for a project in the off season."

"Yes, Martin, I did say that and I'm two days into the off season. Your timing is amazing."

"'Tis, isn't it?" He clears his throat and adds, "Seriously, this one is perfect for you. The author is in Dublin; may need a bit of handholding on the project, perhaps a trip or two to Dublin. It's a retired footballer writing his memoirs."

"Oh, I see. It's an aging footballer and naturally, you thought of me?" Sarcasm drips from my voice.

"Aging, *Oy-rish* footballer, so yes."

"I'm already reading a book." I fib. Technically, I did sit down a moment ago entirely prepared to read a book. I just haven't started it yet.

"No, you're not, I know you. Or if you are, let me guess, is there a picture of a bare-chested Highlander on the cover?"

I glance across the room at the book on the table, "There may be a man on the cover wearing an open shirt and a kilt."

"Ha! I knew it! Come on, Nora, this won't be too hard, and we could really use your expertise and people skills with this client. He's dictated notes and they've been transcribed already. It would just be organizing and piecing it together. There are plenty of pictures too, he was a famous footballer so ya know, lots of photos. Sports fans love pictures of their heroes in books about them."

"If I say *yes*, and that's *if*, when is the deadline? When do you have to have it ready to go to press? And don't say this Christmas."

"No, not this Christmas, but we'd like proofs by March so it's out by the time the new season kicks off. Did you get how I did that there? *Kicks off*?"

"I got it, Martin. This better pay well if I'm giving up my off-season."

"You'll be quite happy with the terms. Mr. Barrett and Mr. Cuthbert are more than happy to generously compensate you for your time." Martin's mocking, serious tone makes me laugh. Especially since Barret & Cuthbert are both deceased, and the company is now owned by a British conglomerate.

"Send me a contract and then we'll talk details. Oh, by the way, who is this retired footballer, anyway?"

"Conall Kelly, the *Great* Conall Kelly. You know the name Conall means *powerful wolf.* I looked it up."

"Stop, Martin. Stop. I said send me a contract, stop selling me on it, you're done selling. Now, make it worth my while."

"Will do, and don't you worry, if anybody can tame the wolf, I know you can, Nora."

"Goodbye, Martin. You better hang up before I change my mind."

"Okay, dear. I'm off now. Hey, *tanks-a-million.* You're the best."

"So are you, Martin. And again, stop making fun of my accent. Talk to you soon."

"Ta!"

And with that, I put the phone down and look back at the book on the table. The bare-chested Highlander will have to wait a little longer.

It wasn't difficult convincing Jeanne to tag along with me to Dublin when I told her I had a room booked at the Shelbourne. "Are ya fecking kidding me? Of course, I can go. For a stay at the Shelbourne? Are ya mad?" She hadn't been speaking to her mother-in-law for months, something to do with a snide comment she'd made about Jeanne's housekeeping skills, so she had to make nice for a few days before she had Jim ask his mom if she could help out with the kids for a couple nights. Now, we're bunk-mates at Dublin's finest hotel.

I stand in front of the full-length mirror and inspect my clothes. I'm wearing my best business blazer and slacks. Since he's a footballer, there's no need wearing a skirt. No doubt he's had plenty of ladies show him more than their legs, and his reputation as a ladies' man precedes him. Not that my legs are that amazing, I just don't want to take chances. My hair is down, touching my shoulders, but I re-think this as well and twist the nut-brown strands into a knot and put it up in a clip.

45

"You look like a librarian, Nora," Jeanne says from behind her coffee cup. She's seated in a large armchair at the table, wearing the complimentary hotel bathrobe, and munching the full-Irish breakfast she had sent up.

"I know. That's intentional. He's a footballer."

She tilts her head in consideration. "So, what? Does that mean he's naturally randy and may go mad, dive across the table and take you for himself right there in the Lord Mayor's Lounge?"

"Don't be silly. It's only breakfast. If we were having drinks in the Horseshoe Bar, that would be a different story altogether." I tease, but she's right. What am I worried about? "I want to look, act, and be as professional as possible."

"For heaven's sakes, Nora. Dylan was a one-off thing and you met like five years ago. One guy out of how many that you've worked with? You need to get over yourself." She takes another sip of coffee, puts the cup down and crosses her arms.

I change the subject. "I don't know how long we'll be discussing the book, so I hope you don't mind visiting Grafton Street alone. Take your mobile and I'll ring if I get done early."

"I've a full day planned, don't worry about me. I'm going to go see that Book of Kells if it kills me. I've begged Jim to take me, but all he ever says is, 'Jaysus what's the point of going all the way to Dublin and queuing half a day to see some dusty old book?' Well, today's the day. I'm going to see that dusty old book."

I put on a pair of pearl earrings, turn away from the mirror, and look at her. "Thanks for tagging along, Jeanne. I've not had a girlfriend to do girl things with in ages."

"I'm having fun, too. Honestly, did we ever do girl stuff when we were kids? You were always so quiet, with your thick glasses and nose in a book. I tell you; you've changed since that laser eye surgery. "She snorts at her own comment.

"Yes, that's what's changed. I treated myself to laser eye surgery for my thirtieth birthday and boring Nora instantly became tons of fun."

"Crickey, what will you give yourself for a fortieth birthday present?"

I pick up the leather briefcase leaning against the foot of the bed, grab the key card and tuck it in my purse before I answer. "I bought an early present - an old house and a new life for myself." I pause for a moment, look around the room to make sure I've not forgotten anything I need for my meeting. "Now, I'm off. Have fun. Be careful and remember your mobile. Call if you need me."

"I will. Oh, and if it's not too much trouble, can you get me an autograph for Des?" She smiles and waves as I close the door behind me.

Chapter 5

November 12th – In Dublin to meet retired footballer who's writing his memoir. Doing this one as a contractor for my old publishing company. Jeanne Buckley's traveling with me, staying like royalty at the Shelbourne. Meeting with 'client' for breakfast and hope to have some girl-time later today, if all goes to plan.

The hostess is seating another diner, so I wait for her to return. I look down at my watch and see it's nine-o'clock sharp – right on time. The hostess picks up a menu as she greets me. "Will it just be one then, love?" Her bright pink lips part as she smiles, revealing prominent, white teeth. Their size distracts me for a second before I find my voice. "No, I'll be joined by a gentleman for a breakfast meeting. If it's possible, I'd like a table that's relatively private as this is a working breakfast."

She nods in understanding and looks back at the seating area before we're interrupted by a dark-haired gentleman. He looks familiar as he approaches, and the hostess speaks to him as he reaches us. "Mr. Kelly, is everything satisfactory?"

"Oh, yes, Patricia. The table is perfect; however, I believe this is the person I'm meeting." He combs his fingers through his hair before turning to me. "Ms. Fallon?"

Darn it, I like to be the first to arrive at a restaurant for a meeting. Selecting the right table, being seated facing the entrance, and setting the expectations with the waiter or waitress are crucial for meetings in restaurants.

I look down at his extended hand. I reach out, clear my throat, shake his hand, and coolly say, "Mr. Kelly, I'm Nora Fallon."

The hostess, whose name I now know is Patricia, says to me, "Oh, so *this* is your business meeting? Conall Kelly?" Her excitement gets the best of her for a second before she adds, "Let me take you to your table."

"Don't worry, Patricia. I've got it." Conall turns to me and says, "Join me, I've got a quiet table in a back corner. We'll be free to talk a little more openly over there." He turns and walks back toward the table.

The Lord Mayor's Lounge is one of the most elegantly decorated restaurants in all of Dublin. I act like being here is the most natural thing in the world, but inside the shy girl from Boyle is giggling at the thought. *Nora Fallon is having breakfast at The Lord Mayor's Lounge*!

He guides me past diners seated at mahogany tables in exquisitely upholstered winged armchairs to a private table tucked to the side of the grand piano and next to the fireplace. The fire is putting off heat but not overpowering the room. I'm glad for this, because I'm feeling nervous.

As Conall reaches the table, he pulls out my chair and asks, "Is this table okay?"

I'm taken with his chivalrous gesture. Maybe I've made some assumptions about football players that don't necessarily apply to them all. "Yes, it's perfect." I also note he's seated me facing the entrance.

"I hope you don't mind being tucked out of the way. We shouldn't be bothered here, but I still have people approaching for autographs from time to time. I don't mind, but since we're trying to get some work done..." He winks.

He's humble and apologetic so I decide it's a good moment to humble myself. "Speaking of autographs, before we get started, would you mind? My friend's son is a huge fan."

He laughs as he pushes in my chair, walks to his seat and sits down. "I tell you what, I don't live far, I'll come by before you leave with a couple signed eight-by-ten photographs."

"Brilliant! His name is Des, and he'll be absolutely thrilled."

A tall, slender man in his forties approaches the table and speaks to me, "Hello, my name is Gerard and I'll be your waiter this morning. Mr. Kelly has ordered some tea; will you be having tea as well or would you care for something else to drink?"

"Tea is perfect, thank you."

When Gerard departs, I look across at Conall Kelly. He's an attractive man with straight, jet black hair brushing the top of his collar. A bit long and shaggy, but if memory serves me, he was a fan of the man-bun when he played. His eyes are big and bright blue. He's a few inches taller than I am so I'd estimate he's close to five foot ten or eleven. He's casually dressed in jeans, a blue polo shirt and a tweed blazer.

"Do I meet your expectations?"

The best approach is the direct approach, so I answer, "Not exactly. I wasn't certain what to expect of a famous footballer. I'm not really familiar with the sport so I thought I might find an arrogant jerk waiting for me."

He laughs and slaps the table with his right hand. "I think we're going to get along grand, don't you?"

I like his smile and he's definitely got charisma. He's more intelligent than I had presumed, so maybe writing his memoirs won't be too difficult, after all. "I'll reserve judgement a little longer, but we're off to a good start."

I pick up the menu and begin reading as Gerard returns with our tea. I feel Conall's eyes on me. No doubt, he's sizing me up, perhaps wondering if I'll be an ally or adversary in this venture. I put the menu down and catch his gaze still locked on me and ask, "Are you ready to order?"

He smiles, nods, and gestures toward me with his hand, "Ladies first."

The breakfast conversation goes well. Conall's eager to open up about his playing days, his childhood, and what he's been doing since he retired a few months ago. He enthusiastically shares his ideas and thoughts on the direction the book should take. He provides me with a glimpse into him and his background, which will be a tremendous advantage in piecing the book together. As Gerard removes our plates, I pull a notepad from my briefcase, remove my pen from its case, and jot down a few notes.

Another employee is busy adding wood to the fire, and Conall watches him as I continue writing down tidbits of our conversation. When the young man finishes, Conall speaks to him. "We're going to be working for a while, if you could let the staff know we don't wish to be disturbed."

He nods in understanding and departs.

I'm curious. "Are we about to discuss some top-secret information?"

"I don't know. It's just a self-defense mechanism I've had to develop over the years. You'd be amazed how many conversations I thought were private weren't private after all."

I nod as I take a sip of tea. "You needn't worry about confidentiality with me. Discretion is part of my contract."

"You're a contractor? I thought you work for Barrett & Cuthbert?"

"I did. I was a vice president, but I took very early retirement, if you will, a couple months ago and moved back to Ireland to open a new business. I'm coming out of retirement to help a friend."

"Should I take that as a compliment? Are you here because B&C thinks I'll be a handful, or are you here because I'm a big deal?"

"Which do you prefer?" I smile and add, "I live in Ireland, they know me, trust my work, my discretion, *and* you're a big deal."

"Very diplomatic, aren't you?" He gives a charming grin as he strokes his hair.

I return to discussing the book, the story flow, topics to cover, and pictures to include. Finally, I ask, "How much of your personal life would you like included?"

"How much is useful?" He cuts me off before I answer. "I've lived my life in the public eye since I was a teenager. There's not much left to add."

I'm picking up a note of defensiveness, so I adopt a casual tone. "I'm more interested in learning about your day to day life. Sure, we might want to sprinkle the story lightly with a few relationship notes but getting to the essence of who you are is what's more interesting to readers. What's it like to be Conall Kelly? That's what we're looking for."

He doesn't speak. He's running something through his head, but then comes back with his own question. "What's the new business?"

"I beg your pardon?" I heard him, but he's lost me.

"What's the new business? It must be something amazing to make a sophisticated publishing VP leave her London gig." He drums his fingers on the table. "I'm sure whatever it is, it's something special."

I don't want to make this meeting about me and my business, so I need to tread lightly in order to keep him talking about himself. I give a quick reply. "Oh, it's a farmhouse B&B in Boyle. Something I've always wanted to do."

From his expression, this hasn't satisfied him; it's only given him more questions to throw my direction. "That's different from publishing. Fecking off-the-charts different."

"I'm not going to get you back to talking about yourself until I talk about myself, am I?"

He gives a defiant grin. "Nope."

"Why the sudden curiosity?"

"You're pretty uptight. I've never met someone who's this *all business*."

My jaw tightens and I glare at him. He lifts his hand and adds, "Before you turn all *angry feminist* on me, that's not a pejorative comment. It's a compliment. Your professionalism is refreshing."

I tip my head and respond. "Refreshing, huh? Thanks, I think."

"What I mean is, usually, not always, when I meet professional women, they still find it hard to stop themselves from flirting with me."

I roll my eyes and exhale. Here it is, here's the typical *footballer* I was expecting. "Are you saying all other women find you irresistible and somehow, I'm the one woman who's impervious to your charms?"

"Not in those words, but..."

I'm frustrated. This had been going so well. Now, I'm tiptoeing through the minefield. I take a deep breath, regroup, and veer back to his original comment. "I started working in a Barrett & Cuthbert bookstore when I was at university here, in Dublin, when I was still a teenager. I worked hard, climbed my way up the ladder, saved, invested, and planned until ultimately, I was able to accrue the resources I needed to change gears entirely. I had a plan, and I worked the plan."

He sits quietly considering what I've said, then raises his hand, gesturing for Gerard to return. Gerard arrives and Conall says, "We're ready for the check, please."

He's got a poker face so I've either offended him royally or I've satisfied his curiosity. I can't decipher which it is yet. He's speechless even when the bill arrives, and I insist on paying. He lets go of the bill in a grand gesture as I grab it and remind him, "This will be picked up by B&C."

Unable to take his silence any longer, I ask, "Are we done here? Have I got enough material to piece together your book? You tell me, because you've gone quiet and I can't read your thoughts yet."

He pushes his chair back, walks around and politely pulls my chair out. I stand and face him – still not a word. He lifts his hand, directing me toward the exit, and says, "Got an hour or so?"

"I'm in Dublin for you. *Yes*, I've got an hour."

There's a flash in his eyes as he says, "Follow me."

I follow Conall outside. The sky's gray and filled with heavy clouds weighing it down. The cool air hits me in the face as I brush past the doorman and a strong gust of wind opens my jacket. I instinctively reach to button it and fend off the cold. This unexpected departure from the hotel has me regretting I don't have a heavier coat. I catch up to Conall who sees my discomfort and immediately walks to the cab stand. I watch as he commandeers a ride and waves me over. He holds the door as I climb inside then hops in the backseat with me.

"Where are we going?"

He glances down at my feet, "It's not a long walk, but those shoes aren't right for the distance. Besides, you're not dressed warmly enough."

Still not sure where I'm being taken, I watch him lean forward and tell the cabbie to drive us to Albert Place Grand Canal.

"What's at Albert Place?"

He puts his pointer finger over his lips and gives a shushing gesture.

I shake my head and whisper, "Okay" as I turn to look out the window to my left. The car circles around St. Stephens Green and towards the Grand Canal. I observe the homes and neighborhoods as we move away from the Green and Grafton Street area into a more residential one close to the canal.

The cab ride lasts a matter of minutes, when Conall calls to the cabbie, "Oy, right here's good."

Our heads jerk forward and back as the cabbie pulls over and hits the brakes. Conall hands him a twenty-euro bill, opens the door, and reaches for my hand to pull me out of the car. Once I'm standing on the curb and the cab's driven off, he lets my hand go and again says, "Follow me."

I trail close behind for about a block before he makes a sharp left turn and enters a courtyard in front of a brick home with a black, Georgian door. Noting the style, I blurt, "I have one of those."

He looks back. "One of those, *what*?"

"A Georgian door. My front door is a Georgian door, but it's red."

"Well, finally!" He says in mock excitement. "Finally, we've found something this serious businesswoman and the arrogant footballer with the inflated ego have in common."

Before I can protest, he walks ahead, pulling keys from his pocket and opening the door. "This is my house. I thought you could look around and see how I live when I'm in the city. It's nothing flashy, just a basic house, but you'll get an idea of the life I live here."

"Are you sure this isn't an intrusion? I've got plenty of material, we don't have to delve too far into your personal life. This isn't a spread for Hello Magazine; it's *your* book. You tell me."

"Come in. You're letting the cold air inside."

I follow him to the back of the house and into the kitchen. It's a high-end kitchen with top quality appliances and abundant cabinet space. No doubt it's been renovated in recent years. The walls are white, the cabinets are white, the counters are white, and the tile backsplash is white as well. The room's bright, cheerful, and obviously decorated by a professional. I wonder if he cooks in here or if it's all for show.

He walks to the cooker and picks up the kettle. "Care for a cup of tea?"

"Sure, why not?"

He fills the kettle and places it on the stove before removing his jacket and hanging it on the back of a chair. "Follow me."

"What's with the *follow me* bit? You've got me here, I'm not leaving."

He runs his fingers through his hair as he walks, tilts his head and laughs as he leads me to the front room. We step inside and he spreads his arms. "This is what I want you to see. I've never shared this before, not with anybody. This will be something readers have no idea about."

I look to my left and begin scanning the room. Canvas upon canvas of landscapes, still lifes, and portraits adorn the walls from top to bottom. In the center of the room an easel stands on a drop cloth dotted with drips of paint. Next to the easel, a pedestal table holds paints as well as brushes of all sizes and shapes. A blank canvas sits on the easel.

I'm shocked, and he's right. I had no idea he's an artist.

He sees my surprise. "I started painting in my early twenties. I was looking for an outlet. You'd think running around after a football would be enough of a release, but with so much pressure to perform and win, I needed something away from the game."

I walk over to one of the paintings. A landscape. "This is gorgeous, where is it?"

"That's one I did while on holiday in Kilkee a few years ago. Well, it's a painting of a photo I took while in Kilkee. I painted it from the picture. That's how I did most of these. I take a picture and then in the off season, when I've got some free time, I put it on canvas."

"You're incredibly talented. Have you ever considered selling your work?"

He snorts in disbelief. "What, me? Sell art?"

"Yes, you're good." I point at the walls. "These are good."

"Nah, I just paint to relax. I'm showing them to you, so you won't think I'm one dimensional."

His words cut me. I feel terrible. In my zeal to appear professional, I've managed to come across as a snob. "Oh, Conall. I'm so sorry. Did I give the impression I think you're one dimensional? I'm too serious at times, but I don't want you to think I'm a snob."

He joins me where I'm standing and puts his hand on my shoulder. "You didn't come across as a snob. It's my stuff." He sighs. "I always feel the need to prove I'm more than a dumb jock. That's why I brought you here. A sophisticated lady such as yourself; I don't want you to think football is all there is to me."

I twist my mouth to the side, wondering how to reply. "Conall, I don't think you have anything to worry about. You're obviously not one dimensional. If you're comfortable and want to proceed, I think we'll work well together. I'm pretty sure your book will be a tremendous success. Not because you're a famous footballer, but because you're *more* than a famous footballer."

The concerned expression on his face evaporates and he grins. He looks completely relaxed for the first time since we met at the restaurant. "Okay, let's write a book then." He heads for the door. "Let me get you the manuscript I've written notes on." He looks back with a devilish grin. "Follow me."

Chapter 6

November 13th – Spent most of yesterday working with Conall Kelly. Met Jeanne for tea at the hotel, then we walked to Grafton Street and found a pub. Stayed for the music and craic before calling it a night. Spending today in National Museum then taking Jeanne to catch O'Connor's bus back to Boyle. I'm staying on in Dublin to continue work on book.

I'm sitting at the desk, trying not to make a sound. After a full day of shopping, touring the National Museum, and all the walking, Jeanne's exhausted. We were going to spend more time at the museum, but her first trimester is proving to be tiring. As she said, "I feel as if I've spent eight hours digging a ditch before I've even gotten out of bed."

We came back to the room, so she could take a short nap before catching the bus to Boyle. I didn't mind if she wanted to stay with me a couple more days, but two nights away from home was plenty. Jeanne doesn't want to owe her mother-in-law any more than necessary since she may need to call in favors down the road.

Rolling over in the bed to face me, she props herself up on an elbow, "What are you writing?"

"I'm writing some notes for my meeting with Conall, later."

"You're really working hard on this, aren't you?"

"No, no more than usual. Though I am kind of excited. I've loved working on the B&B, but I always love doing this, too." I smile and look over at Jeanne. She sits up, yawns, stretches, then gets up and walks to the bathroom. As she closes the door behind her, she mumbles, "Just be careful."

I pause and shake my head. I'm not sure what she's telling me to be careful of or about. "I always am."

She returns a few minutes later having brushed her hair and fixed her face. "How do I look? Good enough to take a bus ride home?"

"You look beautiful."

"Aw, thanks. I know I've got dark circles under my eyes and I look like shite, but thanks." She walks to her suitcase and begins packing. "When will you be coming back to Boyle?"

"I'm meeting with Conall this evening for a few hours. I'm hoping we'll get enough accomplished tonight, so I'll be able to catch the bus home tomorrow, but if not, I'll catch the train the next morning."

Jeanne's busy stuffing a Book of Kells t-shirt she purchased into the side zipper pouch of her suitcase. She folds it small then rolls it, stuffs the shirt into the compartment, and zips it shut. "Voila! I've proof I've finally seen the Book of Kells." She smiles and turns to me. "Are you meeting Conall in the restaurant again?"

I don't know why, but I feel a little defensive. "No, we're working at his house for a few hours tonight." I keep my eyes fixed on my notes, but I suspect she's standing behind me processing what I've told her.

"His house? Is this a professional meeting?"

I knew it. "Yes, Jeanne. He has a giant kitchen table. We'll be able to spread out and get to work without interruption."

"Oh, okay. Well, let me know if you discover he has a *giant* anything else, will you?"

I turn back and glare at her. She giggles and returns to her packing before adding, "You know I'm only playing with you, right?"

"I know. I suppose I'm a little defensive, especially since I told you about me and Dylan. You're the only person I've ever told about Dylan. I'm not proud of myself, and I certainly didn't intend to turn a working relationship into more, nor do I ever want to do that again."

Her eyes are sympathetic as she approaches and puts her hand on my shoulder. "Dylan must have been special to get you to give him your heart. He was just the wrong guy and the wrong situation. You shouldn't close yourself off from the possibility of a relationship because of one bad situation. You've been alone so long; wouldn't you like someone in your life again? Someone you can count on. Someone who will stay with you. Someone you won't have to keep a secret."

I consider her questions before answering. "I don't know anymore, Jeanne. I'm not sure I have the energy or the desire. Everything's wonderful when love's new, but then the excitement fades and it becomes life. Life becomes busy and filled with the minutiae that bogs couples down until eventually they forget why they're together at all." I look ahead and think about what I've just said before quickly adding, "Present company excluded. You and Jim have it all. A good life, great kids, you're still in love as evidenced by your growing tummy."

"Nice catch, Nora, but I know what you mean. That's how you know it's real love, when you somehow manage to find each other despite the minutiae. It's work and you really have to make each other a priority, but it's not impossible."

"I suppose you're right, but I've been on my own so long, I'm afraid I'm entirely too independent and set in my ways to make room for a man." I turn and see the clock on the night table. "We should probably get you to the bus stop."

Conall answers the door in his stocking feet wearing a pair of blue jeans and a long sleeve t-shirt. The navy shirt brings out the blue in his eyes as he smiles and greets me. He takes my coat and leads me to the kitchen. He's got a fire going in the fireplace and there are papers and pictures spread across the table.

I walk over to the fire and stand warming my hands. "I love a fireplace in the kitchen. That's one thing I don't have at the B&B."

"You do have fireplaces, though, don't you?"

"Yes, it's a big old house and last time I counted, there are four downstairs, alone. I have one in my library, which is my favorite room. I intend to spend most of the winter there." I laugh and turn to see him standing behind the kitchen counter uncorking a bottle of wine.

"Will you join me?"

"I guess one glass would be okay."

"Okay? It's an exquisite Cab Franc from Bordeaux; it's more than okay." He brings two glasses down from the cabinet and begins pouring before adding, "We'll let it breathe a few minutes."

Conall leaves the wine and joins me by the fire. "Nora, thanks for coming over. I know you would much rather be back home in Boyle than strolling down memory lane with a retired football player, but it means a great deal to me."

I turn to face him. "Believe it or not, I'm enjoying this. You've had an impressive career, and from the look of things, you'll be successful in your next one too. Do you know what you want to do yet?"

I watch as he returns to the wine and pours two glasses. He hands me one. "I've had a few coaching opportunities as well as broadcasting, but I'm taking my time deciding. I love the game but sometimes feel like it's time to move in a different direction."

"Art is a completely different direction. Is there a way you can combine the two?"

He lifts his glass and touches mine with it. "Cheers." He takes a sip, then combs his hair back as he collects his thoughts. "Art and football? I haven't a clue. Let me get back to you on that one."

69

I take a sip of the wine. He's right, this is more than okay. I'm no connoisseur when it comes to wine, but this, *this*, is fabulous.

Conall walks to the table. "Come on, let's get started. I don't want to keep you out late."

After an hour of sifting through pages and pages of his manuscript Conall looks at his watch. "Do you like pizza? I'll ring Mizzoni's and have one delivered."

"I love pizza, sure." I'm hungry and feel a little light-headed from the wine.

He calls Mizzoni's and I return to the manuscript. Just as he sits back down at the table, my mobile phone rings. However, it's a ringtone. A ringtone I didn't set, but that Martin set. Upon hearing my phone blaring the Queen song, *Get Down, Make Love,* Conall roars in laughter. "Who the bloody hell is that calling?"

My internal thermometer is on fire and I feel my face turning crimson as I answer the phone in my most agitated tone, "Hello, Martin."

"Ouch, gee. Calm down, why so surly, Nora?

"It probably has something to do with the embarrassing ring-tone you loaded to my mobile. Every time you call me that song plays, and it's wildly inappropriate for mixed company."

He's laughing into the phone. "I forgot about that. Why don't you change it if it bothers you?"

"You know I'm clueless when it comes to technology. I'll have to have my friend's twelve-year old fix it." I take a sip of wine. "What do you want?"

"I'm just checking to see how the book is going. Everything okay with you and Conall?"

"Yes, he's here now. We're going over the manuscript and we're close to having a working outline pieced together. I might even be able to send it to be revised early next week."

"Awesome! That's my girl."

"Yes, Martin. That's your *Oy-rish girl,*" I joke.

"Well, I'll let you get back to your…" he clears his throat and says, "*footballer.*"

"I'm not sure what that was about, but okay, Martin. I'll be in touch if I need anything. Otherwise, I'll call you when I get back to Boyle."

"Okay, sweetie. Have fun."

"You too, sweetie. Ta!"

I put the phone down on the table and make my apologies to Conall. "I'm so sorry. That was Martin Wilson checking our progress."

Conall nods in recognition and we return to the work in front of us when we're interrupted again by my phone. This time there's a text message so I grab it and look. Conall asks, "Is it important?"

"No. It's my neighbor, Mick. He's letting me know a package was delivered to the B&B and was left on the doorstep. He didn't want to leave it there because it would let people know nobody's home, or it might get rained on, so he brought it to his house."

I type a note back. *Thanks, Mick. I appreciate you looking out for me and the house. I'll call by when I get back and pick up the package.*

"So, wait. Your neighbor knew you had a package on your front step? Gee, he keeps a close eye on you. Is he a love interest or just a neighbor?" Conall is grinning at me now.

"How do I explain Mick?" I take a deep breath. "Mick owns the farm that borders my property. He was a year ahead of me in school and was one of the smartest kids. He could have gone to university, but instead he stayed and farmed like his father. He was always kind to me, so I leased my front field to him for his sheep. He gets to graze his sheep and I get the sheep for atmosphere.

One of the fringe benefits of him leasing the field is he's always around and looking after the place." I exhale, "Phew, is that a satisfactory explanation?"

Conall begins laughing but before he can tell me what's so funny, the doorbell rings. It's our pizza. Conall goes to the door. I can hear him and the delivery guy talking football as Conall pays him. No doubt, the guy recognized Conall and is hitting him up for an autograph.

Conall returns carrying a pizza in one hand and tucking his wallet into his back pocket with the other.

"Did you have to give an autograph before he'd leave?"

"Worse. He recognized me, so I had to give him a big tip. You have no idea how fast news of one bad tip spreads across social media. Giving autographs is easy and inexpensive, but heaven forbid I'm short on cash. I'd be branded as cheap the rest of my life."

Conall gets two plates, a stack of napkins and hands them to me. He gathers our wine glasses, tucks the wine bottle in the crook of the same arm and with the other hand balances the pizza box and says, "Follow me."

I follow him out of the kitchen, past the dining room, and down a hall. "We're not eating in the kitchen?"

He flips a light switch, so we can see where we're going. "It's a clear night, follow me. It's my favorite room on a clear night."

We reach the end of the hall and he turns to me. "My hands are full; can you turn the doorknob?"

I reach around Conall, turn the knob, and open the door. Conall enters the room ahead of me, stands still for a moment allowing his eyes to adjust to the darkness, then places the pizza down on a bistro table by the window. My gaze goes upwards as I walk across the room and join him, place the plates and napkins on the table then turn to examine the room.

"It's an atrium," Conall brags as he retrieves a box of matches from a credenza in the corner. He lights the candle on the table and says. "Have a seat, we'll eat in here. It's a clear night so we can see the stars." Pointing upwards, "It's why I bought in this neighborhood. Not as much light noise here by the canal. The stars are still visible. Not as visible as in the country, but enough for me to see 'em."

I sit down at the table. Conall sits across from me and I study him in the candlelight. His eyes are kind. His smile is warm. His body language exudes strength and confidence. My mouth curls into a grin.

"What's so funny?"

"This. Is this how you ensnare women? Come on, a famous, good looking footballer. You bring them to your *atrium* lair to look at the stars. Is *look at the stars* a euphemism?"

He picks up a napkin, places it on his lap, and stares at me. "I'm hurt. After all this time we've been working together, I'm hurt you would think I'm that shallow."

He picks up a slice of pizza and puts it on my plate. I take a bite and swallow before answering him. "Funny thing is, I don't. I don't think you're that shallow. I believe you're being sincere. You really love this room. You enjoy looking at the stars on a clear night."

"I'm glad. I don't know why, but I really care what you think of me. I'd be disappointed if you thought I bring girls here as part of a game or method of scoring an easy shag."

"Oh, this could still all be your chick-magnet, but I decided to give you the benefit of the doubt when I saw the telescope over there."

He smiles and takes a bite of his pizza. "And here I thought I'd convinced you." He swallows and continues, "So, I've managed to convince you I'm not one dimensional, but I bet you're not as one dimensional as you like to pretend you are either."

"What do you mean by that?"

"You've made it very clear you're a tough, independent businesswoman, but within a matter of minutes, that fiercely independent façade was shattered." He takes a sip from his wine glass and adds, "Not just one, but two men checked in on you tonight. Martin, who thinks so much of you he assigned his own ringtone on your mobile, and your neighbor, Mick. Let me guess, they're both single?"

"Martin's divorced and Mick is a bachelor." I answer curtly.

"Just as I thought. They're both infatuated with you."

I rear back in disbelief. "They are not! Martin is like a brother and Mick is like ...." I trail off because, again, I was going to say, *a brother*.

Conall pounces and finishes my thought, "A *brother*? Interesting, you've somehow managed to relegate all single males who adore you to the brother-zone. That's worse than the friend-zone. Poor sots."

"No. Brother's just a polite way of saying they're friends."

"Would you ever or have you ever shagged or wanted to shag either?"

His bold question throws me for a loop. Simmering to cool off, I attack the slice of pizza and tear away a bite before answering. "First off, that's a very personal question. And second, I never thought about either of them that way."

He sits up straight in his chair, raises his finger and exclaims, "Ah ha! You never thought of either one of them that way because you're too busy thinking of someone else that way!"

He's wearing a smug grin that looks sinister in the candlelight, but he has no idea how correct he is. I don't reply. I keep eating, which only confirms it in his mind. "Yep, I nailed it. Who is he?"

I try a different maneuver this time. "If I tell you, promise to never mention it again?"

He sees my somber expression and leans in closer, almost touching the flame with his nose. "Of course, I promise."

I'm going for brutal honesty. "My father cheated and drank and ultimately died when I was eight. He was in Dublin for work, got pissed, and fell off a curb into the path of a bus. My father's drinking and death was more than my older brother could handle so he took off, leaving me and my mother alone. My mother had to work hard her whole life and I'm positive that's why she died young of an aneurism when I was twenty. I never thought much

77

about men because the men in my life never thought much about me, in fact, they were the cause of most of the struggles in my life, so I chose to never need any man. Then one day, I met a man who got me to tear down the barriers I'd built up."

Conall's expression has changed from concern to shock, but I carry on. "The man was married. I'm ashamed of my behavior, but when I sit and think about it, a married man makes sense. He was unavailable so there were no promises made and we were both free to exit the relationship whenever we needed to leave. No strings, no broken promises, no disappointment."

Conall is quiet for a moment. He looks at me, then tips his head back to see the stars overhead. "I'm so sorry about your family. Do you still see this married man?"

"No. I ended it. I knew it was a lie. I *did* care. I *did* want it all with him. One night, I was lying in his arms and he started talking about the house he purchased in the Seychelles. A vacation home that one day he's planning on retiring to with his wife. A beach home with ocean views from all rooms. He was talking so matter of fact, I questioned him, *when did this come about?*"

Conall whispers, "What did he say?"

"He thought he told me about the house. Could have sworn he mentioned it." I pick up my napkin, dab the corner of my mouth, and place it beside my plate. "It hit me like a bolt of lightning. I loved him, but I didn't love me in this situation. He's never leaving his wife. He's planning their future together. Meanwhile, I'm sneaking around, lying, pretending it's all good and that I don't need more than he's willing or able to give me." I look down and collect my thoughts, before adding, "Most of all, I was ashamed. My mother worked hard to give me all she could. She'd be so disappointed in me." Tears burn my eyes, but I take a deep breath and push them back.

"How'd you end it?"

"The next day, I called my friend Jeanne. Her husband is an estate agent in Boyle. I bought a farmhouse and I haven't looked back."

He doesn't speak for a minute. The silence is deafening, but Conall breaks it. "Come here." He hops off the chair, walks to the telescope, and begins fiddling with it, pointing and focusing. "Look up there."

I lean in, put my eye to the lens and squint to see what he's found in the sky. "What am I looking for?"

"Venus. It's fairly easy to see in the night sky, but tonight it's especially bright."

He's right. Venus is radiant. I study it and the stars close by for a moment. Backing away from the telescope, I turn and look at Conall. "Thanks for listening. The only other person I've opened up to about this is Jeanne."

Conall's blue eyes are sincere as he reaches for my hand, lifts it and kisses my fingertips. "That story won't leave this room. You can trust me."

My hand is warm inside his as he gives a light squeeze and holds it tightly for a moment before letting go. "I wanted you to see Venus, Nora. Venus is the goddess of love. Promise me you'll keep looking for love. You didn't look in the right place before. Keep looking."

Chapter 7

November 14th – Last evening was productive.
Accomplished a great deal on the book, also got to know more
about Conall Kelly. He's convinced me to remain in Dublin an
extra day to attend a charity event for which he is the honorary
chairman. He feels it will give some insight into his off-the-field
interests and concerns.

I never travel without my LBD, little black dress, and with good reason. It's a wardrobe staple and a lifesaver should there be the sudden addition of a funeral or formal event to the itinerary. Conall's suggestion that I attend the Children's Cancer Relief Charity Gala was last-minute, but will no doubt give me a clearer picture of the man away from the football pitch.

I carefully guide sheer black stockings over my ankles, pulling them delicately over my thighs, trying to avoid putting a ladder in my only pair of hose. I slip the sleeveless, Sabrina-neckline dress over my head and reach back for the zipper. I'm able to tug the zipper partially up my back but can't quite finish pulling it closed. These are the frustrating moments, where having a man around to zip me up would be nice. I exhale and try again – finally, I'm zipped.

I put on the pearl necklace and matching earrings I bought myself for my twenty-first birthday then sweep my hair into a twist and stand back to look in the mirror. After giving myself the once over, I slip into the pair of black four-inch heels I bought on Grafton Street earlier in the day. My business black shoes were too *all business* for a night out. As I slide a few items into the matching black clutch I spent entirely too much money on, I hear a gentle tapping on the door.

I open the door a tiny crack and see Conall smiling and holding a single rose. He whispers, "May I come in?"

I forget how guarded he is. As a man who's spent most of his adult life in the public eye, something as innocent as picking up a friend at a hotel can turn into a tabloid feeding frenzy filled with photos and speculation. I swiftly recognize his uneasiness and open the door wide and silently gesture to him to enter. Once the door shuts behind him, he hands me the rose. "You look gorgeous, tonight. Thanks for hanging around for me."

I inspect his dark suit and admire his hair, which tonight is slicked back with copious amounts of styling gel before saying, "How could I resist a night out with one of Ireland's most famous footballers? Besides, it's for a good cause. I want to go."

I watch as he walks to the table, picks up a glass, and carries it to the bathroom where he fills it with water.

He returns and takes the rose from my hand and places the flower in the glass. "There, now it won't die while we're out." He grins and gently places it in the center of the table by the window. It's a simple gesture, but I find it endearing so I ask, "Where did the flower come from?"

He picks up my clutch which is on the table and hands it to me. "There was a lad outside the hotel with a basket full of em, so I thought it's a nice thing to do. You don't mind, do you? I know you're the consummate professional so if you in any way interpret this as sexist or inappropriate, I've meant no offense."

"No, no offense taken. I have interpreted this as a random act of kindness slash friendship. Besides, I like roses." I turn to the door and Conall reaches for the knob and opens it before murmuring under his breath, "Phew, I took a risk there and it paid off."

The cab drops us in front of the Grand Canal Theater. I survey the arriving crowd and am reassured that my major purse and shoe purchase was a wise move when I notice the slightly more formally dressed attendees arriving alongside others who are less formally attired. I let my relief be known as Conall shuts the cab door and pays the driver. "Thank goodness. I was afraid I'd be underdressed." Conall takes my elbow, leading me to the entrance and says, "Nah, you got it just right I'd say. Too dressy and it looks like you're trying too hard. Not dressy enough and you look like you're not trying hard enough."

I turn to see his expression to decide whether he's serious or not. If he's joking, I'm not able to detect it so I decide he's being sincere. As we reach the entry of the theater, I stare up at the soaring glass façade. It's moments like these I feel the small-town girl I've kept tucked inside begin to reemerge. Conall sees my mouth agape in wonder and smiles. "Pretty fecking amazing, isn't it?" I keep staring up at the incredible structure and manage to mumble, "Aye." He laughs at my momentary trance and brings me back to earth when he says, "Are you ready?"

I snap out of my wonder to look at him. He's got a serious, determined look on his face. "Ready for what? It's a charity event, right? I've been to dozens of these, you forget what I do, or used to do, for a living."

Shaking his head, he softly chuckles. "No. Are you ready to be seen on the arm of a footballer? Look, I know this is a *professional* outing, but once a reporter or photographer spies you and me as much as standing next to each other, everything will change. There's a strong likelihood you'll be mistaken for a *WAG*."

84

I raise my eyebrow. "*WAG*? What's a *WAG* and why would I be mistaken for one?"

Conall lifts my hand and gently pats it. "You really need to watch a couple football matches before we go much further with this book. But in answer to your question, *WAG* is a term which stands for Wives and Girlfriends. It's very common among footballers."

I detect he's deriving some pleasure in knowing my appearance with him tonight could be misconstrued so I bite back. "Well, this is strictly business and you better make sure you point that out at every opportunity."

He snorts with laughter before raising both hands in a defensive posture. "I'll do my best but keep that sour expression on your mug and we won't have to worry about anybody misinterpreting our situation."

The moment we enter the grand foyer, Conall is surrounded by well-wishers, football fans, attractive women and the generally curious attendees. I manage to stay beside him but ultimately, I'm nudged aside when the charity director approaches and sidles up next to him. Conall glances back at me with an expression that conveys an apology. I smile, wave, and give the universal gesture for *drink* and point to the bar. He raises his brow in recognition before he's herded to meet a large cluster of people affiliated with the charity.

I pivot towards the bar and on my way over decide to have a glass of white wine. Ordinarily, I wouldn't drink at a business function, but something tells me this could be a long night. The bartender is a tall, dark haired fella with a ponytail and Clark Kent glasses. "What will you have?" He beams as I approach.

"I'll have a glass of Chardonnay, please."

He lifts the open bottle, begins pouring and says, "Did you see Conall Kelly's here?"

I'm busy digging through the clutch in search of my money but answer distractedly, "Aye, I did."

Before I can tell him I'm here with him, he adds, "He's absolutely, brilliant, isn't he?"

I look back towards the crowd where Conall is standing surrounded by smiling faces then back at the bartender. "He is, indeed."

As he picks up a cocktail napkin and wraps it around the wine glass to hand to me, he continues, "Sure enough, indeed. When I heard he'd be here tonight, I told the catering company I absolutely had to work this event. I think the world of Conall Kelly."

"Are you a big football fan?" I say before taking a small sip.

"Oh, I guess I'm a football fan, but I'm more of a Conall Kelly fan."

"Oh, really? Just what makes you a Conall Kelly fan?"

I'm half expecting him to tell me he admires his athleticism or his prowess with the ladies, but instead he exuberantly replies, "It's his charity work that makes him my hero. He gives so much time and money to kid cancer research, but not only that, he really cares about the kids he's helping."

The bartender is smiling ear to ear and I'm surprised with his unabashed praise of Conall. "Is that right? I had no idea he was so philanthropic."

The bartender looks down for a second and collects himself. He seems to be a little choked up, so I read his nametag and ask, "Ted? Are you alright?"

He looks me in the eye. "Yes, ma'am. Sorry, it's hard for me to not get emotional when I think of it."

I'm completely perplexed now. "Think of what?"

"My younger brother, Jamie. He was sick with leukemia two years ago. Conall Kelly met him in the hospital when he was there for a charity visit. Well, anyway, he met Jamie when he was in hospital for treatment. Oh, boyo Jamie thought it was the greatest thing in the world. To be honest, for an 11-year old, it was!" He nervously wipes his hands on his trousers before finishing, "Not only did he make a fuss over Jamie in the hospital, praise Jaysus, he kept in touch with the lad. Sure enough, this big important footballer took the time to keep in touch with a dying child. Now *that*. That's why Conall Kelly is my hero." His voice breaks and tears fill his eyes behind the glasses as he chokes out, "You can be sure, there's few men in the world that would be so caring as to take the time to bring joy to the final days of a child like he did."

I see the anguish on Ted's face, so I softly say, "Ted, that is the most touching story I've ever heard about Mr. Kelly. Thanks for sharing it with me and I'm so sorry for your loss."

He collects himself and looks me in the eye. "Right, so. Forgive me prattling on; I just feel strongly about Conall Kelly."

"And with good reason. Thanks, Ted." I pat his hand, tuck ten euro into his tip jar, and turn to find my way back to Conall.

As I scan the busy room, I see a circle of people near the string quartet playing beside the theater entrance. Though the theater is dark tonight, the lobby is filled with people milling about. I hang back a bit from the crowd and sip my drink as I watch Conall in action. He catches sight of me for a moment and waves, so I smile and wave back. I have a new appreciation for him so I'm content letting him be while I observe from the perimeter.

Conall is chatting away with a stout woman in a red dress. The dress is two sizes too small and the fabric is stretched, struggling to contain her ample bosom. He's oblivious to her dress and its difficulties, but deeply engrossed in conversation. His eyes are intent on her as he listens to what she's saying. Clearly, this is one of his greatest characteristics: he can make the person he's speaking with feel they're the most important person in the room, even if it's only for a moment.

I'm admiring Conall's gift when I feel a hand on my arm. Surprised, I whip my head to the left and see a tall man standing beside me. Startled, I choke on the wine I'm trying to swallow and begin coughing uncontrollably. I'm gasping for air and my eyes fill with tears as the man, seeing my distress, begins patting my back which only serves to further alarm me. I finally manage to clear my airways of wine and draw in a large breath before murmuring, "You frightened me."

I'm still reeling with surprise when he speaks. His deep voice is low and soothing, "I'm sorry. I didn't mean to startle you. I'm just…. I'm just so surprised myself…seeing you here…"

His piercing blue eyes lock with mine and I feel a wistful pang deep inside as I softly utter, "Hello, Dylan."

My knuckles are white as I clutch my wine glass to steel my resolve and brace myself for his response. "Nora, how are you, darling?"

His deep, smooth tone and the way my name mellifluously flows from his mouth make my knees weak, but I manage to squeak out my reply. "I'm great, Dylan. How are you and *Kimberly*?" The added emphasis on her name doesn't go unnoticed. Dylan grins and nods his head. "We're both doing well, thanks."

I've recovered from the wine-choking, near death experience and regain my wits, but still can't help admiring his immutable good looks. There's a bit more salt in his salt-and-pepper hair, but he wears it well. His angular jawline is accentuated by his broad smile, and I detect a hint of fading suntan which can only mean one thing: he's been to the Seychelles recently. Though I admit feeling a tinge of jealousy that Kimberly's the one traveling to the tropics with him, I can't be icy towards Dylan. I love him, this much I know. I didn't leave London angry. I left because staying there was unproductive, and I needed to put space between us. Now, after months of moving on with my life, here he is standing in front of me in the last place I ever imagined I'd encounter him. I swallow hard and ask, "What brings you to Dublin?" *There, I've regained composure. I'm a pro at this. See? A piece of cake.*

Clearing his throat, he responds, "Kimberly's nephew is marrying a girl from Dublin, so we came over for his wedding. His fiancée's father is involved with the CCC and asked if we'd come to the gala tonight."

With that, my knees once again turn to jelly with the realization that not only is Dylan here, he's here with her. Kimberly. Kimberly, the woman he doesn't love enough to remain faithful to, but enough to stay married to. I take another sip of wine to process this new piece of information and do what all good Irish men and women do in polite society: talk about the weather. "Well then, you're fortunate the weather hasn't been terribly wet. We've had some lovely sunny spells the past couple of days. Should be grand for the wedding. Every bride wants the sun shining on her big day..."

Dylan looks puzzled by my sudden interest in the weather but plays along. "Oh, yes. Yes, it has been mild since we arrived. We're hoping for a sunny day Saturday, when the wedding takes place." He looks down at the floor and then back up at me. He couldn't possibly know how those small motions have me melting inside, but then again, he probably does. He knows me so well. The corners of his lips lift into a tiny smile and he says, "I thought you were the proprietor of a B&B. You can imagine how surprised I am running into you here." He makes a sweeping gesture with the cocktail glass in his hand before continuing, "I was flabbergasted when I saw you across the room. Flabbergasted and thrilled, all at the same time. You left London so... so, abruptly...there was more to... to say." He looks forlorn and I feel like a heel for having bugged out without so much as an explanation to why I departed.

Purposely avoiding his comments about me fleeing London, I circle back to his original remark about the B&B. "I am very happily doing the B&B thing, but Martin has me taking on the odd assignment for him. I'm helping put together Conall Kelly's memoir now. That's what has me in Dublin, tonight."

He lifts his eyebrows in recognition, fixes his eyes on mine. "I have to know. Why did you leave London so... unexpectedly?"

I investigate my wine glass and run my index finger around the rim, searching for the right words, then look up, take a deep breath, and exhale. "Dylan, it's complicated... I... I wanted to talk to you, but I knew you'd only try and talk me out of my plans." Our eyes connect, and I see he's wounded, but I persevere, "I had to go, and I think deep down inside, you know I did too. You and Kimberly are *You and Kimberly*, there was no future in you and me and it was time." I sense I'm failing miserably at conveying to him that I needed to leave to preserve my sanity and integrity, but I think he gets it. He's a smart man, a millionaire former MP, after all.

I'm about to tell him I'll always love him and how he will always be the man of my dreams, but someone approaches and prevents me from either professing my undying love or from making a complete fool of myself. It's Conall. He's broken free from the adoring throngs to join me. He bounds over, stands between me and Dylan then interrupts, "There you are! Jaysus, I'm sorry, Nora. Talk about terrible manners. He faces Dylan and adds, "I left a beautiful woman. A woman I practically begged to come with me to this gala and lo and behold, I think she's still speaking to me." He winks, takes my hand and gives a squeeze.

I'm not sure how, but he's read the situation and is playing along. Conall Kelly, the man I thought was a shallow, one dimensional footballer a mere forty-eight hours ago, is perceptive enough to have pieced together I need him to fawn over me at this very moment. I smile coyly. "Conall, you know I could never be upset with you. Besides, this charity is important to you. I expected you'd need to work the room. I'm only happy to be the girl on your arm for the evening." He lifts my hand and gives a small kiss. His fawning is a bit over-the-top, but it gets a reaction from Dylan, so I keep up the ruse.

"Dylan Cooney, I'd like to introduce you to Conall Kelly. Conall, this is Dylan Cooney. Dylan is a former MP.

I worked with him on a book a few years ago in London, much like I'm working with you, now."

Conall runs his hand through his hair before reaching to shake Dylan's hand. "Pleasure, mate."

At this moment, I want to hug Conall. He's got Dylan rattled and I'm loving every moment of this. Dylan tentatively reaches out to shake Conall's hand which undoubtedly is now covered in pomade from his slicked back locks. "Conall, I always enjoyed watching you when you played in the Premier League. How smashing of you to be so benevolent to the folks back home in Ireland."

Dylan isn't prone to condescension, but we all note the hint of condescension in his words. Conall retorts immediately, "I'm Irish. Not benevolent at all, simply caring for the folks at home. No different than any other Irishman who's thankful for his blessings."

His words trip me momentarily. I know he's playing out this little *scene,* but he's sincere. His words are the truth. Conall's an Irish boy who has made it big and is giving back, no, *sharing* his good fortune. I tilt my head and smile at Conall. He grins at me and I note the twinkle in his eye.

Seeing this exchange of glances, Dylan clears his throat and comments, "Well, Nora. I'm glad to see you're doing well. It's been a delight running into you and I wish you well…. If you'll excuse me now, I'll need to rejoin

Kimberly." There's sadness in his eyes and his voice is morose as he turns and offers his hand to Conall. "Mr. Kelly, it was nice meeting you and I wish you all the best with your charitable endeavors. Good evening."

Dylan looks at me for a split second and says, "Goodnight, Nora."

My throat tightens, but I manage to utter the words, "Goodbye, Dylan." My words hang in the air as he tilts his head and gives me a wounded look before he nods, turns, and walks across the grand foyer of the theater. Once Dylan's a safe distance away, I turn and face the windows and let out a long sigh. I'm not certain what I feel, I only know I've weathered a storm. I gaze out the window through the tears puddling in my eyes and study the unusual artwork the waterfront is renowned for; red poles reaching skyward, scattered about the courtyard. I tilt my head to study them, but I'm really reviewing the unexpected events that have just played out inside the theater.

Conall's hand is warm as he begins gently rubbing my back. I keep staring out at the grand canal through tear-filled eyes until, finally, Conall whispers in my ear. "So, am I correct in assuming Dylan Cooney is the MP you fell in love with?"

I don't reply, the lump in my throat prevents words or sound from leaving my mouth. Conall's hand on my back is soothing so I stand there letting him comfort me before turning to face him. I push the tears back and choke out the words, "Thank you, Conall. You were perfect." No further explanation is necessary... he knows. He appeared at the right moment and he played his part brilliantly. He helped me keep my composure. He helped me keep my resolve. He helped me finally and definitively say, goodbye to Dylan Cooney.

Conall puts his hands in his pockets and looks me in the eye. There's compassion in his blue eyes which reminds me why we're here. I take a deep, lung-filling breath, put my hand on his shoulder, usher him towards the bar, and say, "Conall, have you met Ted? You're his hero. I think you two need to chat."

Chapter 8

December 1ˢᵗ – Preparing Cara Maith for Christmas. Decorations inside and outside, professional photographer coming to take publicity photos, and posting invitations to holiday open house.

I throw a piece of turf on the fire and watch the sparks kick up as it hits the flames. Gently stoking the fire, I integrate the dark brown peat into the deep orange pieces burning in the fireplace, return the poker to the stand on the hearth, and walk back to my desk. I draw in a deep breath of the turf's sweet aroma as I sit down behind my computer. The office is toasty this chilly, early morning. I proudly survey the shelves of books surrounding me in my favorite room while I wait for the computer to boot up.

It's been an interesting couple of weeks since my trip to Dublin. I've weathered the storm that ensued after a photographer at the Children's Cancer Charity Gala captured a few candid moments Conall and I shared that evening. There was one of Conall kissing my hand - Dylan had conveniently been cropped out of that one. Another of Conall stroking my back as I gazed out the window, and finally, one of me with my hand on Conall's shoulder at the bar.

I awoke the next morning to my mobile phone ringing repeatedly. First, Martin called, followed by Jeanne, then Mrs. Flood – all wanting to know if it was true. Martin was naturally the most direct. "You're a WAG? Did ya shag?" Not even as much as a hello.

Jeanne wanted to know if he was a good kisser, because she had for some time thought if she were to kiss a footballer, Conall Kelly would be the one she'd kiss and that his kisses would be soft, lingering, and unforgettable.

Mrs. Flood, on the other hand, was concerned about my reputation. "Mind yourself, now, Nora. I know you're a grown woman but mind yourself. 'Tisn't easy to repair a reputation once sullied."

She's protective of me and I think that has to do with her friendship with my mother. On some level, she's taken it upon herself to stand in for her departed friend from time to time. I could tell she was uncomfortable phoning me, but the relief in her voice when I assured her it was all quite innocent was touching.

It's amazing how a single frame of an innocent moment can be taken so wildly, inaccurately, and completely out of context. One minute, I'm helping with an autobiography, the next I'm, *The Mystery Woman Who's Stolen Footballer Kelly's Heart*.

I bought a copy of the *Irish Times* and caught the first train back to Boyle. I practically snuck out of Dublin because of the pictures of me and Conall.

Conall phoned as I stood on the platform at Heuston Station, waiting for the train. "How's it feel to be a WAG?"

His delivery was a little too exuberant, so I lashed out in reply. "Do something about this! You better fix this... set the record straight or I'm done working on your project. You got that? I don't fecking need this shite."

"Calm down, darling. Let's not get into our first fight over such a silly little thing as a sweet photo or two or three." He laughed into the phone before finishing, "Not to worry, I'll give a call to the paper and let em know they've got the wrong end of the stick. *Though*, now that I've been exposed to Nora Fallon's wicked temper, I'm a little turned on."

Hearing the delight in his voice, I snapped back, "I'm boarding a train. Fix this and fix it fast. I'm not a WAG nor will I be mistaken for one."

Conall, in his most patronizing tone said, "Okay, Okay. Just teasing. You must admit, it's good craic. Here I was consoling the MP's former lover, with the MP in the picture. I suppose it was a natural mistake, what, with him being so much older than you. The photographer probably thought Dylan was your Da."

"You're enjoying this, aren't you?... Have your fun... then fix it!" I shouted into the phone as the train entered the station. "I'm leaving now."

"Don't worry, it will all blow over. But if it makes you feel better, I'll sort it with the newspaper."

The warmth in his voice reminded me of how kind and sweet he'd been up until the pictures surfaced, so I modulated my tone and added, "Thanks, Conall. I enjoyed learning more about you. You're a nice guy."

He responded by once again promising he'd fix the whole WAG misunderstanding and wishing me a safe journey home.

That was a couple of weeks ago, and it seems to have worked, though I heard some whispering when I was in Boyle at the Farmers Market. But that could have been my imagination running away with me.

Returning to the task at hand, I wrap my sweater around me tightly and focus on email. As I'm reviewing the proof the printer sent of the holiday party invitations, I hear a light tapping on the kitchen door. I'm not expecting Mrs. Flood or Imelda today, so I look at the time on the bottom corner of the computer screen. 6:11 am. I glance out the office window and notice it's still dark, but then I hear the tapping again. Someone *is* at the door. Rather than ignore their knocking, I walk to the kitchen, picking up my brother's old Boyle GAA hurling

stick I keep in the umbrella stand by the kitchen door...
just in case.

I approach the door as the tapping subsides.
"Hello?... Who's there?" I lean close to the door and grip
the hurling stick with my right hand.

"'Tis me, Nora. Mick."

I relax my grip and unlatch the door. "Holy shite,
Mick. Ye scared the feck out of me...come in outa the
damp."

He steps inside. Spotting the hurling stick in my
hand, he mumbles, "Early match this morning?"

Knowing I must look ridiculous standing at the
door in my pajamas ready to defend myself with a
hurling stick that's at least twenty-five years old, I
chuckle. "No, just practicing."

His face brightens as he flashes a broad grin and
removes his cap. Running his fingers through his hair he
looks down at his wet boots. "I'll just stand here then.
Don't want to muck up the floor." He looks back up
meeting my eyes. Tiny copper flecks brighten the deep
brown irises. I've always wondered how a man with such
gorgeous, expressive eyes manages to remain single.

Realizing I'm staring, I cut my eyes to the floor. I
notice the mud on his boots and immediately appreciate
his courtesy, though his tall frame filling my doorway is a

bit awkward, so I add, "It's early. Take off your boots and have a cup of tea with me." Before he can answer, I'm at the sink filling the kettle. "Besides, it will be nice having company." I look down at my flannel PJs and over-sized cardigan. "Hope you don't mind my...*casual*... attire." I let out a nervous laugh as he removes his muddy Wellies and places them on the door mat.

"Aye, ye always look lovely, Nora. From the time ye were a small girl, you had that natural beauty thing going for yourself." He removes his jacket and drapes it over the back of the chair, then sits down facing me.

Mick was always a serious child and has grown into a relatively somber adult, so I know a compliment from him is sincere. "Thanks, Mick. What a sweet thing to say to a girl first thing in the morning." *I mean it. What girl doesn't want to hear she's pretty when she's just rolled out of bed?*

I put the tea in the pot and sit down across from Mick to wait for the kettle to boil. "So, what has you up this early? You don't typically make social calls at this hour, do you?"

He gently drums his fingers on the table, then answers. "Nah, I was in the front field minding my sheep and saw the light on in your office." He hesitates for a split second then proceeds, "First, it's been a couple weeks and I've still got the box at the house t'was delivered to you when you were in Dublin. I know you said you'd stop to get it, but it's a wee bit heavy so I'll be happy to bring it round for ye."

"No. I'm so sorry, Mick. I completely forgot about the box. I'll stop by later today. I'm going into town, so I'll call by on my way home. That way you can help me put it in the car...if that works for you?"

He shrugs. "There's no rush, but I'll be around any time after four o'clock. It gets dark early these days."

I stand up, walk to the kitchen counter, and lean against it. The kettle is starting to murmur and he's back to drumming his fingers on the table. His hands are large, but his nails are surprisingly well-manicured for a man who works with his hands all day. He's wearing an anguished frown and the finger drumming seems to be a delaying tactic so finally, I ask, "Is there anything else, Mick?" Obviously, there is, but he's more reserved than usual and is struggling with something.

Mick draws in a big breath then exhales before continuing, "I'm not certain."

"You're not certain? What are you uncertain about, Mick?" I fold my arms across my chest and wait.

"You know that incident in Dublin that made the newspapers?" Avoiding eye contact, Mick studies his stocking feet before reluctantly looking back at me. Just as he opens his mouth to form his next word, the kettle lets out a shrill blare as steam surges and water spits out of the spout onto the stovetop.

The ear-splitting whistle interrupts his train of thought and I grab the kettle off the burner silencing its cry. I turn my back and pour the scalding water into the pot as Mick continues, "You know. The pictures in the papers of you and Conall Kelly, the *footballer*." I detect added emphasis when he says the word *footballer*, but he keeps going, "Well, there's people in town who've been saying unkind things about you and I just thought you should know."

I place the teapot in front of Mick and walk back and get two beakers and retrieve the milk. As I place the milk on the table, I ask, "sugar?" He shakes his head, *no,* and I join him.

He pours a cup of tea for me and one for himself before speaking again. "Some people were saying you were always *extra friendly* with the people you worked with and that's how you were so…*successful.*"

His pained expression tells me how uncomfortable he is bringing this news, so I gently place my hand on top of his. "Look, Mick. My entire life there have been people talking about me or my family. My father's drinking gave smaller minds plenty of fodder, but the people who knew us, they knew the truth and they were the ones who mattered most. I learned a long time ago not to let gossip bother me. Especially when I know it isn't true."

He gives a small grin, clears his throat. "I know, Nora. I've always admired your strength. It's just this time, the person doing the most gossiping is telling folks not to promote Cara Maith..." He lowers his head and in a barely audible tone finishes, "because you bought it with ill-gotten gains from being a whore."

His words smack and I'm pretty sure he's startled himself by using the word *whore,* which isn't a cornerstone of his vocabulary. I don't even remember hearing him swear let alone use such a crass expression as *whore.* The word struggled leaving his lips, dragging on the "o" turning it into a protracted monosyllabic *hoooooor...* before freeing itself from Mick's mouth.

I recover from the shock and reassure him. "Mick, I worked too hard to earn the things I've acquired to let some small-minded gossip detract from my accomplishments. Besides, I have a feeling there's only one person who has said that about me, so if you happen to run into Mrs. Roach, please ask her to refrain from saying untrue things and if she cannot keep from slandering me or my business, I'll have my solicitor contact her." *Slander, libel, I can never keep the two straight, but it sounded good, anyway.*

I remove my hand from Mick's, and he takes a sip of his tea before dryly responding, "I thought that's what you'd say." He swallows his tea and mutters under his breath, "That rotten ol biddy."

The rain subsides, but the chill remains in the air as I get in the car, which I've parked on Patrick Street. Jeanne and I had met at Clarke's for tea and talk, like we used to when we were teenagers. One summer, when we both had gotten jobs at shops in the arcade, we were so proud of our *income*s we'd treat ourselves to afternoon tea once a week. It became a habit up until the time I left for school. Now that I'm back, we're lucky if we manage finding time once a month, but as often as possible we pop into Clarke's, ask for a table next to the fire, and remain there for at least an hour, catching up on the latest news. Today, Jeanne was bubbling over with anticipation. She couldn't wait to be filled in on the gala and what *really* happened. I had mentioned to her I'd run into Dylan, but we hadn't spoken in person. She wanted details, more than I wanted to go into over the phone.

"How did he look?"

"What did he say when he saw you?"

"What did Conall say to Dylan?"

"Was Dylan jealous?"

I laughed. "What do you mean, *jealous*? There's nothing to be jealous of."

She giggled, "Right..."

I drive away from Clarke's and wave back at Jeanne who's standing outside waiting for Jim who's across the street showing an empty property to a prospective buyer. She waves enthusiastically as I round the bend and make my way out of town.

As Boyle gets smaller in the rear-view mirror, my thoughts wander to teenage years. Before long, the familiar pangs of missing my mother, my brother, and yes, even my father cast a cloud over me. I have few solid memories of my father. He was handsome, I know that. Why else would my mother put up with his behavior?

Folks in town considered him an interloper. He came from Galway to work on a construction job but stayed. To this day, there are people around these parts who felt he committed the sin of theft. He stole a young Boyle girl who would have made a lovely bride for a better man, a better man from Boyle.

I recall the time Mrs. Roach's daughter, Ava arrived at school one Monday ready to burst if she didn't get to tell me of her father's encounter with my father in the pub Saturday night. Ava sprinted towards me as I walked through the classroom door. I can still see her flipping her long blonde curls over her shoulder and the sparkle of glee in her eyes as she recounted how, "Once again, your father was loud and drunk at the pub until my father had enough and told your father in no uncertain terms, 'Jack Fallon, it's bad enough you come here and poach one of our women, but by God, do we have to listen to you as well?' "

I had stood silent for a moment before pushing past her to get to my desk. At this point, Sister Ursula arrived in the classroom and caught the tail end of Ava joyfully telling how her father put my father in his place. Sister Ursula loudly cleared her throat as she walked to the front of the room. "Right, so. Let's all find our seats... I thought we'd start the day with a little lesson called THINK... THINK is an acronym to help us remember to THINK before we speak." Jeanne cut her eyes in my direction as the rest of the class settled in their chairs. Once we were quiet, Sister Ursula began, "The "T" reminds us to ask if what I'm about to say is Thoughtful. The "H" reminds us to ask if what I'm going to say is helpful or honest. Next, the "I" stands for intelligent. Followed by the "N", which is for necessary. Finally, the "K" reminds us to question if what we're about to say is kind."

She turned and wrote *THINK* in big bold letters on the board then spun back around and looked directly at Ava Roach. She projected her voice like she was speaking to everyone, but we all saw to whom her next comment was directed. "Class, I expect *and* require everyone in here to rely on this code of conduct. T-H-I-N-K." She drew out and enunciated each letter so there would be no uncertainty. "If I find anyone in my class, in the hallway, in the lunchroom, or on the playground; I don't care where, but if anyone isn't following this simple guideline of loving your neighbor, as our Dear Lord commands us to, there will be consequences. Is this understood?"

We all replied, "Yes, Sister" in unison, but Sister Ursula never stopped staring at Ava. I almost felt sorry for her; being called out in front of the entire class, especially by the nicest nun at the school. It was humiliating, but then I remembered the glee in Ava's eyes as she humiliated me. I also remember feeling grateful I hadn't lashed out at Ava. Sure, I wanted to and had I been faster with the comebacks, I would have, but by walking past Ava to my desk, I got to claim the high ground for the moment and for a girl who often felt less-than, it felt tremendous.

I come to the crossroads, which jolts me from my memories long enough to remember I'm supposed to go to Mick's and retrieve the package he's been holding for me. Rather than taking the left that leads to Cara Maith, I continue straight towards St. Coman's Farm, Mick's place.

I seldom drive this way and though it's almost half-four, I stop at Eastersnow since it's on the way to Mick's. I pull off the road and open the gate before driving through the entrance to the ancient church and graveyard. The old stone structure is the remains of what hundreds of years ago, was a beautiful church. The church was the Church of Ireland, but the graveyard belongs to the Catholic parish of Croghan. Today it's one of Ireland's iconic graveyards. I'm still in awe of the old church building.

When I was a child, the structure had fallen into terrible condition; covered with vines, weeds and nettles. It was in such a sad state, finally folks did something about it. I step out of the car and admire how beautiful it is and decide I need to make the effort to visit my parents' graves more often.

The grass is still damp from the rain, so I tread carefully to the spot where my mother and father are buried. There's a gray stone with FALLON engraved across the top and a Celtic cross below the family name. I read the inscription, *John "Jack" Fallon*, then look beside Dad's name and read, *Katherine Brennan Fallon* followed by her birth and death dates and *Beloved Mother.* It still bothers me I didn't think to put "Kate" on the stone. That's what she went by, and that's how everybody knew her. I imagine someday, years from now, a long-lost relation doing ancestry research will come stand right here and not know this was *Kate* Fallon, not *Katherine*. I shake my head and murmur, "sorry, Ma."

I stand still for a few moments. The distinct braying of a donkey in the distance is the only sound. I've never been at ease in the graveyard. Should I talk to the deceased? That always strikes me as a bit pointless and a touch mad. I wouldn't be expecting a reply and since they're dead, will they really hear what I'm saying?

I could cry and have cried in the past when visiting, but it feels a little self-indulgent. I remember Jack Jr. chiding me after an emotional boo-hoo-hoo session, "Wipe the sour off your mug! *You're* not dead!"

I decide to pray instead and mumble a few *Hail Marys* and one *Hail Holy Queen* before patting the top of the stone and choking out, "I miss you, Ma." I shut my eyes squeezing them tightly trying to picture her face. I have photos at home, but my mental picture is fading. I so want to see her, but time has eroded the clarity of her picture in my mind. Her face is blurry and expressionless. I think I recall her voice, but even that's uncertain in my memory, so I give up trying to recall. Instead, I touch my fingers to my lips, kiss them, softly place the kiss on top of the cold granite stone, and walk to the car.

It's nearly five o'clock when I reach the driveway to Mick's house. He took over his father's farm a few years back and when he did, he had a new house built for himself behind a patch of trees. Jeanne said he did it so nobody could spy on him. I wasn't sure what she meant when she told me that, but as I drive beyond the patch of trees, I get what he was going for. *Privacy.*

Mick is a very private and quiet man. He's been that way since we were kids. I remember thinking he'd make a wonderful Colonel Brandon when I was reading Jane Austen's, *Sense and Sensibility* in school. He's got this tranquil exterior, but I've always sensed he's a sensitive soul. His cool, controlled exterior belies his deep emotional side. Unflappable on the outside, tender on the inside – he's the uttermost combination of feeling and logic – a genuine grownup.

I approach the house in awe. Having never been here before, I had no expectations of his home, but this place catches me by surprise. The home is a sprawling, white bungalow with a slate roof. The expansive front windows are adorned with overflowing flower boxes filled with dahlias and purple asters cheerfully holding their blooms well into late autumn. Inside each window, delicate lace curtains hang in true Irish fashion.

The front door is tucked inside a small alcove and above it is a rustic wooden sign with *St. Coman's Farm* burned into the wood. St. Coman is the Irish saint for whom County Roscommon is named, *Ros* meaning wooded, and *Coman* for the first bishop of Roscommon. Mick's father always had a fondness for St. Coman and renamed his family farm for the saint when it was passed to him by his own father. I smile up at the sign aware Mick is honoring his father in keeping and embracing the name.

I ring the bell and stand studying the large brass ram's head door knocker and regret not giving that a go instead of the bell. If he doesn't come in ten seconds, I'm going to give the ram a solid pounding, but alas, my fun is denied as he opens the door to find me giggling.

"Well, now, Nora. What's the craic?"

He opens the door wide and I walk past him into the foyer and point up at the ram on the door. "Nice knocker."

He looks at the knocker before closing the door behind us and says, "Ah, t'was a gift from me Da. Do ye like it?"

"I do like it. The ram reminds me of an old expression."

Mick holds his hands up to halt me from continuing, "Don't bother, Nora. As a sheep farmer, I've heard em all."

There's playfulness in his eyes, so I continue, "*Heard* em all or *herd* em all?" I joke, adding, "You know what rams do?"

He groans and shakes his head, "do tell."

"Feck ewe." I laugh until I let out a tiny snort.

He looks at me, sighs and asks, "There, now. Do ye feel better."

"I do." I grin and notice he looks like he's just gotten out of the shower. His hair is wet, he's wearing a plain white t-shirt, blue jeans and is in his bare feet so I ask, "Did I come at a bad time?"

He gives me a warm look. "No, not at all. Will ye stay for a cuppa or something a wee bit stronger? My Da and I are just about to sit down."

From somewhere down the hall I hear his father shout, "Join us, Nora. We'd love the company of a beautiful lady."

I've always liked Mick's father. He coached Jack Jr. the year he tried hurling. He was so kind and patient, I think he felt sorry for Jack. Jack was athletic, but hurling wasn't his sport. Maybe because at the time our home was in such turmoil with Dad being away *working* in Dublin and Ma working all hours to keep us fed. The hurling season had just ended when Dad was killed, but Mr. Reynolds kept coming by to say hello, or bring a meal.

Salt of the earth, my mother would say. *The Reynolds are salt of the earth, they are.*

Mick reaches for my coat and begins helping me out of it before I can answer, "I can't say no to your father, Mick."

He grins. "I know, that's why I've already got ye out of your coat, my lady." He puts my coat on a hook by the door and I follow him down the hall to the kitchen where his father is seated at the table, which has three place settings awaiting. He stands and warmly greets me with a small peck on the cheek. "Sure, if you're not a sight for sore eyes, Nora. My, how's it possible you get prettier day by day, doesn't she, Mick?" He says this rhetorically, but Mick answers him.

"Aye, Da. I don't know how she does it, but she does." He points to one of the place settings and says, "Have a seat, Nora. We're just about to have tea. Nothing fancy, just tea and scones, hope that's alright with ye."

He pulls out the chair for me and I sit down. "That sounds lovely. I could use a cuppa to warm up. I stopped at Eastersnow before coming here." I decide not to mention I already had tea in town with Jeanne since judging by the third place setting, they were expecting me to join them.

"'Tis beautiful altogether, now, Eastersnow, isn't it?" Mr. Reynolds sits back in his chair and continues,

"Sure it's a national treasure, indeed. Like something you see in all those holiday brochures for visiting ancient Ireland."

I nod in silent agreement as Mick places the teapot on the trivet in front of us and a basket of scones beside the tea. Mr. Reynolds pours the tea for me and Mick passes the scones. It's been five years since Mrs. Reynolds passed away and Mick invited his Da to live with him. There's a genuine closeness the two men share, and I watch their rapport; they're not just father and son, they're friends too. I feel a familiar twinge of jealousy; how I longed for that kind of relationship with my own family. Mom and I were close, but I didn't get to enjoy an adult friendship with her. My father and Jack Jr. were never close. "Water and oil," Ma used to lament.

Mick sits in the chair next to mine and as soon as he's seated, pops back up. "I've forgotten the clotted cream and jam." He opens the fridge and while his head is deep inside, searching for jam, I return my attention to Mr. Reynolds whose eyes are locked on me. He has the same deep brown eyes as Mick, but they're fringed by bushy gray brows and he hasn't nearly as many copper flecks, so I attribute the beautiful copper flecks to Mrs. Reynolds.

Once Mick returns, I say, "You have a beautiful home... I've never seen it before."

Mick's busy spreading jam on a scone so his father responds, "Aye, Mick had it built about seven years ago. You were off in London back then. He'd been thinking and planning a while and once he sold the rights to the apps he developed, he started construction."

"*Apps*? What *apps*, Mick?" This is the first I've heard of *apps*. I always knew he was into computers, but I'm stunned. Why is this the first I'm hearing of Mick's apps? I already have the topic of conversation for the next time Jeanne and I have tea at Clarke's.

Mick's cheeks redden slightly before he answers, "It's just a couple farming apps I came up with."

Mr. Reynolds slaps the table so hard our teacups rattle in their saucers, "Just a couple apps?! Well, there's an understatement. Why, Mick's changed Ireland's cattle breeding entirely with 'Mama Moo'."

Mick gives a shrug and turns my direction. "It's an app I created to let farmers know the optimum time for breeding. The cows wear collars that track when a cow is in heat and alert the farmer at any hour of the day, thus optimizing the breeding time of the herd."

I lift the saucer from under my teacup and pour the tea Mr. Reynold's table slam sent sloshing over the sides back into the cup, before turning to Mick. "That's incredible. I had no idea. Well done, you."

Mr. Reynolds agrees, "Well done, *indeed*. The next year he came up with a second app called 'Amazing Graze' for managing pastures and monitoring field conditions. That got him an award and his picture on the covers of 'Modern Irish Farmer' and 'Sheep Farmers Monthly'." He pauses to slurp from his teacup before adding, "Then he sold em both and made a fortune."

Mr. Reynold's exuberance over his son's success is touching. Mick's soft-spoken nature would never permit him to brag about his exploits the way his father just did. I turn to Mick and he returns my gaze. "I'm gob smacked, Mick. I had no idea. Congratulations, you deserve all the success in the world."

"Your good opinion and well wishes far surpass any accolades, or financial rewards I've received." He's still looking directly at me and I notice a softness. For the first time, I understand Mick Reynolds values my opinion.

He holds my gaze momentarily and it unleashes a flutter within. I awkwardly reach for my teacup and take a sip as a mechanism of restoring my composure, but his words linger, and nobody speaks. I gently place my cup back in the saucer and from the corner of my eye I spy Mr. Reynolds beaming.

Mick breaks the awkward silence. "After tea, would you like a tour of the house?"

"I'd love that. From the looks of the kitchen and my walk down the hallway, you've got an eye for interior decorating. I can't wait to see what you've done with the rest of the house."

Mr. Reynolds finishes his tea with a loud, *ahhh*, indicating he's reached the bottom of the cup. "I'll be leaving you two to tour on your own. I'm going into town. Tonight's the High Nelly Club meeting. I'm on the board of our bicycling club again this year and we're busy making plans for a holiday party."

His mention of a party reminds me of my own upcoming event. "Oh, save the date of the fifteenth. I'm having a small Christmas party at Cara Maith. I'd love for you and Mick to come. I'll be posting the invitations tomorrow and I don't want you to go and book a High Nelly party first." I smile at Mr. Reynolds as he gets up from the table and carries his dishes to the sink.

"I'll be delighted to attend and thanks for the notice. I'll make sure to steer the High Nelly Club away from the date of the fifteenth."

Mr. Reynolds gives me another peck on the cheek and makes his exit. I hear the front door close and the sound of his tiny Renault creeping down the gravel driveway. I get up to help Mick with the dishes. As he rinses a cup I say, "I didn't know your father still has his vintage bicycle. I figured with his bad knee; he didn't ride anymore."

Mick hands me the cup to put in the dishwasher. "He doesn't ride anymore, but he's still involved with the club. He follows along in the car and carries water or tea to their destination. He keeps a patch kit in case someone gets a puncture, that sort of thing."

I place a saucer in the dishwasher and turn to Mick. "Turn it on or wait till it's full up?"

He glances at the dishwasher then at me. "Let's wait till it's full up, shall we?"

I close the door and follow him out of the kitchen into the hall. He looks over his shoulder and smiles. "And now, for the grand tour."

Mick shows me the living room, the dining room, the bedrooms on his side of the house and we stop at the door leading to the wing of the house where his father lives. Respecting his father's privacy, we go no further, but he describes his father's living quarters.

"Did you design the house with your parents in mind?"

He smiles down at me. "I did. They weren't old and frail at the time, but I knew one day, one or both might need to be with me, here." He turns and continues walking back to his side of the bungalow before saying,

"Mom's heart attack took us all by surprise. Dad had no desire to live in their house once she was gone, so I was glad I could offer him a home, here."

"You're a good son, Mick. Your Dad's fortunate to have you."

We walk into what's obviously his office and he turns to me. "Nah, 'tis me that's lucky. Having Patrick and Sarah Reynolds for parents t'was the best fortune a lad could have in life."

I'm moved by his remark and again feel a pang of jealousy shoot through me. "Again, I contend, you're a good son, Mick."

He runs his hand through his hair, which has fully dried now, and points to the box in the corner. "I brought your package in here and I'll carry it out to the car for ya, no trouble at all."

I see the box but turn back and tease, "Is this your office? Is this where the brilliant technology expert changes Irish farming as we know it?"

His expression softens, "Aye. This is where it all happens." He points to the oak desk with the high back leather chair behind it. "I sit right there and think about cows in heat."

His abrupt humor catches me by surprise, but I like it and comment, "I like when you joke, Mick. You're funny. Your delivery is…dry…very dry… but I like to see you smile."

He opens his eyes wide, raising his dark eyebrows then lowering them. "I'll have to remember that. Like I said, your good opinion is important to me."

I walk over to his desk which is covered in papers filled with notes and sketches. "Are you working on something new?"

He joins me and picks up a sketch. "This is my work on a new app I've been commissioned to design to help optimize sheep shearing." He raises his hand to halt me. "And please, no sheep jokes."

I laugh at this. "You caught me. I was just about to tell one…"

Our eyes meet, and I see a tenderness in Mick's I've not noticed before. There's much more to Mick Reynolds than I'd ever realized.

He breaks the silence and walks back to the box on the floor. "Shall I put this in the boot of your car?"

Stirring me from my new-found appreciation of Mick Reynolds, his words remind me it's getting late. "Yes, perfect. I should get going. You know how dark it is and I don't think I left a light on at the house. I'll be fumbling in the dark with a box in my arms."

He lifts the box and proceeds to the front door. Glancing back, he says, "You should keep a torch in the glove box of your car. 'Tisn't really safe for you to return to a dark house."

I follow behind, grabbing my coat from the hook in the foyer. "You're right. I guess I'm still not used to country living. I spent so many years in London where the lights are always on."

Debby is lounging next to the rear tire of my car. The dog lifts her head, opens her mouth and yawns as Mick steps over her. "You could always get a dog for protection" he says.

"*See*, Mick. That's what I mean. Your delivery is dry. Debby doesn't get that you were being sarcastic."

I pop the boot open using the key fob. Mick puts the box in and says, "What is that anyway? 'Tis heavy as me grandmother's Christmas pudding."

I laugh. "It's new towels for Cara Maith. They've been embroidered with the Cara Maith logo. They're meant to bring class and sophistication to the B&B experience."

"Ah, ye sound like the product description in a catalog." He closes the boot and walks over to me. He's still barefooted so I warn, "You better get in the house or you'll catch your death of cold." I pat him on the arm, open the car door and get in. Mick leans over the open door as I put the key in the ignition.

I look up and smile. "Thanks, Mick. I've always loved your family. Thanks for inviting me to tea."

"You're welcome to tea any time, ya know. You don't have to wait for an invitation. Our door is always open to ye."

I feel a tear puddling in the corner of my eye as a wave of loneliness washes over me. "I know. That's part of why I love your family, Mick."

Mick leans in closer. "…and just so you know, Da and I are as proud of you as can be. 'Tis incredible what you've done and become. Don't ever let small minds make you feel bad. You're a beautiful, successful woman, Nora Fallon. Your Ma would be proud."

He pushes the door closed and I turn on the engine. I drive off as he goes back inside. Wiping tears from my eyes, I guide the car down the driveway and onto the main road. The night is pitch dark as I drive home reflecting on the things Mick said.

Would my mother be proud of me?

Would Mick think I'm a beautiful person inside and out if he knew about Dylan Cooney?

Was Mick Reynolds really the first person I spoke with this morning and the last person I talked to at the end of the day?

And a new question: *Why do I care what Mick Reynolds thinks of me?*

Chapter 9

December 15th – Several people coming to the Cara Maith Christmas party, tonight. Mrs. Flood and Imelda providing buffet and desserts. Weather is dodgy, cold and damp with possibility of snow. Hope it won't upset the party.

Mrs. Flood is arranging cookies on a tray in the kitchen as the doorbell rings, so I call to her from the lounge, "I'll get it, Mrs. Flood," though I don't think she planned to answer it anyway. I open the door to greet four young people holding instruments. "Come in, come in," I say as I open the door wide enough to accommodate the lad carrying a cello and direct them towards the lounge. The musicians come to me via Imelda. I'd wanted to feature a local musical group but didn't know where to begin auditioning let alone finding a string quartet. Imelda is studying Home Economics at Abbey Community College and suggested I ask her schoolmates. She had them send me a demo tape and I was delighted to find such a wonderful ensemble right here in Boyle.

"Right in here," I direct as the musicians follow me into the lounge. "You can set up in the corner to the left of the fireplace, if that works for you."

The quartet make their way to the corner and begin setting up their music stands in front of chairs I've already positioned in a semi-circle beside the hearth. A tall slender girl with auburn hair smiles at me and says, "This is grand, Ms. Fallon. We've been rehearsing Christmas carols for the past month. We're delighted you've hired us for your party."

"Please, call me Nora…" I trail off in a questioning manner and she picks up on my lead.

"Oh, sorry. My name's Caitlin Murphy and I play violin." She flashes a toothy smile before continuing her introductions. Pointing first to a tall dark-haired lad she says, "This is Seamus Dwyer on cello." Next to a short, slightly chubby girl with glasses, "Deidre Shannon on violin. Finally, she nods in the direction of a tall girl with a short blonde bob, "this is Peggy Roach on viola."

The four smiling faces are fixed on me, so I hope my expression hasn't betrayed the inner angst upon hearing the name of the girl on viola. *Roach*? Don't tell me, she's a relation of Nancy Roach.

Before I can ask to take their coats, Peggy offers me her hand and says, "So nice to meet you, Nora. My Aunt Nancy has told me so much about you…"

I force a stiff grin and look at the girl. She seems genuine in her tone, but she's a Roach so I tread lightly. "Oh, you're one of the Roaches, then?" I reach for her coat and she hands it to me before I finish speaking. "I hope your family are well and enjoying the holiday season."

She tucks a strand of hair behind her ear and smiles. "Oh, yes. We're all doing well. Aunt Nancy was a little upset with me when I told her I'd be playing here tonight… with you being the *competition*." She rolls her eyes and gives air quotes as she enunciates the word before giggling.

I reach for the rest of their coats and reply, "Oh, Boyle's a beautiful area, plenty of room for several B&Bs. Isn't it nice that she can offer an in-town experience and I can offer a farmhouse experience? Really, it's grand the town can furnish such a variety to tourists."

"That's precisely what I told Aunt Nancy, though she didn't seem to agree." Peggy leans in closer and whispers, "She can be a bit of a horse's arse at times, but don't repeat that, please."

I give a conspiratorial wink as I leave to hang the coats. I think I'm going to like this member of the Roach clan. I call back to the musicians, "Let me know if there's anything you need. The guests should be arriving in about twenty minutes."

The doorbell rings precisely at eight o'clock and I smile as I make my way to the foyer. I feel certain it must be Mick and his father. Mick is *the* most punctual individual I've ever met. I throw open the door and let out a booming *Happy Christmas* only to find it's not Mick at all. Puzzled for a moment, I stand frozen in the doorway until my guest finally speaks, "Happy Christmas to you too, Nora!"

I'm still frozen as he kisses my cheek and steps inside. Finding my voice, I ask, "What are you doing here?"

"Now, is that any way of greeting a guest?"

Conall's standing wide eyed and unblinking in my foyer. When I hear a squeal of recognition from one of the musicians, I'm forced to acknowledge my holiday party will have an entirely different flavor from what I'd intended.

I lean in and give Conall a peck on the cheek. "Welcome, Mr. Kelly. To what do I owe the honor of your presence?"

His cool blue eyes sparkle, "Now, that's more like it." He removes his jacket and smiles. "Hope you don't mind. Martin Wilson told me about your holiday party, so I thought I'd come to Boyle and surprise you."

"I'm surprised. Well done, you."

Hearing my sarcasm, he takes my hand and pats it gently. "Hope you've got a room I can let for the weekend. I know it's the off-season, but since we're old friends."

I release a long low sigh and, seeing my exasperation, Conall bats his eyes and grins widely, making it impossible for me to be angry with him. "Of course, I've got a room for you." I shake my head and tell him to follow me into the kitchen where Mrs. Flood and Imelda are busily completing the food for the buffet. The pair look up and immediately recognize our unexpected guest.

Mrs. Flood's mouth is agape, and Imelda drops the carving knife she's using on the roast beef. The knife makes a loud crash as it hits the silver service tray below. I wish I had my phone handy to capture a picture of their priceless expressions. They're obviously familiar with Conall Kelly, but I still make the introductions.

"Conall Kelly, I'd like you to meet Mrs. Flood and her granddaughter, Imelda. Mrs. Flood cooks for me and Imelda is in school at Abbey Community College but helps here as well."

Conall offers his hand to Mrs. Flood, who promptly wipes her hands on her apron before extending hers and stammering, "Oh, Mr. Kelly, sure we were all great fans of yours when you were playing."

Conall demurs a bit, "It's lovely meeting you. I hope you're still fans, by the way."

He turns to Imelda who isn't quite as starstruck as her grandmother, but still a little unsteady. She recovers nicely. "Nice to meet you, Mr. Kelly."

"*Conall*, please call me *Conall*." He gives an easy wink and adds, "I hope my surprise visit won't upset things too much."

Mrs. Flood is still wiping her hands furiously on her apron, though she is entirely unaware as she speaks, "Will you be staying the night? I can put you in the *Gaelic Chieftain*."

Conall raises his eyebrows and clears his throat. Seeing his bewilderment and recognizing Mrs. Flood is tongue-tied by his celebrity status, I turn to Conall and say, "The *Gaelic Chieftain* is the name of one of the rooms. Each room is named after a place in or around Boyle. There's a piece of sculpture on the Sligo Road just outside town called the *Gaelic Chieftain*, thus the room."

I turn to Mrs. Flood and ask, "Is the room ready for guests?"

Still wiping her hands, she answers, "The sheets and towels are clean, I'll need to put milk in the mini-fridge for the tea, but there's no fresh flowers."

I look back at Conall who's smiling and focused on me. "Can you live without fresh flowers for the night?"

He holds my gaze briefly before answering, "I'll survive just fine without fresh flowers."

His eyes sparkle and I feel my face warming, but manage to ask, "Have you got a bag with you?"

"It's in the car."

Imelda's gone back to her food preparation and Mrs. Flood is too star-struck and busy wiping her hands to direct Conall to his room, so I say, "Go get your bag and I'll show you to your room before the guests arrive."

Conall retrieves his overnight bag and follows me upstairs. The string quartet are tuning their instruments as we ascend the stairs to the sounds of Good King Wenceslas. Conall trails silently behind me and remains quiet as I put the key in the door and open his room. I watch as he enters, turns the light on and places his overnight bag on the luggage stand in the corner.

As he slowly steps away from the luggage, I break down and ask, "Seriously. What are you doing here? I don't believe for one minute you're here to attend my holiday party."

That sounded harsher than I wanted it to, but Conall isn't upset by my terse remark. Quite the contrary, his face brightens, and he laughs softly before approaching and taking my hands in his and saying, "You're gorgeous when you're angry. Really. It's quite lovely to see the flash of anger behind those beautiful eyes, Nora."

His hands are warm and by the strength of his grip I'm certain it would cause an awkward scene if I try snatching my hands away right now, so I let him hold on as I respond, "I'm not angry, Conall. I wasn't expecting you, that's all."

He smiles and softly says, "I'm on my way to Donegal to see me family for Christmas so I decided to make a stop along the way. I don't want to be of any bother to ye, so if you aren't prepared for a weekend visitor, I understand."

His voice is soft and low, and his eyes look sad, so I feel terrible for my momentary lack of manners. The poor bachelor is only on his way to see his relations for the holidays and stopped to see me. I should be happy he's here, but instead I've behaved as if his arrival is a major inconvenience when it really isn't. I glance down at my hands still in Conall's then back at his clear blue eyes.

"Conall, you'll be the hit of the party, no doubt. It may even turn out to be good publicity for the inn."

He lets out a sigh of relief and finally releases my hands. "I'll just need a minute to freshen up and I'll come down for the party."

I turn to exit the room and glance back at Conall. "Make yourself at home and let me know if you need anything at all. It's a causal get-together. What you're wearing will be fine."

"Grand. I'll only be a few minutes, then." He lifts his hand and gives a small wave as I close the door behind me.

I return downstairs to the sound of guests arriving. Mrs. Flood is happily taking coats as I reach the bottom step. Several guests have arrived simultaneously filling the entry with laughter and conversation, so I slip into the crowd and begin welcoming them.

I usher them all into the lounge where the string quartet is softly playing Christmas carols by the fire and Imelda's boyfriend Robby is standing behind the bar, prepared to serve. He's wearing a crisp white shirt, a smart black vest, and a holiday tartan bowtie. His usually unruly blonde curls are slicked back with pomade giving him just the right look of sophistication for the soirée.

As Robby is pouring Chardonnays for Jeanne, Jim, and a couple of ladies from the chamber of commerce, I turn to see Mick and his father entering the room. Mr. Reynolds is promptly swept away by a fellow member of the High Nelly Cycle Club, but Mick's standing in the doorway inspecting the crowd when our eyes meet. Upon seeing me, he immediately flashes a smile and approaches. He bends down and whispers in my ear so to be heard above the music, "Everything looks beautiful, tonight."

I smile up at him, our eyes connect for a second, and I recognize his familiar heartwarming air of pride. I take him in from head to toe. He's dressed far differently than usual. I'm accustomed to seeing him clothed for farm work. His usual attire for such occasions would be a pair of trousers, a plain shirt, a tweed jacket and the ubiquitous Wellies. However, tonight he's got an air of refinement I've not seen before. He's wearing a soft blue, button-down Oxford shirt, a tailored navy-blue jacket, and slim-cut trousers. The jacket tapers at his waist calling attention to his broad shoulders and the trousers emphasize his long legs. He catches me admiring his clothing choice and remarks, "Do I pass your inspection, my lady?"

My cheeks warm, but rather than concede to having been caught giving Mick the once-over, I match his snide remark. "I see you've eschewed the Wellies tonight and gone with a pair of pointy hipster shoes. Very nice."

Mick looks down at his shoes then back at me with a playful grin. "Aye. They're grand for killing spiders in corners. May I get you a glass of wine, then?"

His dry response followed by the offer of a drink makes me laugh out loud, "Aye, a glass of Chardonnay, my dear *hipster*."

Mick hands me a wine glass and much to my surprise, when the string quartet finishes a lovely version of *Dashing Through the Snow*, he clears his throat and announces, "I'd like to offer a toast to our hostess."

All eyes are on me as Mick lifts his wineglass and exclaims, "I'd like to offer a toast to Nora. She purchased the old parochial house about a year ago, now. I've watched in admiration as she single-handedly turned this lovely old home into the Cara Maith. She's worked very hard, and tonight all we need to do is glance around to see what an outstanding job Nora's done. She's restored the old home to its former glory, she's giving Boyle an outstanding new inn, and she's giving back to the community as well. So, raise your glasses high with me and toast, to Nora, a girl from Boyle who's succeeded in every venture partaken. May the Cara Maith Inn's success exceed her wildest dreams. To Nora!"

The gathering repeats after Mick, "To Nora!"

I'm blushing as the crowd drink their toasts and wish me well. I had planned on giving a welcoming speech and inviting my guests to visit the buffet in the dining room. Instead, Mick has deeply moved me with his thoughtful toast. I gaze up at him and mouth the words *thank you*, before directing remarks to the gathering.

"Thank you, Mick, and thank you all for coming tonight. I'm delighted you braved the rainy weather to be here and help celebrate what I hope will become an annual Cara Maith event. I'd also like to thank the string quartet from Abbey Community College for the lovely music." I give a small applause directed towards the quartet and the others join me." I'd also like to direct you across the hall into the dining room where Mrs. Flood and Imelda have put together a delicious buffet." I lift my hand in direction towards the door at the very moment Conall Kelly enters the room.

Heads turn at my announcement and immediately Conall is recognized. A murmur goes through the crowd and Conall gives a sheepish wave, so I'm forced to add, "Oh, and I almost forgot. We have a special guest this evening. Many of you may recognize him from his days on the football pitch. Conall Kelly is joining us, tonight."

For the moment, the roast beef, prawns and cheese plate are the last things on the guests' minds. Instead, the crowd huddle around Conall. A couple musicians abandon their instruments and scamper to his side. I manage to extract myself from the lounge and retreat to the dining room where the buffet is awaiting. The dining room is empty except for Mick.

"Ah, smart man. Get it while it's hot." I nod towards the plate he's just piled high with sliced roast beef." I stride to the table, grab a napkin, and hand it to him.

Mick balances the plate carefully as he takes the napkin then replies, "Aye, Mrs. Flood and Imelda worked hard on this, I'd hate to let it get cold." He winks before continuing, "If I know you, you've not eaten all day. Why not fix yourself a plate while the others swoon over your football... *hero*."

His snide tone catches me off guard, so I laugh. "Why, Mick. That almost sounded sarcastic. What have you got against the famous Conall Kelly?"

His expression softens, and he says, "Nothing. I didn't mean that to sound the way it did, but since you've asked, I don't know what his business is here, but you've gone to a lot of trouble and expense to showcase the inn tonight. I can't help feeling he's stealing your thunder, so to speak."

Picking up a plate, I take a toothpick and begin stabbing cubes of cheddar cheese and placing them on the plate. I'm focused on the cheese but pondering his remark. I stop, look up at Mick. "He's on his way home for the holidays. His family are in Donegal, so he thought he'd spend a couple nights here on his way. Yes, he's taken me by surprise..." I hesitate as I pick up a prawn and lay it beside the cheese cubes. "However, this could be exactly what I need. Think about the buzz his being here will create. There won't be a soul in town who won't know that Conall Kelly is a guest here, let alone the publicity it will generate all over the county, the country. He's a big name, *right*?"

Mick shrugs, adds a roll to his plate and crosses to the corner of the dining room. He seats himself at one of the small tables I've set up for the party, places his napkin on his lap, picks up a prawn, studies it then takes a bite. Before I can join him to delve further into Mick's opinion of my unexpected guest, Conall bellows my name.

"Nora? Nora!"

I glance toward the corner and Mick then back to Conall as he and the herd approach. "Yes, Conall? What do you need?"

His voice is clear and loud above all the others, "I need you." He wraps an arm around me being careful not to hit the plate in my hand. He squeezes me tight and as he does, I notice Frank Keegan from the local newspaper snapping pictures. Conall raises his free hand and clears his throat. "I want to thank Nora for welcoming me during the inn's off season and I want you all to know what a gem you have here in her. I hope you'll all enjoy this incredible spread of food and that you'll recommend the Cara Maith Bed & Breakfast to all your friends and relations. Now, get some food, have fun and Happy Christmas!"

The crowd is clearly exuberant with Conall's attendance and his ringing endorsement as they rush to the buffet table. Conall leans in and softly says, "There, I hope that helps ye out with the business."

I don't know whether to be angry or thrilled, so I murmur, "Thanks a million" as he leans in and gives me a kiss on the cheek before joining the others in the buffet line. I stand watching him work the room then glance down at my plate. I stuff a cube of cheese in my mouth and chew. The cheese tastes fantastic and reminds me I'd wanted to mention all the food is made with fresh, local ingredients. I'm a big advocate of the whole farm-to-table food sourcing and want to make sure this news gets around Boyle.

I draw a breath to guarantee my proclamation of local produce will be heard over the din but instead of a lung-filling breath, I draw in the cheese. Initially, I'm startled as I process the thought, *I've got a piece of cheese stuck in my throat*. Then panic sets in. I can't breathe, the cheese isn't moving. I gasp, but nothing. No air in or out and perspiration beads are bubbling up on my forehead. I stagger to one of the small tables, drop my plate on top of it and fling myself against it in hopes the force of me slamming into the table will dislodge the cheese, but that doesn't work either.

I'm desperate for air, no longer concerned with making an embarrassing scene but sincerely worried this may be my death scene. I'm going to die, right here in front of half the town and a famous footballer. The thoughts are running through my mind and I have a momentary thought of my mother, my father, Jack Junior. I begin flapping my arms and throw myself against the table one more time in a desperate attempt to free the blasted piece of local cheddar that's about to kill me at this very moment when I'm hoisted from behind by a pair of strong arms. I'm feeling faint, but the arms are strong and tight around my middle. I hear a voice calmly and firmly say, "On three." The words mean nothing to me, but I hear counting. "One...Two...Three" followed by a massive blow beneath my ribs and a projectile flying from my mouth - the lethal cheddar.

Tears flood my eyes as air returns to my lungs. I gasp, cough, and tears stream down my cheeks. The strong arms around my waist slip away and I hear the voice again, "You're alright, love. Just breathe, just breathe."

I do as I'm told, drawing in air in rapid, urgent breaths as I collapse into a chair. The crowd which had gone silent begins applauding. Jeanne breaks through the crowd and kneels in front of me. "Are ye okay, Nora? Can you speak?"

I wipe tears from my face, look into her concerned eyes, and nod *yes*. Jeanne lets out a nervous laugh and exclaims, "Well, that's not speaking but an encouraging sign all the same. Come, love let's go and tidy yourself." Jeanne turns to the on-lookers and says, "Go on now, enjoy the buffet, we'll be right back." She grabs me by the elbow, lifts me to my feet, and leads me out of the room. As we reach the doorway, she calls into the room where the musicians are standing, staring with mouths agape, "Could ya play a bloody carol for feck sake?"

※

"Here, drink some water, Nora. God, ye scared the life out of us down there." Jeanne hands me a glass she's just filled at the bathroom sink as I sit on the foot of my bed. I take the glass from her and stare at it in my hand before drinking. Finally regaining my voice, I clear my throat and sigh, "What in the buggery bollocks happened?"

Jeanne raises her eyebrows and admonishes, "Ye nearly died. That's what."

"I got that part, Jeanne. Thanks... I mean, did I just become the laughingstock of the town? Did I just ruin a pivotal moment in my business?" I hand the water glass to Jeanne, hoist myself to my feet and amble to the vanity and plop down in the chair in front of the mirror. I look at my reflection without seeing at first but then scrutinize this sad expression looking back at me. My hair which had been so neatly pulled into a bun on top of my head is now a tasseled mess with wisps of hair hanging over my eyes. My cheeks are tear stained with tell-tale black streaks from the mascara now smeared beneath my eyes calling to mind Heath Ledger's version of The Joker in *Batman*. Taking in this pathetic mess, I spy Jeanne in the mirror standing behind my shoulder with a look akin to that of someone who's just been told the family dog's been hit by a car.

"Nora, why don't you fix your face and hair and come back to the party?"

"Great idea, Jeanne. I'm sure nobody noticed. I'll clean-up, slip back in the room and we'll all go on as if nothing happened. As if nobody hurled a chunk of cheddar across the room. Ha! Brilliant plan!"

Jeanne draws closer putting her hands on my shoulders. "You didn't really hurl the cheese, love. You had the cheese thrust out of ye."

"Oh, God. That's right. I felt… I felt…" I pause to recreate the near-death experience in my mind. "Someone…someone counted to *three*. Someone had their arms around me…" I put my hands on the vanity top and turn back to Jeanne. "Someone saved my life!"

"Well, technically, *yes*, someone saved your life, tonight." Jeanne lets out a nervous chuckle and pats my shoulders. "Okay, love. I'm going back to the party. You hurry, don't want your guests to rush right out after eating, now do you?"

She hands me my hairbrush and scoots out of the room before the thought I have forms into a question. *Who? Who stopped me from choking? Who saved my life?*

Chapter 10

*December 16th – Woke up to find a dusting of snow on
the ground and large flakes still falling. Feeling mortified about
last night but all in all the party was a success. Conall's
presence, the festive celebration, and delicious buffet more than
made up for my embarrassing choking episode.*

I'm standing on a chair putting clean glasses back
in the cupboard when I hear the soles of Conall's slippers
shuffling down the hall. Seeing me on the chair he stands
in the kitchen doorway and in a groggy voice says, "Good
morning, Nora."

I glance over my shoulder before picking up
another glass, "Good morning, Conall. How'd you
sleep?"

He's motionless for a moment before stretching his
arms in the air and giving an overly dramatic yawn and
grunting, "I slept okay. You?"

I climb down from the chair, reach for a clean
beaker on the top rack of the open dishwasher and hand it
to him. He takes it from me and walks to the coffee pot
and fills the mug. "I slept as well as can be expected
considering." I shake my head as if trying to shake off the

memory of so publicly gagging and hurling a cheese cube across the room.

Conall's eyes brighten with the memory and his first sip of coffee. "Oy, I almost forgot."

He puts the steaming beaker down on the counter and begins handing me glasses from the dishwasher. We work silently as I finish putting the clean glasses from last night away. Finally, he adds, "That was a ludicrous display, for sure." Picking up his coffee he takes another sip then walks to the kitchen table and sits. "Good thing your friend Mick knew what to do. Bloody amazing how fast he darted through the crowd and saved your life."

I reach for a clean coffee cup, fill it and sit beside Conall. His expression is tender as he looks into my eyes and adds, "He was so calm, absolutely brilliant how he wrapped his arms around you and counted. It was like time stood still until that hunk of cheese shot out of ye. I can still see it flying over heads and landing with a thud right smack in the middle of the Christmas pudding. Brilliant!"

I scowl at him before replying, "Conall, I've been reliving that episode in my head over and over. Can we talk about something, *anything* else?"

I'm not sure why I'm so deflated over the incident. Everything else went well and when people were leaving, they made such nice remarks, but I'm letting those brief moments get me down. Conall plays like he's hurt by my admonishment, so I put my hand on his and say, "I'm sorry, Conall. I don't mean to be cross. I'm feeling sorry for myself. I wanted last night to be perfect, and…"

"It was perfect. You put on a smashing party. You've got to stop focusing on the wrong thing, Nora. If I only focused on the times I fell on my arse or missed a shot, I'd have never been any good on the pitch. Stop being so hard on yourself." He moves his hand from underneath mine and wraps it around my hand, "Last night was a gas. You're going to get all kinds of business from this, and if your guests didn't know before, they all know now, the cheese at Cara Maith is from local farms."

I can't stop the smile crossing my face. Conall seizes upon my mood change and says, "So what's on our agenda, today? Can we play in the snow?"

"Play in the snow? Are you serious? I've got to finish cleaning and there's a million projects to get busy with before I reopen in the spring, not to mention the loose ends I have to tie-off on your memoir." I pull my hand away from him, pick up my coffee and take a slow sip.

He looks boyish sitting by me in his pajama pants and sweatshirt. His hair is tossed wildly from sleep, giving him an impish quality, I've not noticed before. His blue eyes pull mine towards his and he pleads, "I'm only

147

here today. Sure, ye can take some time to play with me. You know, you need to loosen up and have some fun occasionally. You don't want me to think you're one dimensional."

He gives a wink and drinks from his beaker. He's wearing a smug grin because he knows he's taken my own words and thrown them right back at me.

I push away from the table and stand up. "Okay, I'll go change and we can play in the snow, under one condition."

There's a twinkle in his eye. "What's your condition?"

I walk to the hall, look back over my shoulder and say, "You've got to make breakfast."

With our stomachs full of Conall's bacon, egg, and tomato breakfast, we venture outdoors and despite the snow only being a couple inches deep, manage to piece together a pretty decent snowman to the right of the front steps of the inn. I can't remember the last time I made an actual snowman. Come to think of it, I'm not sure I ever made one, not even as a kid. As we're silently shaping the snow, Conall takes the moment to get personal. "What ever happened with you and that Dylan fella, anyway?"

I pause and look at Conall who is smoothing the snowman's neck into his body. I'm surprised by his inquiry and consider his question as I wipe a drip from my nose with my pink, woolen mitten. "I told you. I had to quit seeing him. It wasn't going anywhere. It had to end."

Still busying himself smoothing snow. "I know you said that, but you really loved him, *right*? How do you one day just make up your mind you're not going to love him?"

I keep packing the snow, staring straight ahead. I don't know where Conall's going with this so I'm uncomfortable but decide to be honest with him. He's been completely honest with me, so why not extend the same courtesy?

"I didn't just turn it off like a spigot, if that's what you're asking, but I discovered one day I'd been lying to myself about my feelings. When I found out he and Kimberly had purchased their retirement home I was jealous. *Jealous* I wouldn't be the one spending time with Dylan, *jealous* no matter how often or effusively he professed his love for me, loving me was too complicated for him to break away from *her*." I stop smoothing the icy powder and turn to see his crystal blue eyes fixed on me, no longer engrossed in his snowman-making. "I never want to be jealous. It's a terrible emotion. It's self-indulgent, petty, and it makes me feel like a victim. I spent my entire life trying to not be *that poor Fallon girl*, or *poor Nora*, and the moment I let myself be jealous of what

Kimberly had and I didn't, it hit me in the face. I want to earn my way in this world and taking or coveting what isn't mine would only destroy me, so I had to end it."

We're silent for a second, the only sound is birds chirping in the trees. I shiver as the snowflakes land on my cheeks and tears well in my eyes. Conall finally speaks, "Do you think ye could ever fall in love again?"

That's the last question I'd have thought he'd ask me, so I glance sideways at him. "Conall, I wake up each morning and say a little prayer for Dylan Cooney."

He reaches his arm around me pulling me close enough that I can lean my head on his shoulder. "I want to feel love like that, I really do, Conall. I used to think I wanted to be alone, but I can't keep up this façade anymore. I've proven I'm self-sufficient and I'm able to achieve great things on my own, but I'm not so sure I want to do great things all alone anymore." He squeezes my shoulder and I sniff back a tear. "Does that answer your question?"

He moves in and kisses a tear that's escaped down my cheek and whispers, "Aye, that answers it but ye know, you have to stop this tough woman act long enough to let the right guy in. Jaysus, you're a right tough old broad."

He drops his arm from my shoulder, gives me a jesting shove, and we both start laughing. Conall bends down and scoops a handful of snow forming it into a ball. Instantly, I recognize his intent. I squeal and try escaping as he playfully pursues me. Conall's got a devilish glint in his eye. I know he won't relent until he's thrown the snowball, so I make a split-second decision to flee. I scream, pivot, and dart around the corner of the house plowing into Debby who has appeared out of nowhere. The animal whines then barks as I sail over her, landing face first on the snowy cobblestone below. Conall still in hot pursuit, launches the snowball as he rounds the corner. The snowball soars over me and Debby sprawled on the ground, hitting Mick squarely in the breadbasket with a thud.

Seeing his colossal miscalculation, Conall slaps his hand over his mouth then slowly drops it. "Oh, bugger! Sorry, Mick. I was aiming for Nora."

Mick has a wry expression as he brushes snow from the front of his jacket. "Ah, I see."

I can't tell if he's pissed off or if he's suppressing laughter, so I clear my throat and say, "Um, fellas? Hi, yeah, I'm on the ground, here. Once again, I've fallen over your dog, Mick."

Both men look down and reach to help me stand. Mick's large, strong, un-gloved hand with traces of dirt under his nails, and Conall's somewhat smaller but manly hand in its fleece glove meet my eyes at the same time. I stare for a second not knowing which hand to take. There's an awkward moment as I study their extended hands, each telling a different story about the man attached to it. With little thought, I quickly take a hand with each of my own hands. As I grip both Mick and Conall, they hoist me from the ground. Once on my feet I see an exchange between the two men I'm not sure they've noticed. Their eyes meet and connect, but only for a split second before Conall begins dusting snow from my jacket. "Geez, sorry love, you okay?"

"I'm grand. No worries." I look at Mick who's stepped back and is tending to Debby. "Are you okay, Debby? You and I have a habit of running into each other, don't we girl?" I'm talking to Debby but looking at Mick.

Mick continues petting his dog. "Not to worry, Nora. Debby's fine. It's yourself I'm concerned about. Ye hit the stones pretty hard, let me look at your cheek."

In all the excitement, I hadn't felt my cheek smack the cobblestones, but now that Mick's mentioned it, my eye is throbbing. I slip the mitten from my hand and reach up to my right eye gently brushing my index finger over a small goose egg growing beneath my lower lashes.

"Oh, feck! Nora, that's gonna be a shiner for sure." Conall moves in to inspect, nudging Mick as he gets closer. "Ah, sure it's all red now, but there's dark purple coming behind the redness." He gives a wincing expression. "Sorry, Nora."

Mick in his calm command puts his hand on my back and says, "Let's get you inside and find some ice, now, shall we?" Directing me towards the kitchen door he pushes past Conall leaving him to trail behind with Debby. "Come on love, we'll fix you right as rain, not to worry." Mick's low tone is soothing, and I feel like a small child being cared for as he takes control of the situation.

As we enter the house, Conall repeats behind us, "Right as rain."

※

Mick tends to my wound and directs Conall to apply ice for ten minutes on and ten off for an hour. He then suggests the two of us join him and his father for dinner at St. Coman's Farm. He's so sweet nursing my swollen cheek, I find it impossible to say no to his invitation. Conall feels terrible about the whole incident so he's willing to go along with just about anything Mick suggests.

I clean myself up and apply a thick layer of makeup to conceal the black and blue. Then Conall and I depart for dinner at the Reynolds'.

Mr. Reynolds is bursting with excitement over having the famous Conall Kelly in his home and keeps repeating himself. "Are you sure I can't get ya anything, Conall?"

Conall answers politely with each inquiry, "Ah no. Not a thing, I'm grand."

While Conall entertains Mr. Reynolds by the roaring fire with stories of his escapades on the football pitch, I join Mick in the kitchen.

"Pour yourself a glass of wine and hop up on the stool, Nora." Mick points with his head towards an open bottle of Zinfandel on the counter. "We're having lamb shanks; that pairs nicely."

He sees me hesitate, "Ah, go on go on."

I grin and ask, "Where are the wine glasses?"

As he opens the oven door and peeks at the lamb, he answers, "In the cabinet to the left of the fridge."

I select a tasteful stem with a bold "R" etched in the glass of the goblet and pour the red wine until it touches the bottom of the letter. Mick sees me and says, "Ah go on, give yourself a splash more, 'tis the holiday season." He smiles as he turns back to inspect the potatoes boiling on the stove.

I dutifully obey. "I didn't know you're such an experienced chef, Mick. Where did you learn to cook?"

He peeks at the green beans simmering before replacing the lid on the pot. "Oh, you know, Nora, I suppose I sort of picked it up along the way. Being a bachelor all these years it was more out of self-preservation than anything. When I brought Da to live with me, well then I had to make sure it was tasty or the both of us would waste away to nothing." He gives a soft chuckle and begins pulling dishes down from the cupboard.

"Let me set the table, please. It's the least I can do." I point at my black eye, reminding him of how within twenty-four hours he'd managed to save me from choking and nursed an injury.

Tipping his head in acknowledgement, he hands the plates to me. As I take the dishes from his hand, our fingers touch. For a moment, neither of us move. Mick looks like he wants to say something, but instead jerks his hand away and turns to the stove.

There's a long pause before I ask, "Will we eat in the kitchen or the dining room?"

Mick looks over his shoulder and says, "Now, what do you think? My father is entertaining Conall Kelly."

"The dining room. Silly me." I turn and go to the dining room.

The lamb shanks are delicious, and I fill my plate with a heaping second serving of potatoes – something I never do, but it's been a while since breakfast and I'm hungrier than I realized. Conall's entertaining Mr. Reynolds with his stories and Mick is happily listening, taking pleasure in his father's merriment. Finally, after an extensive conversation about great Irish musicians, Mr. Reynolds insists Conall join him in the lounge to listen to his collection of Dubliners records.

"Aye, you've actually got a record player? I thought everything was downloaded these days." Conall teases.

"I don't just have a record player, as you call it, I've a brilliant stereo system. Come join me, Conall, and hear music that was great long before Bono and The Edge came along."

Conall looks at me with plaintive eyes, but I don't save him. "Go, enjoy the music, Conall. I'll stay and help Mick with the dishes. You haven't lived till you've heard The Dubliners singing *Black Velvet Band* on Mr. R's high-fi-stereo."

Conall glares at me then turns and follows Mr. Reynolds. "If you don't have to hurry off, I've got a few of Hal Roache's comedy records too."

"Ah, he's in for a treat, indeed." Mick whispers in my ear as he breezes past me with a stack of dirty dinner plates. His mellow tone as he glides by and the woodsy scent of his aftershave so close to my face distract me momentarily. I quickly recover and turn to gather something, anything, I can take from the table. I pick up the gravy boat as the first notes of *Fields of Athenry* fill the house.

"Oy, he's picked this one specifically for Conall."

Mick returns and scoops up several more plates while I'm still struggling to remove a gravy boat from the table and say, "Huh?"

"*Athenry*. It's what the crowd sings at the matches." He slides past me once again, clearing the table as quickly as a waitress in a London tearoom.

"Oh, right. I've not been to many football matches, but now that ye mention it, I do recall this song being played." I follow Mick to the kitchen with gravy boat in hand. He's at the sink which is filled with sudsy water. His sleeves are pushed up above his elbows as he immerses his hands in the dishwater and begins the arduous task before him. As he picks up the dish sponge, he looks and points with his head. "Go get that stool, bring it over here and sit down." He hands me a dishtowel and adds, "You dry, I'll wash."

I retrieve the stool, sit down and begin drying the wineglass he's handed me. One by one he hands me stemware and crystal. I dutifully dry each one and place it on the counter once I'm done. Mick is quiet as he works. We hear music and soft conversation in the other room but work in silence. Mick is vigorously scrubbing the roasting pan when he finally breaks the silence. "I know it's none of my business, but are you and Conall seeing each other in a non-professional sense?"

"Seeing each other?" I repeat the question because I'm caught off guard. Mick isn't one to get personal and he's never inquired so directly about anything this private. I'm drying a large stainless-steel pot with a dishtowel as I answer his question. "No. Conall and I aren't strictly professional, but it's not a romance, if that's what you're asking." I'd not given me and Conall much consideration beyond our discussions over the book and the handful of times we'd spent in conversation, so I pause my drying and think. I let out a sigh and add, "I think it's more of a friendship. He seems intrigued by me and wants to know what makes me tick." I shrug my shoulders and continue. "We have fun together, and he's a great listener, which is surprising. In a million years, I'd never have thought a footballer could be this..."

"Deep?" Mick stops scrubbing the roasting pan and focuses on me.

"Yeah. *Deep* works. He's keenly interested in me. Beyond that…" I'm stumped, but I don't tell Mick. His brown eyes are on me and the copper flecks are sparkling in the kitchen light. Mick's deep too, but different from Conall. He's about to say something when the volume in the next room grows louder. The Dubliners are cranked to full blast as *A Nation Once Again* booms and Conall enters the kitchen.

"All right you two, Mr. R's getting nostalgic. You can't leave me alone anymore. Out of the kitchen with the two of ye." He grabs my sleeve pulling me along as he belts out, "A nation once again, a nation once again!"

Conall's already dressed and downstairs when I saunter into the kitchen in my robe. The aroma of freshly brewed coffee fills my nostrils and I note his overnight bag on the chair by the door as I cross the room.

"Was it something I said?" I joke as I open the cupboard, reach for a beaker, and fill it with coffee.

Conall leans against the counter as I add milk to the steaming mug. "No, I promised me mum and step-da

I'd be home for Sunday lunch." He takes a gulp from his cup and swallows. "No doubt she's cooking a chicken and making a fuss over her prodigal son coming home for Christmas."

I move to take a sip from my coffee but stop, lower the mug, hesitating before replying, "Wait a minute. You have a step-father?" Placing the hot coffee on the counter I stand unblinking taking in his countenance. "Your life story's about to be published and *this* is the first I've heard of your step-father?"

Conall shrugs and grins. "He's the only father I've ever known so I guess I didn't even think to mention. Since I was a wee one in nappies, Frank Gannon's been my Da. I never knew my biological father and Mum never talks about him."

I shake my head to make sense of his revelation. "You mean your mother, Lucille, isn't Lucille Kelly? She's Lucille Gannon?"

He takes another sip of coffee and says, "Nah. She's Lucille Kelly-Gannon."

I'm more confused than before so I ask, "Your name is her name? *Kelly*?"

He walks to the cupboard, opens it, and asks, "Have ya got a to-go cup? I want to take this with me."

"Aye." Distracted, I reach for the top shelf pulling down a thermos for him. "*Kelly*. Your mother is *Kelly*? That's her maiden name?"

As he pours the hot liquid into the thermos, he says, "Me mum wasn't married to me bio-daddy. She gave me her last name to avoid confusion." He screws the lid on the thermos and adds, "When Frank Gannon came along, she fell madly in love with him. He didn't mind the package deal of Lucy and Conall, so it all worked out for the best."

I stand staring at Conall, not knowing what to say. After months of helping him craft his memoirs, he's thrown a wrench in everything with his off-the-cuff revelation. I sigh and ask, "Don't you think you'd like to tell this part of your story in your book? It's kind of an important fact. Surely, your formative years and the man you call Da played a significant role in your character development. Don't ya think? Won't your fans want to know the *whole* story of Conall Kelly?"

Conall looks at me for a moment before approaching. He places his hands on my shoulders. "That's me mum's story, not mine," he says softly. "How I came to be is her past, not mine. Frank and Lucille are the only parents I've ever known. Out of respect for mum, we'll leave it at that." I stare into his eyes, breathing in the aroma of his cologne mixed with the coffee on his breath. There's a twinkle in his blue gaze as he adds, "You're crafty with words, there's no need going into detail. Just make sure you talk about my wonderful parents and happy childhood in Donegal. *Okay?*"

His hands are still firmly planted on my shoulders. His eyes plead his case. I take a deep breath and release it, befuddled and confounded, I concede, "*Okay*."

Conall drops his hands, grabs the thermos, picks up his overnight bag, and opens the kitchen door in a whirlwind of motion. "Right, so. I'm off to Donegal then my dear, Nora."

I trail behind him as he opens the door of his car, tosses the bag in the back seat, and climbs inside. He's about to shut the door, but I grab it before he has a chance to shut it in my face. I'm baffled by his sudden flight from my home. "Conall, is everything okay? Did I upset you? What just happened?"

I lean into the gunmetal gray Jaguar, put my hand on the steering wheel and repeat, "Conall, is everything okay?"

He places his hand on top of mine and murmurs, "Everything is perfect, Nora. I'm not upset at all. I don't speak of my birth" raising his hands to form air quotes he finishes," '*situation*,' often. I'm sorry if I gave the impression it upset me. On the contrary, it doesn't upset me. It's something I had nothing to do with. It's more for my mother I keep silent." His face brightens as his mouth opens into a large smile. "Forgive me, Nora. The entire weekend was brilliant. You're brilliant, the B&B, your friends - all brilliant."

He lifts my hand from the steering wheel, gives it a gentle kiss and says, "Thank you, darling, Nora. Thank you."

I take my hand from Conall's, he pulls the door closed and starts the engine. I'm bewildered by his capriciousness, so I stand watching as he puts the car in gear. The early winter air hits my face. I glance up at the dreary sky. The icy wind cuts through me. Instinctively, I wrap my sweater tightly around me, crossing my arms, holding the sweater closed as the wind whips wildly.

Seeing my wounded expression, Conall puts the window down. His brows are knit together in thought as he runs his hand through his hair and leans out of the window. "Nora, you look like ye just came from a funeral. I can't leave ya looking sad. Now, cheer up, put a smile on that mug, and send me off proper!"

I shake my head. "I can't figure you out, Conall," I shout to be heard over the car and the howling wind.

"No need, Nora. It's all good. It's how I roll. You're grand. Absolutely brilliant, and I mean that. It's all good. Bye for now, love."

The window goes up, the car shifts into gear, and Conall drives away. I stand waving at his taillights as he departs Cara Maith and enters the N4. I watch as the car disappears, and another gust of wind lifts the front of my sweater shocking my midriff with a jolt of icy air. I clutch the sweater and dart to the open door and the warmth of the kitchen. I stand and look around the room, which only moments earlier had been filled with Conall's energy and take in the void his departure has created. I don't understand Conall, but I *do* understand he's no longer on the outer edges of my life. I'm not certain of his role, but he's a presence in my world – I care what he thinks, how he feels, and I notice the hollowness of things when he's not around.

Chapter 11

March 3ʳᵈ – I'm beginning to get into a routine and have many guests scheduled to arrive in the coming weeks. Cara Maith received a ton of positive PR from Conall's appearance at Christmas. Adding to that, we re-opened with a highly successful Valentine's Day Romance Package which sold out followed by a splashy feature story in a major tourist magazine. We now have multiple sold out dates!

Imelda is pulling a soda bread out of the oven as I return from gathering the eggs. The sweet scent of baking bread hits me the moment I walk in the door and instantly I'm transported back to my youth. My mother's soda bread was the most delicious in the county, and the memory of the two of us seated by the fire enjoying a hot cuppa and a warm soda bread on a Saturday morning is priceless. I watch as Imelda places the loaf on a cooling rack, closes the oven door, and slides the oven mitts from her hands. "Ah, you've a full basket of eggs this morning, haven't ye?" She nods and smiles.

Lifting the basket to show off the bounty, I return her smile. "Indeed. It's as if the hens know we're open for business again."

Taking it from me, Imelda turns to place the eggs on the counter beside the stove in preparation for the morning meal. "What time are the guests expected to breakfast, Nora?"

Before I'm able to answer Mrs. Flood strides into the kitchen. "I've got everything ready in the dining room, Nora." She breezes past me and places a hand on her granddaughter's shoulder. "Now, Imelda, Mr. and Mrs. Harrison, the couple from Manchester, said they'll be down at half past seven. Mr. O'Rourke, from Belfast was less exact. He said he'd be down around eight or half-eight. You'll need to plan accordingly."

Imelda glances at the clock on the wall, back at the eggs, then lifts the basket. "I'd best keep these in the fridge for now."

Mrs. Flood huffs and puffs as she grabs a crystal pitcher of orange juice from the table and carries it into the dining room. She's a tremendous help, but at times her nervous energy makes me feel stressed. I'm not even sure she's aware of the anxious frequency of her huffs, puffs and tuts as she goes about her duties. Sensing my thoughts, Imelda whispers, "Gran is a right mess when she's a wee bit nervous, sorry about that, Nora."

Before I'm able to reply, there's a tapping at the kitchen door. I don't have a stream of regular visitors to the rear of the house, so I'm not at all surprised to find

Mick standing on the straw matt when I open the door. He smiles, removes his cap, and in a soft tone says, "Good morning, Nora. Hope I'm not waking your guests." He looks down at his Wellies and I follow his gaze. The boots are clean with no signs of mud, turf or worse so he proceeds, "May I come inside for a moment?"

"Good morning, Mr. Reynolds." Imelda smiles and Mick waves at her as she exits the kitchen carrying a tray of dishes to the dining room.

"What brings you to Cara Maith this morning, Mick?"

He stands rubbing his thumbs across the tweed of the cap in his hands. "I've gotten an invitation in the post. It's a bit unusual so I wanted to share it with you, first."

Mick reaches his long fingers into his breast pocket, pulls out an envelope, and hands it to me. "It's very formal, isn't it?" he comments.

I take the ivory envelope from him, remove the engraved invitation from within, and begin reading… *Barrett & Cuthbert Publishing Co. and Book Seller request the honor of your presence at the book launch of "Pitch a Fit – The Conall Kelly Story" Seventeenth of April at half-past seven in the evening. Ambassador Event Centre Parnell Square South, Upper O'Connell Street, Dublin 1, Ireland. Open Bar, cocktails and hors d'oeuvres.*

I crinkle my nose, purse my lips, and reread the invitation. I run my index finger across the raised letters before looking up at Mick. "Looks like you've been invited to Conall's book launch."

I haven't received an invitation yet, so I'm taken aback Mick has one before I do, but I keep my surprise to myself.

"Well that's the thing, Nora. You see, there came a handwritten note with the invitation. It's from Conall. He'd like me to escort you to Dublin." He takes a small piece of yellow note paper from his coat pocket, unfolds it and hands it to me. "See, this came with the invitation."

I focus on the Catholic school-style handwriting on the yellow lined paper I'm holding and read, *Mick, please escort Nora to Dublin for the book launch. I'll make reservations for the two of you at the Shelbourne. Your friend, Conall.*

I hear Mrs. Flood and Imelda chatting in the dining room. The Harrisons from Manchester have joined them. I'm focused on the note in my hand and Mick's tall figure in my kitchen but shake off my momentary distraction. "Well, Mick. It would appear you're escorting me to Conall's book launch in Dublin, next month. Now, I must pop in and say hello to my guests. There's coffee in the pot… why don't you fix yourself a cup and have a seat while I greet the Harrisons?"

"That would be lovely, Nora." His expression softens as he slips off his jacket and hangs it on the hook by the door.

I pick up a pot of marmalade to carry into the dining room. I want to make my appearance seem as natural as possible, so things are comfortable and informal. "Good morning Mr. and Mrs. Harrison, did you sleep well?"

Mrs. Harrison is a stout woman with an expansive girth. Her hair is bobbed in a smart, short style that frames her round face. Mr. Harrison is a balding man of about fifty-five years, I'm guessing. Before either has a chance to answer, Imelda excuses herself to begin cooking their eggs.

"Oh, the bed was most comfortable. I do believe I was asleep the moment my head hit the pillow," Mr. Harrison says as he plops a heaping spoonful of sugar into the cup of black coffee in front of him.

Nodding in agreement, Mrs. Harrison affirms, "Oh, indeed. It's so peaceful here in the country, I'd imagine you sleep like a baby all the time. Back home, we live right in the heart of the city, so we're accustomed to the hustle and bustle of city life. It's lovely here in the country." She reaches for a piece of soda bread and begins buttering. "I'm elated our friend, Dylan, recommended your establishment."

169

Her thick Manchester accent halts me in my tracks as I plunk the marmalade in the center of the table. "You come to Cara Maith based upon a recommendation, do you?"

I pose the question as casually as possible, though I'm certain I sound as if the wind has just been knocked out of me.

Mrs. Harrison is stuffing the soda bread into her mouth, so Mr. Harrison jumps in, "Yes. Yes, we do. Our friend Dylan Cooney, he's a retired MP, he'd read good things in a travel magazine about your B&B and suggested Cara Maith would make a wonderful stopping point in our journey." He takes a sip of coffee, swallows and adds, "I have to say, Dylan gave us a wonderful tip. Everything has been spot-on. Yes, yes. We shall sing your praises, Ms. Fallon."

The blood has left my brain, but I feel my mouth moving. "That's lovely. I appreciate referrals. Please, enjoy your breakfast, I'll leave you to it, now." I back out of the room withdrawing as if leaving the presence of royalty, but I'm backing out of the dining room to escape. I want to run. Run from anyone or anything having to do with Dylan. I bolt down the hall practically sprinting into the kitchen where I find Mick sipping coffee, reading the financial newspapers I'd left there earlier, and enjoying Imelda's soda bread.

Mick looks up from the paper, sees my expression, and puts the cup on the saucer. "Geez, Nora. You look like you've seen a ghost. Is everything okay?"

I let out a long, heavy sigh. "Fine. Everything's fine." I run my hands through my hair and take a lung-filling breath. Not knowing what to do with myself, I place a hand in each back pocket of my jeans and look at Mick. "Mick, can you stay for breakfast? I'm starving, and I don't want to eat alone."

I'm finishing a bowl of muesli and Mick's mopping the last of his egg with a piece of toast when Mrs. Flood comes tutting into the kitchen, looks at the clock, and turns to me. "You know, Nora, it's half-nine and still no Mr. O'Rourke. Not a peep. Mind you, I'm not being unaccommodating, but he should have informed us if he was going to be a lie-about." She brushes her hands across the front of her apron and sighs before muttering," It's a bed and *breakfast*, not a bed and lunch."

I swallow the cereal in my mouth, but Mick interjects before I'm able to, "You seem irritated, Mrs. Flood. Is everything okay?"

His mollifying tone softens her irritability and her face reddens as she replies, "Yes. Forgive me, I'm so eager to help Nora, I guess I get a little put-out when things don't go precisely to plan for her."

I place my spoon in the bowl and push back my chair. "Oh, Mrs. Flood. Don't you worry. If it were the middle of summer and we had a house full of guests, then maybe I'd be concerned, but we aren't expecting new guests until Friday." I place a reassuring hand on her shoulder. Imelda enters and informs me Jeanne has arrived and is now tending to the Harrisons as they are leaving. I turn back to Mrs. Flood and add, "See, everything is right as rain."

Imelda asks, "Nora, I've got classes shortly and will need to leave in a few minutes. Will you be able to handle breakfast for Mr. O'Rourke when he's ready?"

"That won't be a problem. Your grandma and I should be able to handle *one* breakfast by ourselves." I smile at Imelda who's removing her apron.

Imelda hangs up the apron and turns to me. "Shall I tap on Mr. O'Rourke's door to get an ETA when I go up to clean the Harrisons' room?"

"Brilliant! Perhaps he's overslept. A courtesy tap on the door may be in order."

I leave Mick and Mrs. Flood in the kitchen and walk with Imelda to the foot of the stairs. Imelda proceeds upstairs, but the Harrisons are in the vestibule with their bags about to depart so I stop. "I hope your stay was satisfactory and that you have a safe journey, today."

Mrs. Harrison turns and smiles. "Oh, Ms. Fallon, everything was delightful. I'll be certain to go online and write a rave review."

"Oh, yes, indeed!" Mr. Harrison jumps in and as I'm about to bid them farewell, he announces, "I will call Dylan Cooney later today and tell him how wonderful the Cara Maith B&B is. He'll simply have to try it out for himself."

Jeanne pops up from her chair behind the desk and waddles over to our gathering. Her eyes are like saucers as she locks hers with mine and says, "Oh. So, you were referred to the B&B. How thrilling! Referrals are the best advertising of all, isn't that right, Nora?"

Jeanne's standing shoulder to shoulder with me, so I turn awkwardly to face her, "Yes, Jeanne, referrals are the bread and butter of the business. I'll be most grateful." I turn back to the Harrisons who are now departing the front door and say, "Thank you and come again."

The Harrisons drive away, I stand waving, then turn slowly to find Jeanne and Mrs. Flood who have now been joined by Mick. The three expressions vary; Jeanne looks about to burst with questions, Mrs. Flood looks relieved to have two satisfied customers on their way, and Mick is as always, hard to read – a mélange of calm, kindness, and a touch of pride is my best guess.

I close the door behind me and am about to encourage the gathering to disperse when there's a screech of horror above us. In an instant, all eyes which were focused on me look upward to the stair landing where Imelda has emerged. Pale and trembling, her usual self-assuredness replaced by a look of terror. Wordlessly, Mick lopes up the steps, three at a time gently patting the terrorized girl as he brushes past her and to the open door at the top of the steps.

Jeanne, Mrs. Flood, and I are statues, frozen in the entry. Finally, I find my voice, "What is it, Imelda? Is Mr. O'Rourke ready for breakfast?"

She's trembling, but manages to sputter, "The door... I knocked, and the door opened when I rapped...so I called inside." She slowly moves down the steps to join us at the bottom, "He didn't answer so I stuck my head in farther... and...and..."

"And *what*? *What*, dear child? *What*? Mrs. Flood says as she eases by me to wrap a comforting arm around her granddaughter.

Imelda is about to answer when Mick appears at the top of the steps and calmly commands, "Mrs. Flood, take Imelda into the kitchen and fix her a cup of tea. Nora, I'm going to need you to join me up here. Jeanne, I'll need you to call for an ambulance, please."

Without question or a moment's hesitation, we all do as Mick has directed; Imelda and Mrs. Flood scurry to the kitchen, Jeanne toddles to the phone, and I mount the steps meeting Mick just outside of *The Connaught*, Mr. O'Rourke's room for the night.

Mick's height advantage is more pronounced than ever at this moment as he places his hands on my shoulders and smoothly intones, "Now, Nora, I'm afraid your guest has passed away in his sleep. You needn't enter and see him as such, but I want you to brace yourself should you wish to go in the room."

Mick's eyes are sympathetic, and I return his gaze. Bewildered, I ask, "Are you sure he's not just sleeping?"

Gently shaking his head, "No, Dear. He's most certainly deceased. Perhaps hours ago, but he's no longer alive."

Mick's hands on my shoulders are firmly planted so I lift my hands and begin rubbing my temples as I look down and mumble," This isn't happening. This isn't happening. This just isn't happening."

Mick lets me continue my denial of the events for a moment before interrupting, "Now, Nora. This is a shock, but you're a strong person and no doubt this is a part of doing business, albeit an unpleasant aspect of dealing with the public, but nonetheless, these things happen."

I look back at Mick and focus on his reassuring voice and concerned eyes and finally find the wherewithal to respond, "Yes, you're right, Mick. I must remain calm." I fill my nostrils and breathe deeply to steady myself then add, "I don't want to see Mr. O'Rourke as he is, now. He is or *was*, a refined gentleman from all I could tell from our brief encounter, so I think out of respect, I'll not intrude."

Mick's hands are still on my shoulders as he softly murmurs, "Excellent decision, Nora."

Jeanne has climbed the steps and unconsciously has her hand at the small of her back, supporting her protruding baby bump. She stands next to me, wrapping her free arm around my shoulders. Mick lets his hands slip from my shoulders now that Jeanne is here, but my eyes are fixed on his.

Jeanne gives my shoulder a squeeze and says, "Why don't we get ye downstairs, Nora. I've called the Garda and an ambulance will be here any minute. Come, dear. Let's get ye a cuppa with Imelda. Shall we?"

Jeanne leads me to the top of the stairs, but I turn back and look at Mick's troubled expression, "Mick, thank you. I'm glad you're here. I don't know what I'd do."

Chapter 12

April 17th – I have survived the loss of a patron and the ensuing attention. According to his wife, Mr. O'Rourke dealt with sleep apnea, poor circulation, and a heart condition for years. Sadly, it was the sleep apnea that got him, and his final moments were at the Cara Maith. That didn't stop the gossip. Mrs. Roach started a rumor that Mr. O'Rourke had been poisoned by eating bad eggs from my hens. And naturally there were jokes, this is Ireland after all. Hence, I am looking forward to Conall's book launch in Dublin. It will be nice to take a small break and spend time in the city.

I stand beside Mick on the platform as the train pulls in and the door opens. His tall frame blocks the sun from my eyes as I look up, "Well, we're off." He collects both our bags and nods for me to board. I lead us midway through the car before stopping at our pre-booked seats. Mick tosses our bags on the rack above before plopping down next to me. We'd both decided the train would be the best travel option for our trip; we can sit back and see the countryside and not have to deal with a car in Dublin. Though the mystery of why Conall wants Mick with me, I still haven't solved that one. I had no idea Conall and Mick were more than acquaintances, but maybe it's a guy thing.

I lean back in my seat and gaze out the window watching Boyle pass by. A flash of Mrs. Flood, Jeanne, and Imelda running the inn while I'm away stirs me for a moment, but I shut my eyes and push it out of my head. Mick sensing my anxiety whispers, "Don't worry, Nora. Things will be just grand at the inn while we're in Dublin."

I open my eyes and see his countenance and feel a grin lifting my lips, "How do you do that Mick? Seriously? I'm beginning to think you're a bit psychic."

He gently pats my knee and in his velvety deep tone says, "No, not psychic, just a keen observer."

"I suppose, but Mick, ever since I returned to Boyle, you've been my rock. I'm not sure you know this, but it seems like everything or event that's been the least bit troubling for me, you've been there. Not so much to take over or spare me, but you've eased me through the difficulties."

He looks down at his hand still resting on my knee then removes it with a sigh. "Ah, you've been grand all on your own, I'm just being neighborly." A darkness covers his face.

"Mick, is everything *okay*?"

He lets out a soft sigh, "Aye. Everything's brilliant. I was just thinking of how far you've come."

I know what he's referring to and it's not the B&B. He's speaking about my family situation and my childhood. I reach across and take his hand and give a squeeze. "You've always been so kind to me, Mick and you're right. I've come a long way from where I was, but I'm a grown woman, now, and although I appreciate your protection and friendship, you needn't feel so protective."

Looking at his hand in mine, he cuts his eyes up from under his strong brow. The sun's hitting the gold flecks in his eyes and he's somber. "Oh, Nora, I don't mean to be overbearing or intrude because I know you've got this. You're no longer that awkward shy child. You're capable of anything ye set your mind to and by gosh you're fiercely independent. I've never wanted to seem like I'm looking over ye. Quite the opposite."

Realizing others on the train are listening to our conversation, he lowers his voice and continues, "Nora, if I'm around and nearby it's only because I enjoy your company and I love watching you work. I marvel at you. You don't see how brilliant you really are, do you?"

I squirm in the seat a little now that the focus has turned to me, but Mick squeezes my hand and carries on, "Nora, I learn so much from you, and you're sweet and kind and funny, that's why I'm always around. I think you're incredible."

He releases my hand, turns to look straight ahead, and eases his head back on the seat then shuts his eyes.

Are you kidding me? You tell me I'm incredible and brilliant and then put your head back to take a nap?

I sit for a few seconds pondering his remarks then look at him resting beside me. I shake my head and turn to the window. The train is passing a sheep farm. Fluffy black-faced muttons with giant red patches on their hind quarters remind me of Mick's sheep in my front field at Cara Maith. *Bugger, I hope everything will be okay while I'm gone.*

I shut my eyes to halt my thoughts and try to nod off. I'll follow Mick's lead and nap my way to Dublin.

Conall has graciously reserved adjoining rooms for me and Mick so we open the doors between the two and order tea upon our arrival. I notice how effortlessly Mick makes the transition from the shy Boyle farmer to an erudite gentleman as we sip the hot beverage and he regales me on the many locations in and around Dublin James Joyce frequented. I determine we must make another trip to Dublin after Cara Maith is closed for the season and find those Joyce haunts for ourselves. We agree to make plans, but knowing how that often goes, I don't consider our plans set in stone. Mick places his cup back in the saucer, looks at the clock and nods. "I guess we should get ready to go to this book launch."

I'd lost track of time sitting here in these splendid environs drinking tea with Mick. I smile considering how much I'm enjoying his company, "Yes, let's do this." I get up and walk to the passageway between our rooms, turn back and say, "Thanks, Mick."

I close the door behind me and return to my room to change clothes knowing the thanks wasn't only for the tea and conversation. The thanks are for standing by me ever since I was a kid and for being my friend.

❈

There's a soft mist coming down as Mick holds the cab door and I dash from the curb making my way inside the Ambassador Event Centre. Mick catches up with me in the entrance. "Can I take your wrap and check it?"

There's a chill in the air so I've brought a pale blue pashmina to wear over my dress. I got it on a trip to Italy when I was working with an Italian chef on a cookbook. It's a favorite and really sets off the silver satin dress I'm wearing. I grin as I think of how fitting I'd pair my

181

beautiful Italian pashmina with a spaghetti-strapped dress. "No, I think I'll keep it with me, but thank you."

Mick places his hand on the small of my back to lead me through the crowd. I see a cluster of people near a giant cardboard cutout of Conall's book and can hear his voice booming in the thick of the crowd. As we're weaving through the people, I hear Martin Wilson above the din calling, "Nora! Nora!"

Martin is crossing the room carrying a glass of champagne in each hand. He approaches and hands me one. "Oy, my favorite Oyrish girl." He tips his head back and laughs at his own joke. Mick clears his throat, extends his right hand, and says, "I'm Mick Reynolds. Nora's friend. Nice to meet you."

Martin's laughter stops abruptly, and his eyes widen. "Well, hello." He gives a conspiratorial nod to me and continues, "I'm Martin Wilson. Nora's longtime co-worker at Barrett & Cuthbert."

Martin begins sizing up Mick, so I interrupt, "Mick owns the farm directly behind the Cara Maith. Conall's invited him to the launch." Martin nods in recognition, but his eyes are dancing with curiosity, so I add, "He's a big football fan as well." With that they both look at me as if to say, *really?*

Martin slugs back his champagne and asks, "Nora, how are things at the old B&B? I hear you already lost a customer. Poor ole chap."

"Yes, Martin. I thought it best to get the dead customer out of the way early on in my business. He checked in, went to bed, had a bout of sleep apnea and that was that." I feel a tinge of guilt for saying it so matter-of-factly, but I really don't want to go into detail or dwell on my first and hopefully last client death.

Martin takes another sip and replies, "Ah, brilliant idea. Now you can add that to your advertising."

I tilt my head to question. Martin swallows another mouthful of champagne and says, "Oh absolutely, you know just a couple blurbs on your brochure, 'Nobody Poisoned Yet' or 'A Night at the Cara Maith is To Die For.'"

I begin to chuckle and even detect a wry grin cross Mick's face but Martin's laughing hysterically. He continues laughing at his own joke until finally he gives forth a giant snort followed by a small burp. "Oh, now look what you've done, Nora. You've made me forget my manners." He leans in, subdues his tone, and puts his hand on my shoulder. "I can't thank you enough for working with the great Conall Kelly on this book. I'm so glad he requested you for his editor. You're the best!" He gives my cheek a small peck though I don't notice because I'm focused on what he's said.

"Wait. Conall Kelly *requested* me?"

Martin gives a look that says, *well dah*. "Yeah, he asked for you specifically or he was going to another publisher." He puts down the glass in his hand, grabs my glass, takes two giant gulps and continues, "So natch, I had to convince you. Why do you think you were paid so handsomely for an easy editing contract?" He tips back the champagne flute to catch the last drips before adding, "I just figured you'd shagged him some time back in the day. He's known as a *player* and you're always so tight-lipped about your personal life."

A waiter passes, and Martin puts the empty glass on his tray. "Well, I'm off. I'm introducing Conall and he's going to do a short reading… so…. only one glass of champagne for me. Nice meeting you Mick, cheers, Nora!"

"Just the *one*? How can you tell if he's had too much to drink?" Mick mutters over my shoulder.

I turn and see him grinning down at me. "Good question, Mick. He's definitely a high-energy bloke."

We move closer to the small stage set up at the front of the room as Martin's about to begin speaking. Conall's standing behind him wearing deep charcoal dress slacks and a light blue shirt that's been tailored to fit his athletic build. Clearly, this man's been told blue makes his eyes stand out because when they meet mine in recognition the vibrancy and sparkle of azure flashing my way is like looking at two swimming pools. His entire face brightens, he smiles, and gives a tiny wave so I wave back.

Martin's not the most gifted public speaker but he does a proper job introducing Conall, especially considering I wasn't sure of his sobriety only a few moments earlier. As he wraps up his introduction and turns the microphone over to Conall, he moves a stool closer to the mic stand and hands Conall a copy of the book. Conall leans back against the stool, pulls the mic closer, and opens the book to a page he's marked.

Conall's not one to shy from the limelight so I'm surprised to see a trace of nervousness as he begins reading. I gaze around the room and note all eyes are on him and there's a silence he's commanding that I've never experienced before. He's reading, but I'm not hearing him. I'm too fixated on the crowd and how he's enthralled them. Men and women alike are riveted to his words. The wait staff is standing like statues in the back. No whispers, no clinking glasses, not even a cough – complete and undivided attention until finally, a light-hearted moment in his story furnishes a ripple of

185

laughter. I'm watching Conall and once again, I'm astonished.

I've come to learn he's much more than a jock but also a thoughtful generous man. Tonight, though, tonight… I see just how much he's admired. I scan the room again taking in the expressions of those in attendance. He's not only admired, he's *loved*. Conall Kelly is loved.

I note Mick's presence next to me and glance up. He's absorbed in Conall's reading as well but takes notice of me looking at him. He smiles and lightly places his hand on my shoulder but only for a moment before slipping it back into his trouser pocket.

I direct my gaze back towards Conall who has finished reading. "I'll be delighted to answer any questions." He grins as hands shoot into the air in front of him. My head is dizzy with a whirlwind of thoughts: Conall, the crowd, our friendship, well I think it's a friendship. I look again at Mick and consider his strength, his loyalty, and his friendship. Well, I think it's a friendship.

My thoughts are interrupted when Conall announces, "I'll begin signing books in five-minutes, but first, I need to go say hello to my amazing editor, Nora Fallon." He jumps from the stage, bounds through the gathering and plants a wet kiss on my cheek. "Oy, Nora, you're looking gorgeous, tonight. Aren't ye a fine thing?" Conall turns to Mick and adds, "Howaya, ye big bollix?"

For a second, I'm not certain Mick's okay with this gross display of over-familiarity but he dryly retorts, "I'm just grand, ye muck savage." Mick's expression is deadpan but Conall roars with laughter and slaps him on the back. "Ah, Jaysus, you're brilliant, Mick. Absolutely brilliant!" Turning back to me, he whispers, "Are your accommodations at the Shelbourne to your fancy?"

His eyes are sparkling and his energy's kinetic, so I respond with an enthusiastic, "Indeed!"

From across the room Martin appears and interrupts. "Hate to break up this little cozy chat, but the place is jammers with people wanting autographed copies of *Pitch a Fit* so before folks start pitching a fit" … he winks and pulls Conall by the elbow towards a table covered with books stacked in piles ten high.

Mick leans in, "Looks like he'll be busy for a while. Why don't we find a glass of wine and visit the buffet?"

Mick leads me through the buffet, and we snag an open table to sit down and eat. Once I'm seated, he looks towards the bar. "Ah ha, perfect timing. A glass of Chardonnay for the lady?"

I see there's nobody at the bar, so I smile and answer, "I'd love one, thanks, Mick. Brilliant!" He strolls over to the bar as I inspect the offerings on my plate. As he returns bearing two glasses, he sees me scrutinizing the hors d'oeuvres and teases, "No cheese cubes on yer plate, I hope."

He puts the glasses down and sits beside me. I'm unaccustomed to his teasing so I feign indignation and say, "No, I'm off the cheese. I think it's unwise to take any chances on Conall's big night. Don't want to make it all about me by staggering around the room, convulsing and gasping for air." He reaches over, places his hand on mine, and looks me in the eye. "Good decision. Good decision."

His voice is serious but there's playfulness in his eyes, so I let out a giggle breaking his solemnity and we both laugh heartily until he pauses. "Stop the lights! Is this Nora Fallon laughing out loud? In public, no less?"

I stop laughing. "Are you saying I've forgotten how to laugh?"

"No. Not at all. It's just been a while since I've seen you do it."

I take a sip as I consider what he's said. "I suppose I've been a little serious lately, but I've had a lot on my plate."

He's pushing a squiggly piece of pasta salad with his fork then stops, looks at me, and says incredulously, "A *little* serious?! There's a fecking understatement."

My mouth is full, but I've learned from experience to finish chewing before I respond. Holding my index finger in the air, I finish the cracker in my mouth, swallow, and say, "*Fecking* understatement? Look here, Mr. *Somber Sheep Herder*, if anybody's a little tense and closed-off from the world, he's sitting right here beside me."

Mick doesn't respond. He shrugs and jabs another piece of pasta salad. I had hoped to finally engage him about why the heck he's always so serious and alone but his silence and sudden interest in the plate before him signals this part of the evening is over. We keep munching in silence until two musicians hop up on the stage. A tall red bearded fella holding a fiddle steps up to the microphone and says, "Conall asked that there be some trad music tonight. I'm Seamus, and this is my buddy Donal on the guitar." With that, he places the bow on the fiddle, and they tear into a jig. Now I know our conversation has ended so I take a sip of wine and tap my foot to the music.

When we leave the launch party, Conall is obscured behind a pile of books pen in hand giving autographs to adoring followers. He manages to take a break long enough to bid us goodnight and give me a hug and a small kiss on the forehead before returning to his fans. Mick's his usual silent self on the cab ride back to the Shelbourne so I'm reticent to ask if he'd like a cuppa before bed, but I blurt it out on the lift. "Cuppa before bed, Mick?"

His eyes are on the numbers above the lift door. "Aye would be lovely. Why don't we get comfy first? I'll tap on the door." His tone is soft and I'm relieved. I'm afraid my earlier observation and moniker of *Somber Sheep Herder* sounded dreadfully caustic. I'm never sure if I've gone too far with him because he's utterly unflappable. I, on the other hand am most certainly flappable and tonight, I flapped – big time.

I pull my hair into a ponytail and put on a pair of fleece pants and an oversized sweatshirt then fill the electric kettle with water and plug it in. I hear Mick's gentle knock on the door between our rooms, so I open it and let him in. He's wearing heather gray t-shirt and sweatpants, so I comment, "Aren't we a sporty pair?"

He enters the room and smiles. "Aye, hope you don't mind the informality."

"As long as you don't." I grin back at him and return to the kettle to pour the water into the teapot.

"Nah. Hey, I hope you're not upset with me, Nora. I wasn't intending to criticize ye earlier. I was only trying to point out you're much prettier when you're smiling and happy and that lately you've seemed so tense. That's all…"

I carry the tea over to the table where he's seated, put it down, and have a seat beside him and he continues. "I think you're doing a fantastic job and I …." He hesitates before finishing, "I worry you're so hell-bent on proving something and being successful that you're not enjoying life the way you should."

He pours the tea into both cups as I study his face. His angular jaw and smoothly shaved cheeks are both strong and gentle and I find myself reaching a hand up and stroking his cheek. As I do, the words come to me. "Mick. I don't know what happened between you and Ava Roach. I hope someday you'll tell me… but she was a fool. You're a kind, caring, and gentle soul. I love knowing you're close by and I love how you care about me…" I'm now awkwardly aware of my hand still stroking his cheek and yank it away completing my thought, "I'll try to relax more."

I reach for my teacup not so much to drink but to break my discomfort. He interrupts my reach, takes my hand, and holds it in his. I dip my head, looking down at his hand and mine when I feel his other hand cup my chin lifting my gaze to meet his. "Fair enough, Nora. One day I'll tell ye how she broke my heart when she met that bollix in Westport and how ever since I've had to encounter that cow of a mother of hers and hear her brag about how grand things are for Ava in Mayo." The pain's written in his eyes and I understand how deeply wounded he was, but he tightens his grip on my hand then looks directly at me. His gaze is penetrating, his voice stern, there's fire behind his words as he adds, "I only hope you'll reciprocate and tell me about whomever it is in London broke your heart so badly you came home with a piece of ye missing."

Chapter 13

May 12 - Cara Maith is starting to receive more guests. Busy travel season is almost upon us! We're booked solid through early August and I expect we'll get more bookings soon! Today is the last free day I'll have for a long while so I'm going to Strandhill Beach in Sligo.

I tuck an apple into the picnic hamper Mrs. Flood has insisted I take with me. "Why waste a penny on lunch in a restaurant when you've plenty of delicious food here you can take with ye?" she mutters as she brushes me aside to place a mug and a thermos of tea into the hamper.

"You make an excellent point," I concede. "That's an awful lot of food for just me. "I look in the hamper and wonder for whom she thinks she's packing.

"Better to have too much and bring it back than not enough and be starving later." She tuts as she walks to the sink to wash her hands.

"Are you sure you'll be alright without me for a few hours?"

Mrs. Flood stands still, tucks her hands into her apron pocket, and looks at me. "Nora, I'll be fine. Besides, Jeanne is coming for a couple hours as well. This is the last day you'll have no guests for quite a while. Go. Take some time to yourself. 'Tis good for the soul."

Her eyes sparkle for a moment before a thought pops into her head. "Napkin! You'll need a napkin!" She turns and goes in search of a napkin, so I slip out the kitchen door and go to the garage in search of a folding chair. It feels a little indulgent of me to traipse up to Sligo to sit on a beach and read a book, but I've been so consumed with the day-to-day running of the B&B since re-opening for the season, I need to unplug and relax, even if it's only for a couple hours.

The bare bulb dimly illuminates the neatly organized garage filled with stuff I have no use for inside the house. I walk to the left side of the car and locate hanging on a hook on the wall the black folding chairs I'd gotten to take with me when Jeanne and I go to watch Des play football. I brush away a cobweb and put one of the chairs in the boot of the car. Once I've secured the boot, I sense I'm no longer alone. There's a cold wet sensation on my hand and I turn to see Debby below, nudging me with her nose. I distractedly pat the top of her head as I know, when Debby appears, Mick can't be far behind.

Something happened in Dublin and ever since, things are a bit uneasy between Mick and me. I'm not sure why and I certainly cannot put my finger on it, but whenever we speak, there's an awkwardness that hadn't been there before. I suppose that conversation over tea after the book launch has something to do with it. We were both pretty direct with each other. The next morning on the train back to Boyle, he was quiet, but that's not unusual for Mick so I thought little of his silence. It was just Mick being Mick.

He clears his throat as I turn away from the car. Debby darts to his side, tail wagging, and looking up as if to say, *here she is, I found her!*

"Are ya going somewhere, Nora?"

"Aye, taking a short daytrip to Strandhill. A little breather, if you will."

He knits his brow in thought. "Strandhill? What's in Strandhill?"

I don't hesitate. "The beach. The breeze. A good book."

Still puzzled. "You're going alone?"

His look is tender and filled with concern, so I pat his arm and reply. "Yes, unless that is, you'd care to join me." I have no idea why I've uttered this and there's a flash of anger at myself for potentially spoiling the last of my alone time but then I remind myself, this is Mick. He's got a million things to do around his farm and it's springtime for goodness sakes. I know he likes hanging out with me but there's not a chance he's free to take a day in the middle of the week to spend sitting on the beach.

He rubs the back of his hand across his chin and asks, "Have you got another chair?"

I turn and look back at the other chair still hanging on the hook. "Yeah. Should I put it in the boot?"

"You sure I won't be disrupting your plans? I'll be quiet so's not to disrupt the breeze and the book." He smiles brightly and his eyes sparkle as he brushes past me to retrieve the folding chair.

And just like that, Mick and I are spending the day on Strandhill Beach.

"What made you choose Strandhill?" Mick says as we cross the sand with our beach gear searching for the perfect spot to situate ourselves for the day. He's insisted on carrying both chairs slung over his shoulders as well as the picnic hamper, so I feel a tad guilty with only the beach bag and thermos weighing me down.

"I have a fond memory of Strandhill." I pause and think of the framed snap my mother kept on her dresser of me sitting on a blanket between Dad and Jack Jr. I couldn't have been more than six or seven-months-old, but I had a big grin on my chubby face and sweet curls peeping out from under a floppy sunbonnet. Jack and my father were like book ends propping me up between the pair. "Well, not really my memory. I was too young to remember the day."

Mick stops, looks around, then skyward before putting the chairs down. "This a good spot?"

Behind us is the village and the towering cliff, Knocknerea hovering above it. To the right there are rocks and to the left a wide expanse of sandy beach. I consider the sun's current position and the direction the wind is coming from before putting the beach bag down and agreeing, "Perfect."

Mick sets up the folding chairs as I take the plaid beach blanket from my tote bag and stretch it out in front of the chairs. Placing the picnic basket on one corner and the thermos on another, I anchor the blanket to keep the breeze from carrying it away. Next, I take a paperback book from the beach bag and plunk down on the blanket.

"Aren't you going to sit in the chair?" Mick looks perplexed standing above me blocking the sun.

"Not now. I will later, but I think it's fun sitting on a beach blanket, don't you?"

He doesn't answer but removes his shoes and socks and deftly collapses his long legs and flops onto the blanket beside me. Seeing the smirk on my face he's defensive, *"What?* You didn't think a lad this tall could get down to the ground?"

He rolls towards me a bit in his awkward landing, so I steady him with my hand, pushing him until he reaches an upright position. "No, Mick. Honestly, I've never doubted you for a moment. I've always believed in your ability to do whatever you make up your mind you want to do."

His expression softens and the seriousness leaving his face is replaced by a small grin. "Now, I know you're having a laugh at me." He pats my knee and leans forward to reach the thermos. *"Tea?"*

"Yes, please."

He pulls two teacups from the picnic basket and the small jug of cream and carefully pours from the thermos. Steam rises from the cup he hands to me, so I give a small blow across the top of the mug before sipping. He closes the thermos, returns it to the edge of the blanket, then leans back on one elbow stretching his long legs in front of him before taking a drink. The sun's bright so he squints as he scans our surroundings. There's a small group of kids with surf boards and wet suits on the far end of the beach. Nearby there's a couple with a toddler playing in the sand. The weather is mild but still a slight chill when the breeze blows, though that doesn't stop some of the heartier souls from swimming. I look to the water where Mick's directed his eyes to see a few heads bobbing in the surf.

"Crazy, aren't they? It's too cold to get in that water!"

He juts his chin upward in recognition. "Aye, but you know what they say... If the sun's splitting the rocks..."

"I suppose, but I'm fine sitting on the beach, thank you very much."

Mick takes a drink and looks at me. "So, tell me about this Strandhill memory."

I place my teacup on the book in my lap and hesitate before a smile crosses my face. "Oh, that. My mother had this framed photograph she kept on her bureau of Dad, me, and Jack Jr. It was from a day at Strandhill when I was still in nappies."

His eyebrows rise with his smile. "You must have been a cute babby."

"I was a chunk, my mother used to say." I won't tell Mick that Jack Jr. used to call me a Mullingar Heifer when I was little. "I was a chubby baby, and Jack Jr. liked reminding me of that long after I lost my baby fat." I take another sip before continuing, "Anyway, my father had taken a construction job in Donegal and was letting a flat with some work mates up there. He had a Sunday off, so he rang mum and told her to bring me and Jack Jr. to meet him in Strandhill for the day." My mind flashes to the thought of Granny giving my mother her "pin money" to hire a car to drive us clear up to Strandhill and another to retrieve us. The silly things we'll do for love.

"We all spent the day on the beach. Mom had her camera, so she took a snap of me and Jack Jr. with Dad, and that snap remained on her bureau until…" my throat catches as I finish the sentence, "the day she died."

"That's a lovely memory, Nora." Mick's looking into his teacup studying its contents somberly.

"Yes, I just wish *I* could remember it. I like to think there was a time we were a happy family. A time when Mom wasn't worried, or Jack Jr. wasn't angry at the world or my father wasn't out catting around and as drunk as a lord."

Mick winces. "Your mum obviously thought that was a special day or she wouldn't have kept the snap all those years."

I feel a little ashamed for taking a swipe at my father that way. "Aye, of course there were happy

200

memories. My mother was a smart woman; she must have seen something brilliant in the lad."

Mick nods, places his empty teacup in the picnic hamper, and lies back on the blanket. He folds his hands across his chest, his long legs extend beyond the end of the blanket and he shuts his eyes signaling this conversation has ended and it's nap time. I open the book on my lap, take a final sip of tea, and rest the cup beside me on the blanket. The cool breeze coming in from the water blows in my face, so I shut my eyes, letting the wind and sun bathe me as I breathe in the sea air.

"Ya, know, Nora. You've got to balance what you hold onto and what you let go of."

Snapping my eyes open, I look down at Mick who's still stretched out with his eyes shut.

"I beg pardon?"

"You've got to strike a balance, Nora. You've just told me a beautiful story about a happy day at the beach with the family."

"Yes, *so?*"

"So, cut it off right there. I'm not saying overlook all the sad memories, I'm just saying you've got to allow yourself to enjoy the good memories, too." He fills his lungs with the sea air before letting out a long breath. "You're exhausting yourself holding so tightly to the bad memories, Nora. Nothing will weigh you down or hold you back more than carrying the baggage of sad memories."

"You know, Mick. That's what I adore about you. These little flashes of wisdom you impart." There's a shortness in my tone I hadn't expected.

Mick opens one eye. "Aye, and there's the girl I adore. The one with a spark of fire who isn't afraid to stand and fight instead of moping about feeling sad over things she can't do a twit about."

I can't hold in the guffaw. I'm not even sure what I'm laughing at. "Okay, Mick. I hear ya, just take your nap, now, would ya?"

He smiles, closes his open eye, and is silent. I detect a slight twitching as he's about to fall asleep when he softly asks, "How long was your Da working in Donegal?"

"I don't know, six months, maybe more, maybe less." I look at Mick, waiting for more, but nothing. His mouth slips open and a soft snore emanates from his nostrils. *You've got to be kidding?* I let out a deep sigh and scan the beach. To the left of us, a family arrives lugging chairs, blankets, an umbrella, and sand pails. I watch as they set up their gear on the beach. The mother and father are arguing as the four kids charge towards the surf. The mum's holding a fifth on her hip as she scolds the father directing him where to place the umbrella. I let out another sigh and wonder if my mum and dad argued the same way on this very beach that day long ago.

I glance back at Mick on the blanket. He's softly breathing in and out. Reflecting on what he said, I sigh. *He's right.* I'm trying so hard to not make the same mistakes my mother made, I've made my own set of missteps. I'm forever focusing on bad memories. I don't give good memories any attention at all.

I give another deep sigh. *When did I become this woman? Is that how the world sees me or just Mick? Am I a bitter woman? Am I so uptight I repel people?* I've got a million questions, but Mick's sound asleep, his soft rhythmic breathing too peaceful to disturb so I keep my questions to myself and resolve to focus twice as much on happy memories. Two-to-one, that's my new and improved outlook. I fill my lungs with sea air and release a long, slow, breath.

"Jaysus, Mary, and Joseph, Nora. Give it a rest."

Mick's eyes are still closed. "I thought you were sleeping."

"Who can sleep with this Moaning Michael sitting by me?"

I bite back, "Moaning Michael? Who's a Moaning Michael?"

"That's another thing, Nora. You obsess." He rolls over on his side turning his back to me pulling his knees into a semi-fetal position.

I remain silent and in seconds he's snoring softly once again. *Am I a Moaning Michael? Do I obsess? Am I obsessing, now?*

My eyes are beginning to burn from reading, so I tuck the Cara Maith business card I'm using as a bookmark between the pages and close the book. I study the picture on the cover. There's a castle in the background and standing prominently is a beautiful ginger-haired damsel wrapped in a tartan cape. Her hair is windswept and she's looking up into the eyes of a barrel-chested Highlander in a kilt. His cream-colored blouse is opened practically to his navel and he's got one hand on his hip and the other on the hilt of his sword, ready to draw in order to protect this damsel, no doubt. I'm not sure why I love these terribly predictable stories, but I do and always have.

I remember the first one of these I read. I must have been only ten years old at the time. I'd finished the book I was reading, and it was Sunday, the library was closed. I found a paperback novel on the shelf in my mother's room. The handsome Highlander with his chiseled features and muscular chest intrigued me. I plucked it from the shelf and scurried into the den. It was winter, so I sat on the sofa with a comfy throw blanket across my lap. The house was always chilly in winter. I used the blanket for warmth and to hide the cover in hopes Mum wouldn't see it and scold me for reading a book I wasn't ready for.

I always loved reading; it was my escape. Sometimes, the school librarian, Mrs. Flynn, would let me stay in the library reading until she had to go home. I think some days she pretended to be busy just so I could stay in the library reading a little longer and not have to go home to an empty house. I remember her sympathetic eyes peering at me over the half-moon glasses she wore on a beaded chain around her neck. I know she was being kind, but her compassionate expression always made me feel like I was an object of pity. I often wondered if the teachers and sisters talked about me in the staff lounge. *Did you see that poor Fallon girl? You know her life is so hard since her father was killed. Or, you know, they don't have a penny to spare. Will ya look at the threadbare jumper on her?*

Odds are they weren't talking about me at all. Nonetheless, I was convinced each glance, each warm expression was laced with a subtext of *Poor Nora*.

I shake my head to interrupt the thought stream that's flowing back to painful childhood memories and remember Mick's admonishment. He's right. I'm doing it again, staring at the bad memories but not focusing on the good. Couldn't I just remember with gratitude Mrs. Flynn's kindness? Did I ever stop to think maybe she just liked me and was happy I enjoyed reading so much?

I look at Mick who's sleeping soundly on the blanket beside me. He's kind of cute when he's sleeping. I don't think I've ever seen him asleep before, so I study the back of his head which is towards me. His brown hair has a slight wave in the back. The deep brown has a strand or two of silver, but not enough to say he's starting to go gray. He keeps it closely cropped above the collar.

Turning my attention from his hair I look at his shoulders. They're quite broad and strong under the soft plaid flannel shirt. I giggle inside as the plaid reminds me of the bare-chested Highlander and his tartan kilt. I could see Mick being one of those heroes in a novel. He's all about helping the damsel in distress. I curl my lip and scrunch my nose at the idea since that would most likely make me the damsel in distress. The very thing I've fought so hard to avoid, I've become.

He rolls over, faces me, opens his eyes, and tilts his head towards the book on my lap. "Ye finished?"

I look down at the book and then back out to the water. "Nah, just resting my eyes a minute." I follow a bird hopping on the sand and watch it take off and land on a rock farther down the beach. "You get a good nap?"

He sits up, raises his arms straight into the air and yawns. His mouth is wide open, and his lanky arms and slim hands extend skyward. "Aye. Didn't realize I was so tired."

"Then you must have needed it. You do work awfully hard. I was surprised you said yes to this." I gesture my head in the direction of the water.

Mick moves towards the picnic hamper and opens it before answering, "I was too, but I've got Bobby Hannon helping on the farm for the summer, so I figured, *why not?*"

He lifts two sandwiches from the basket, one in each hand studying them to discern what Mrs. Flood prepared for lunch. "You can have a ham sandwich or a cheese sandwich, but you can't have a ham and cheese sandwich."

I give a snort of laughter remembering Mrs. Taylor from the café in town. A group of us from school would go there for lunch from time to time. She was a sweet older woman with a stern face and a voice that matched. We were all there one day and Mick asked for a ham and cheese sandwich. He'd seen an American program on the tele the night before and one of the characters had ordered a ham and cheese sandwich and Mick thought that sounded pretty good, so he ordered one.

Mrs. Taylor stood behind the lunch counter in her apron, hands on hips, glaring through thick glasses, and bellowed, "You can have a ham sandwich or a cheese sandwich, but you can't have a ham and cheese sandwich."

Mick was deflated and the rest of the kids in the café roared with laughter. It became a catchphrase. That afternoon and for several days thereafter, the entire student body was imitating Mrs. Taylor. *You can have a ham sandwich or a cheese sandwich, but you can't have a ham and cheese sandwich.*

I never understood why it would have been so out of the realm of possibility for her to combine the ham and cheese on the same sandwich. To this day, you cannot order a ham and cheese sandwich in the café.

Mick nods at the sandwiches he's holding. "I'm not kidding. There's one ham and one cheese. Mrs. Flood and Mrs. Taylor must have been mates in school.

I laugh and snatch the cheese sandwich from his hand. "Well, then, I know which one I'm having."

He looks bereft as he opens the ham sandwich and mutters, "Maybe, *I* wanted the cheese sandwich."

I climb up into the chair and Mick does the same. "My bum was tired of sitting on the ground," I add after swallowing a mouthful.

"Aye, this is a pretty nice chair." He puts his free hand on the arm and begins pulling on it, testing its sturdiness. "I should be okay; don't think I'll come thundering down to the ground." He smiles at me and takes another bite of his sandwich.

I watch the children from the angry family playing in the surf as I chew my food. "I'm thinking of purchasing a bunch of chairs for the inn. Good to have for guests in the warmer months if they want to sit outside and watch the sunset with a glass of wine or port in hand."

"Brilliant. Another brilliant idea, Nora."

"I thought so. Wouldn't it be romantic, sipping wine, watching the sunset over the front field while the soft baaing of your beautiful Roscommon sheep can be heard in the distance?" I take another bite and chew before adding, "Though I'm not sure about the pop-up style chairs. May not be fancy enough. Perhaps I should make an entire outdoor deck area with paver stones and wrought iron tables and chairs."

"Sounds expensive." He's finished his sandwich and has pulled an apple from the basket and is polishing it on his sleeve.

"Yes, but if this summer is as successful as I hope it will be, then maybe I can splurge and do it right."

Mick gives an approving nod before taking a bite from the apple. He starts chewing and then stares at the water in front of him. I note his hard swallow as he stands up straight and drops the apple. He lifts his hand to his brow, shielding the sunlight, and squints before running.

I'm still facing where Mick stood only a second earlier, but now I'm aware of shouting and screaming children near the water's edge. Mick is sprinting towards the commotion. Others on the beach are now aware of the disruption and are walking towards the clamor.

As I take my first steps towards the uproar, I see Mick dart past the screaming children and into the water. He's fully clothed but doesn't hesitate to plunge into the icy tide. In my periphery I see the angry father lumber towards the water with the wife and crying baby on her hip screaming in terror, "Which one? Who is it? Help!" She trots after her husband as others crowd towards the scene.

I push my way through three or four onlookers to get a better view. Mick's long arms are cutting through the water as he swims towards a small blonde head. I think it's a boy, but it's hard to tell. The child is screaming and waving its arms wildly as Mick reaches him or her.

Mick tries grabbing the child, but the towhead is flailing violently and choking on sea water. I squint to get a better view of what's happening. I can see Mick's mouth moving, he's saying something to the youngster, but the child just keeps on in his or her panic. Mick's wrestling with and trying to calm the child. Their heads are bobbing up and down and soon they both disappear.

The crowd gathered gasps in horror as both Mick and the child are no longer to be found. I feel the blood drain from my face and my stomach lurches. *Where's Mick? Surface! Surface, damnit!*

The mother with the screaming baby on her hip along with her other children are all standing at the water's edge crying. She lets out a plaintive wail, "Fidelma!!!!! Fidelma!!!"

Her anguished cry for her daughter puts a lump in my own throat as I see neither head has surfaced. My heart is racing and inside my own cry starts, *Mick! Mick!!!*

More people are gathering around us. One of the surfers is beside me with his board, "Is someone in trouble?"

I can't take my eyes from the water, but I snap, "Yes."

He tucks the board under his arm and lurches towards the water. As he paddles through the waves,

Mick's head reappears. I release the breath I've been holding, and the crowd follows suit with a collective sigh when the little blonde head pops to the surface. Mick has the child, who I now know is Fidelma, tucked under his arm and is cutting through the water towards the shore, pulling her behind him.

The surfer spots them, paddles ferociously and when he meets Mick, lifts the child onto his surfboard. When Fidelma is safely on the board, she sits up and the crowd breaks into applause. The sight of Mick, the surfer, and the tiny towhead is blessed relief. The mother standing still with the baby on her hip, drops to her knees and gasps, "Oh, thank God. Thank God" as her husband splashes into the waves to meet the trio.

The surfer drags the board from the water and Mick is pushing from behind. His clothes are hanging like sodden rags from his limbs, his hair is slicked back, and his cheeks are flushed. His eyes catch mine and for a split second I see the tell of how terrified he was, but in a flash the tell is gone and his usual cool expression returns.

The faint sound of a siren grows louder. Someone has clearly dialed for an ambulance. *I'm terrible in a crisis, never even crossed my mind to call 999.*

The surfer drags the board across the sand until it's far from the incoming tide, stands straight with his hands on hips, and smiles. His blue eyes sparkle under wet eyelashes, his hair is a short spiky patch, and his trim limbs are slender in the skin-tight wet suit. Turning to face Mick, he extends his hand. "Major props, Man."

Mick is dazed and looks like he's just heard a new language and hasn't a clue what's been said but instinctively takes the surfer's hand, shakes it and says, "Thanks."

Fidelma is still lying on the surfboard and is surrounded by her brothers, sisters, and parents. An onlooker barks, "Backup and give the child some air." Fidelma's mother throws a hateful glare towards the onlooker, but Mick steps closer and places his hand on the mum's shoulder. "She's right. Poor child needs some air, and look," he nods in the direction of the approaching medics who are traipsing across the sand with their apparatus.

She looks into Mick's eyes, and her tears spill over her cheeks. The baby is handed to an older child as the mum stands, wipes a tear with the back of her hand, and throws both arms around Mick's neck. "You saved Fidelma." She sniffs back tears and repeats, "You saved Fidelma." She hangs on Mick a moment before he stiffly wraps an arm around and pats her back.

The medics arrive and go to work on poor Fidelma who is lying flat out with exhaustion on the surfboard.

"Whose child?" Calls one of the medics. "Who's the mum and da?"

Freeing herself from Mick, the mum turns to the medic. "She's mine, her name's Fidelma and she's seven years old." She joins the medics beside Fidelma as the father approaches Mick.

I feel sorry for the bloke; he's dazed and awkward but juts his hand at Mick. "I can't thank ye enough. It all happened so fast. Didn't see her out there till ye were after saving her." He shakes his head side-to-side trying to rid himself of the image. Mick returns his handshake, and softly replies, "T'was nothing. She got out a little too deep. Couldn't stand; she panicked. Go be with your baby, now."

People are approaching Mick asking questions. There's a garda taking notes on a pad, and a photographer from the newspaper office in the village joins the group, enthusiastically snapping pictures of the soggy hero and the surfer.

I'm a bystander watching in disbelief. The medic announces authoritatively in the mother's direction, "She's breathing fine and hasn't taken in too much water, but we're taking her into Sligo General for observation." Her proclamation causes a few moments of discord between the parents and children. But it's finally agreed the mother will accompany Fidelma to hospital in the ambulance and the poor dazed dad will follow but will stop at gran's with the kids first before stopping home to change and gather clothes for mum so she won't be in her swimming costume in the hospital.

The frenzy of activity slows as the medics carry Fidelma from the beach with the rest of the family trailing behind. Fidelma pops her towhead up from the stretcher and waves at Mick and calls to him, "Thanks, sir. I couldn't swim anymore."

Mick smiles at her as the stretcher passes by. "And I wanted to swim in me clothes, so it all worked out fine, didn't it?" Fidelma waves her little fingers at him and in a split second the sweet exchange is over and Mick steps away from the noisy throng to join me.

Mick's clothes are water-logged, his hair is a wild wet mess, and there's a small scratch below his right eye and a trickle of blood sliding down to his cheek. "You're bleeding."

"Aye, little one's got some mean fingernails, God bless her." He lifts his arm and wipes his face on the soggy sleeve.

The crowd begins dispersing, the surfer nods at Mick and says, "Great work, dude" as he returns to the part of the beach near the rocks. A short stocky man walks over and places his hand on Mick's back. "I don't suppose you're wanting to spend the rest of the day in those." He tips his head at the saturated clothes which are now causing Mick to shiver a little underneath them. "Come with me, I'm Owen McGarry. I own McGarry's Clothing up in the village. We'll get ye some dry clothes."

Mr. McGarry still has his hand on Mick's back as he starts walking. "Come now." Turning over his shoulder, he calls to me, "I'll have your husband back in two shakes of a lamb's tail."

I watch them cross the beach and climb the steps until they disappear into the town before retreating to my chair and book. I try reading but am too distracted, so I stare at the water for what feels like hours before Mick returns.

He has a bag slung over his shoulder with "McGarry's Fine Clothing" emblazoned on the side and is carrying a takeaway tray with two large paper cups. He's sporting a pair of jeans that are not quite, but close to what I'd call skinny jeans. They fit his form nicely though they're not tight at the ankles like hipsters wear them. The tired plaid shirt has been replaced with a cobalt blue button-down he's wearing untucked, and on his feet, soft tan boat shoes complete his new look.

His expression is animated, and his eyes are dancing. He lifts the tray with the cups and smiles as I take it from him, "The lady working at Mammy Johnston's Café insisted I take a couple teas and scones in reward for my heroics." He laughs handing me the tray with the cups as he reaches into the McGarry's bag and produces a small white bag containing two monstrous scones.

He plops into his chair, stretches his legs in front of him, nods at his legs and says, "Well, what do ye think?"

I scan the new attire and approve, "I like it. Very modern without being a cliché." Taking a tea from the tray, I hand it to him.

Removing the lid from the cup, he gives a small blow across the top before sipping. "Aye, apparently when someone saves a life on the beach, it's a bit of a big deal in town."

I chortle, "Yes, I'd say so." I take a bite of my scone. To my surprise, it's still warm. The raisins are enormous and it's not too dry like some scones are. "Oh, my goodness, it's delicious."

"That's grand. Especially since I've been given a voucher for a dozen free scones." He bites into his and nods as he chews. "Brilliant."

We eat our scones in silence for a few minutes before I inquire, "How much did this new look set ye back?"

He takes a sip of tea before replying, "Well, like I said, it's apparently a big deal in town when ye save a life on the beach. Mr. McGarry said not to worry about it. My wallet is sodden, so he told me my money is no good in his store with it being so wet. Then he gives a wink, shakes my hand, and sends me on my way."

I give a smile, pat his hand, and say, "I know where I'm coming to shop for your Christmas present this year."

"Do you like it, really? It's not too modern?" His eyes telling me he wants my approval.

"Absolutely, you look terrific. The blue shirt sets off the brown in your eyes." I catch myself searching for the beautiful gold flecks and he fixes his gaze on mine. I continue. "It's a winning look, indeed." I turn and take another bite of the scone and we don't speak more than a few words for the rest of the afternoon. He's gone back to his silent self, and I've buried my nose in the book with the Highlander on the cover.

Chapter 14

June 1ˢᵗ – The busy season has arrived! Lots of visitors and guests booked. Thank goodness Jeanne is efficiently taking reservations. Don't know what I'm going to do when she goes out on maternity leave. Have promised to attend Des's GAA match this afternoon. Need to find something burgundy I can wear to support his team. Must be home before 5:00 to greet guests.

Imelda brushes past me in the hallway, her arms full of clean linens. "I'm going to change the last bed upstairs." Before I can ask, she answers my next question as to which room: *"Castle Island."*

She's halfway up the stairs as I say, "Wonderful, thanks a million." I sling my purse over my shoulder and walk to the kitchen where I find Mrs. Flood placing cups and saucers neatly on a tray.

She looks up from her work and beams. "It's ready for the next crew to arrive." Turning she reaches into the cupboard and pulls down the cream and sugar and adds them to the collection of china cups and saucers on the tray. "There, now all we'll need to do is make the tea and warm the lovely banana bread you've made." She wipes her hands on her apron, looks me over, and asks, "You going somewhere?"

"Yes, I promised Des I'd watch his match." Sighing, I add, "I have so much to do around here, I hate leaving, but he looked at me with those big puppy dog eyes. I couldn't say no."

"Oh, God love him. He's a sweet child, hard to say no to the lad." She pivots to the counter and places her hand on the freezer bag containing the banana bread. "Should be thawed in time for tea. Want me to take another out of the freezer, just in case?"

"No, that should be plenty. If we need more, I can always put it in the microwave for a few minutes."

She gives a silent nod, removes her apron and puts it on the hook by the door. "Well then, if that's everything, I'll leave ye to it. Imelda said she'll stay and tidy up until about 5:00. Will ye be back by then?"

I begin rummaging through my purse, looking for the car keys. "Aye, I've told Des I have to leave at half-four and no later." Finally, I grab the large shamrock keychain from the depths of my bag. "He assures me they'll win outright in regulation time."

"Will Mick be going with ye?" She's in front of the kitchen door so I'm facing her, trying to leave. "He's not been around much lately. There for a while he was a bit of a fixture." Tilting her head in a prying manner, she asks, "You've not had a falling out of sorts, have ye?"

"No. It's just a busy time of year for him."

She reaches for her handbag which is hanging on the hook beside her apron, turns the doorknob to leave, and casually adds, "Ever since he was the hero in Strandhill, he's been a bit scarce. Could be because of that shop girl."

And there it is. She's telling me something while she's asking me something. It's a great skill of Mrs. Flood's, but I already know. Jeanne told me the other day that Jim had run into Mick and a pretty blonde having a pint at Clarke's last week. I think I'll let Mrs. Flood have the satisfaction of telling me her gossip.

"Oh, a *shop girl*?"

She spins on her heels and her eyes light up. "Yes! Apparently while he was in McGarry's shop in Sligo getting his stylish new dry clothes, there was a cute blonde girl working in the shop." Still holding the doorknob and blocking my passage, she continues, "Apparently, she asked for *his* number. Well, in my day that was unheard of." She shakes her head in disapproval but goes on, "So, word around the bush telegraph is her name is *Reagan. Reagan!* That was a surname in my day." She gives another disapproving head movement and finishes, "and they've gone out on a couple of dates, though that's quite a distance to travel, if you ask me."

Strandhill is about forty minutes from Boyle, not exactly geographically undesirable, but I agree with her, "Aye, that is a fair drive for a date."

She's pleased I affirm her point of view and waits for me to say more, so I add, "But, if she's attractive and nice, and he likes her, isn't it grand he's met someone." I add the word, *finally*, in my head.

She takes a deep breath and thinks for a moment before walking out the door. I follow her and pull it closed behind us. We walk across the gravel and I stand with her as she climbs into her car. Before she closes the door, a wistful expression blankets her face, "'Tis good he's met someone. Just too bad he couldn't find a nice girl closer to home."

She pulls the door closed, starts the car, and I wave as she rolls down the drive. I walk into the garage, retrieve a folding chair from the hook on the wall, and place it in the boot of my car. Slamming the boot closed, I think of the last time the chair was used. That was the day Mick and I went to Strandhill. That was the day he saved Fidelma from drowning in the Atlantic. That was the day he became the hero. That was the day he met the shop girl. *Reagan*.

Jeanne is seated on the sidelines and waves her arms to catch my attention and call me over. I tip my head in recognition and trudge over to her. The grass is damp from an earlier shower, so I take each step gingerly to avoid slipping with my chair, my purse, and umbrella. I'd hate to land on my bum in a public setting such as this since the town already thinks I'm accident prone after the choking incident and the dead guest.

"How's my favorite geriatric maternal aged woman feeling this day?" I tease as I unfold the chair and sit down beside her.

She gives a stern look and says, "Oh, not you too. I've had about enough of this geriatric maternal age nonsense. I'm not exactly Old Mother Hubbard." Laughing, she goes on, "I'm exhausted, my ankles are cankles, and I can't get comfortable for more than two minutes at a time, which means I've not had a good night's sleep in weeks. Other than that, I'm brilliant." She gives a mocking growl and we both laugh.

I nod towards the pitch and ask, "Is this match going to be any good or am I in for a snore fest?"

Jeanne shifts in her chair and inches closer. "They're actually pretty good this year. If they win today, they move on into some big tournament. Des is so excited.

223

I think he's invited practically everyone he knows to come watch. Jaysus, I hope he plays well. Would be heartbreaking for him if it doesn't go well."

Rolling to the other side of her chair and sliding back, she continues, "He's even invited Conall Kelly."

"What?" I sit forward and ask again, "What?"

"Sure, ye know he'd been telling all his mates how his mum knows Conall Kelly and that we're good friends with him, so he wrote Conall a lovely email inviting him to his big match."

I'm dazed momentarily but inquire, "How did Des get Conall's email address?"

Jeanne lowers her chin, tucks her lower lip in and looks at me sheepishly before responding, "I may have given Des his email address."

"How did you get Conall's email address?" Before I finish my question, the light comes on in my head. "You got it from our client records, didn't you?"

Before I can tear into Jeanne and remind her our client records are private and under no circumstance do we share information, let alone how unethical it is, I detect tears forming in the corners of both her eyes. As a tear escapes and rolls down her cheek she whimpers, "I'm sorry, Nora. I know how improper it was to give Des Conall's email, but you two are friends first and the lad was so excited, I didn't think you'd mind." She wipes her cheek on her sleeve and adds, "Damn these pregnancy hormones. I turn into a puddle over the slightest thing."

She pulls a tissue from her pocket and dabs her eyes. "Can ye forgive me, Nora? I'll never do something like this again, I promise."

Jeanne's pitiful as she blows her nose into the tissue. I look at her hands and see her swollen fingers, her gold wedding band so snug it appears to be restricting blood flow to the rest of her hand. If this baby doesn't come soon, I'm afraid she'll either have an emotional breakdown or explode. Taking pity, I'm about to give her absolution when some kids blaze past us shouting, "He's here! He's here!"

I don't have to look, I already know. It's Conall.

He's striding towards us surrounded by kids that are yapping like a pack of dogs, "Mr. Kelly! Conall!" He tries navigating through them but stops and throws his hands in the air before calming them. "I tell ye what, if you all focus on the match, I'll hang around for twenty-minutes afterwards for questions, photos, autographs – the lot. But only twenty-minutes and only if ye stay focused on your match, *deal*?"

A tall slender boy with a shock of red hair jumps in the air and shouts, "Yes!" Another kid adds, "Sweet!" This seems to placate the kids and when Conall points towards their coach, they hurry off practically skipping at the thought of hanging out with the great Conall Kelly after the match.

Conall raises his chin towards me and Jeanne in recognition and walks to where we're sitting. I don't know whether to stand and greet him since I know Jeanne will try and do the same but fail miserably to hoist herself from the chair, but Conall jumps in, "Stay seated ladies, stay seated!" He bends down giving each of us a small peck on the cheek. Although the kids are on the pitch kicking a ball around in pre-game drills, all eyes are on Conall. One of them calls out, "Oh my gosh, Des! Conall Kelly kissed your mum!"

The kid's remark causes Conall to laugh loudly. Jeanne and I join in but as suddenly as the laughter began, Jeanne melts into tears once again, adding, "I'm so sorry, Nora."

Conall's eyes quiz me about Jeanne's unusual reversal of emotion so I shake my head and mouth the word, *hormones*. Nodding in understanding he ignores the tears and says, "Haven't brought a chair. Have ye another I might sit down with ye?"

Jeanne has an extra in her car, so she tosses him the keys and sends him on his way to retrieve the chair. She whispers, "I never in a million thought he'd actually come."

I direct my eyes to the pitch where the match is about to start, "Well, he did."

Conall returns, places the chair beside mine, and sits down. He's wearing a pair of khaki twill trousers, a white polo shirt, and loafers. I'm not sure if it's cologne or deodorant, but he's got a fresh woodsy scent about him that's pleasant and manly. His skin is bronze, so I ask, "Have you been to the beach?"

Keeping his eyes on the pitch he replies, "Aye. I spent a couple days at the Jersey shore in America."

A pack of kids on the pitch charges past towards the goal, the tall lad with the ginger hair strikes the ball hard towards the net but misses. The crowd, including Conall, lets out a collective *Ugh!*

"America? What were you doing in America?"

There's a whistle on the pitch and a break in play so Conall turns to me and answers, "I was in New York for a couple days working on a project, so I thought to meself, *why not hit the beach?*"

Play resumes and he's back into the match and clearly not going to be forthcoming with more details so I let it drop. As he and Jeanne closely follow the ball and the kids chasing the ball, I'm running scenarios through my head, thinking about what kind of *project* he could have in New York.

227

Maybe it's something for charity. He's very philanthropic. *Or*, maybe he's being coy and it's really a girl or someone he's dating. *Or*, what if he's moving to America to be a sports announcer over there. Do they have football? I think they do, only they call it soccer. As the possibilities fill my head, I catch out of the corner of my eye a tall male figure escorting a diminutive blonde in our direction. As they near us, I see. It's Mick and the shop girl.

Jeanne struggles to straighten herself in her seat as Mick and the shop girl approach. Mick towers over her petite frame. She's got long golden curls tied back in a smart ponytail and the pair of aviator sunglasses shading her eyes confer an aura of Hollywood glamour. Jeanne whispers, "Do you think she's over 21?"

I give a muffled snicker. "Let's hope so for Mick's sake."

Mick raises his hand in a semi-wave and as they reach our spot on the side of the pitch, he greets us. "Alannah Reagan, I'd like you to meet Nora, Jeanne, and Conall." She lifts the sunglasses from her eyes and places them on top of her head, smiles, and says "Hi, so nice meeting you. Mick's told me so much about you all." Before any of the group can respond, there's a shout from the pitch and the ball comes hurtling at our little gathering. Conall instinctively reacts, jumps in front of me, and catches it just as it's about to slam me in the face.

The crowd breaks into applause as Conall tosses the ball to the referee. Perfect. Absolutely perfect. His face reddens, and he bends slightly and says, "You're welcome, Ms. Fallon."

I bite my lower lip to keep the grin from my face. "Thanks, Conall."

Jeanne exclaims, "Oh, my gosh! Conall, you saved the day. That ball was heading straight for Nora's face. That could have been a broken nose or a pair of black eyes at the least."

The whistle sounds and play resumes. Most eyes return to the pitch, but I feel Alannah's gaze on me. "So, Nora, Mick tells me you were with him at the beach the day he saved the child from drowning." She's now standing beside my chair and leans down, places her hand on my shoulder and adds, "Wasn't he simply amazing?"

I look up at her over my shoulder. Her pale pink lip gloss accentuates her youthful appearance, but up close I can see she may be slightly older than my first estimation. I want to hate this cute shop girl, but I can't. She seems sweet and charming. I look up at Mick beside her. His eyes are directed towards the pitch but no doubt he hears us speaking. "Yes... Mick was amazing that day. He always amazes me. He's one of those special people

229

who runs towards trouble when everyone else's instincts tell them to head the opposite direction."

Alannah nods in agreement. "I can so see him being like that."

I hadn't noticed Conall focusing on the conversation between me and Alannah when he contributes, "Aye, ye know I read about his heroism clear up in Donegal." He gets up from his chair to stand closer to Alannah and is now directly behind my chair, so I must crook my neck to see him.

Alannah smiles at Conall. "You live in Donegal?"

"Aye. Not full-time. I've got a place in Dublin where I spend most of the year, but I grew up in Donegal and my parents are still there so that's where I go when I want to go home."

She smiles and asks Conall, "So do you work in Dublin and commute to Donegal?"

I smirk because it's apparent Alannah has no clue, she's speaking with the famous Conall Kelly, hero of the pitch, athlete extraordinaire, and ladies' man.

Before Conall can answer her question, Mick says, "Conall played football. He's just retired so he's able to live in Dublin, Donegal, or wherever his new endeavors take him, which lately seems to include Boyle."

We're all quiet for a moment until Conall breaks the silence. "Indeed. I'm between places for now, but I'm doing some charity work and I've got an opportunity to be a color announcer for my old team, and the possibility of a small art exhibition in New York so there's lots happening in me life."

Alannah comes back with another question, "So, what brings you to Boyle?"

Mick is standing next to Alannah rocking back and forth with his hands in his pants pockets. He's looking at the pitch, but his expression tells me he's more interested in the conversation. I can't tell if he's angry or not, but there's a vein on the side of his jaw bulging and pulsing. I've never noticed it before, so I'm riveted on Mick as Conall answers Alannah's question.

"Des brings me here today. He wanted me to come watch his match. However, it was Nora who brought me here originally. She edited my biography, which went on sale in April, by the way."

Alannah looks at me, then at Mick, and finally at Conall. "Wait. I thought Nora owns a bed and breakfast."

Conall opens his mouth to explain but Mick jumps in first. "Nora worked for a major publishing company before buying the Cara Maith. She's a hugely successful businesswoman. The door on the Cara Maith is painted red. Tradition says a red door represents a house that's

231

paid for in full. That's our Nora, so successful she bought the place outright."

Alannah is quiet at first but finally adds, "Wow, Nora. That's so cool. You worked for a publisher? I love books."

That's what she got out of Mick's answer? Really?

I hear Conall behind me give a muted, *heh, heh, heh.* Mick shouts, "Kick it Des, kick it!" Jeanne is looking wide-eyed at me and whispers, "What in the buggery hell?"

I shrug my shoulders and we both look at the pitch just in time to see Des score.

The rest of the first half is a blur of inane conversation interrupted occasionally by action on the pitch. At half-time Mick and Alannah leave us to sit in the bleachers. I'm not certain if that's because she's bored, tired of standing, or he's done making small talk. I look at Jeanne and ask, "Do you want to go get some crisps?" She's got both legs stretched in front of her and begins rocking forward trying to get enough momentum to stand. I jump from my seat, take her left hand and pull her forward.

"Success!" Conall exclaims.

"Can we get you anything Conall? We're going to the snack bar."

He shrugs. "Maybe a bottle of water."

"Got it." Jeanne says.

We pass the bleachers where Mick's sitting and I call to him, "We're going to the snack bar. Can we get ye anything?"

Mick stands and calls back, "I'll go with ye." Turning he looks to Alannah, "Would you like anything?"

She smiles up at him and gently replies, "Maybe a Diet Coke."

Mick lights up at her soothing voice and sweet face. "Diet Coke it is my lady." He lumbers down from the top bleacher to join us.

I feel guilty for wanting to dislike Alannah. She doesn't come across as a scholar, but she's kind and he's clearly smitten. So, I say as we cross the grass and progress towards the snack bar, "She's lovely, Mick."

In support of my assessment, Jeanne adds, "Oh, yes. Lovely, Mick. Absolutely lovely."

He stares ahead and just as we reach the snack bar says in a hushed tone, "She is lovely, isn't she?" He puts his hand out to direct me and Jeanne to go in front of him to the counter. Jeanne steps up and I hang back with Mick.

"Any long-term relationship potential?"

He gives a blank stare as he studies the menu hanging over the snack bar. "Oh, who knows. She's lovely, but a wee bit young and it's early days."

Jeanne stuffs two packets of pickled onion flavored Taytos and two bottles of water in the pockets of her jumper. She moves to the side so I'm able to place my order and so is Mick. The three of us are moving away with arms and pockets filled as it happens.

Mick sees her first because he's no longer walking next to me but has dropped a step behind us. Jeanne having just crammed a crisp into her mouth coughs, as if she's having difficulty swallowing. My mouth drops open. Standing in front of us are Nancy Roach and her daughter, Ava.

There's no way of avoiding each other. The entire group has recognized each other too late to permit evasion strategies. We're all set for an unavoidable face-to-face encounter. I decide to manage the situation. "Hello, Mrs. Roach."

She haughtily lifts her chin. "Hello, Nora." She nods and adds, "Jeanne… *Mick*." She practically spits out Mick's name, which forces a soft chuckle from Jeanne. We all stand frozen before I interrupt the silence and reach out my hand to the slender blonde beside her. "You may not remember me, but I'm Nora Fallon. We were in school together." Of course, she remembers me, but I'm letting her off the hook and giving her a fresh start as an adult. Perhaps time in Westport paired with the fact we're adults has made her a little kinder.

Ava juts her hand into mine and shakes it quickly before shoving her hand back into her jacket pocket. She regains composure and flashes a smile. "Oh, of course I remember you, Nora. Mother tells me you've bought the old parochial house and made it into an inn. How industrious of you."

"Yes, that's me. Industrious Nora." I glance at the hotdog in my hand, trying to think of something to say. "So, what brings you to the match?"

"I've come home for a visit."

Mrs. Roach interrupts, "Yes, she's home from Westport on a visit so naturally we wanted to come support her nephew who plays for Boyle."

Jeanne adds, "Oh, that's right. I forgot the Roach boy on the team is your grandson."

No, she didn't but I admire Jeanne for pretending she did.

Mick finally speaks. "Hello, Ava. Long time no see."

Ava places an awkward semi-smile on her face and agrees. "Yes, it's been a long time, Mick. Nice to see you."

The unease and awkwardness of this moment are more than I can take. I clear my throat to speak but Mrs. Roach intercedes, "Well, we've got to be leaving you all now. We don't want to be late for the beginning of the second half." She practically shoves Ava to the side, and they walk by us towards the snack bar. The entire encounter lasts maybe thirty seconds but feels like an hour. A long, icy hour. The rest of the way back to our seats is eerily silent. Mick, being a man of few words to begin with, is mute and Jeanne, who ordinarily would be chirping like a parakeet, is restrained.

Mick takes the Diet Coke and lopes to the top bleacher, hands it to the unaware Alannah, and sits down beside her. Jeanne and I simultaneously return our attention towards the pitch before she finally breathes out, "Well, that was brutal." She stuffs a few crisps into her mouth, chews, then swallows before completing her thought. "Thank goodness he's got that bitta fluff to soften the blow of running into that lot." She tips her head in the direction of Mick and Alannah in the bleachers.

Returning to our seats and Conall, he asks, "Did ye get me water?"

Jeanne pulls the bottle from her pocket and hands it to him. He opens it, takes a long sip, replaces the cap, and says, "So what did I miss?"

My first thought is to not go into what just happened by the snack bar, but then I decide, *Why not?* I direct him with my index finger to come closer. Conall leans in close and I quietly recount, "We were walking back from the snack bar and ran into the only woman Mick ever loved. His ex-fiancée is here with her mum watching her nephew play."

"Ouch, that's got to hurt." He glances up at the bleachers then back to me. "Good thing he's got that young blade with him to keep him distracted. Where is she? His former fiancée?"

I discreetly point at Ava. Conall shrugs then turns back towards the action on the pitch. "Who broke it off? Him or her?"

Jeanne answers, "I've heard he did, but I've also heard she did. No idea what happened."

I sit quietly watching the match, but my mind is focused on Conall's question. *Who broke it off?*

If it was Mick, which I've always thought it was, he must have had good reason. He's as loyal as they come, no infidelity on his part, that's for sure. So, *if* he did break it off, it was either because he was brutally honest and felt she was completely wrong for him, *or* ... I turn to the left to get a better look at Ava and her mum who are seated on the sideline at the far end of the pitch. Ava's hair falls in soft curls landing on her shoulders. She's wearing a pair of dark sunglasses hiding her eyes from the sun and perhaps more. She's attractive and has certainly aged much better than her mother had at thirty-seven.

I angle myself to see Mick and Alannah engaged in conversation. He's pointing to the goal and then back at one of the fielders. I can't tell if he's having fun or not - most men I know prefer not to have to explain the game while watching - but he's such a patient soul he'd never complain. Furthermore, she's an attractive young lady. I'll bet if she took her hair down from that ponytail, she'd look a great deal like Ava.

My mind races as I swivel my head from Alannah, then towards Ava, and back again. Oh, my goodness, Alannah is Ava's doppelgänger. She's not an exact replica, but the resemblance is extraordinary. I give another contrasting glimpse of each woman, turn my eyes towards the pitch and sigh.

Conall bends to my ear and whispers, "Took ye long enough to figure that one out, didn't it?"

Flustered and marginally embarrassed that he's deduced what I've been thinking, I bite back, "You know, you really should have brought your own chair with you."

He roars with laughter, places his hand on my shoulder once again, and leans in. "God, you're brilliant, Nora."

Jeanne turns to us and asks, "What? What's so funny?"

I'm too frustrated to go into what I've been considering, nor will I give Conall the satisfaction of telling her how he surmised Mick's young lady is almost the spitting image of his ex-girlfriend, Ava, long before I did. So, I fume. "Tell ye later. When we get home." Which only causes Conall to guffaw again.

"Brilliant, absolutely brilliant." I glare at him. He's sitting with his shoulders vibrating up and down, mouth open, eyes sparkling – all at my expense.

"Go ahead, Conall. Laugh it up. Glad I could be so entertaining." I feign anger, but his warm laughter lessens my ire and I find myself playing along. "Glad you find me so hilarious."

He bends forward again to whisper in my ear, "Aye. You've no idea just how entertaining it is watching you." I turn, and our eyes connect as he straightens, puts his hands in his pants pockets, and gives an admiring grin.

I think I've been paid a compliment, but I'm not one hundred percent certain. I evaluate his expression, but it's changed. He's shouting towards the team running down the pitch. The moment is gone.

Des's team wins the match, which leads to exuberance, celebration, and fizzy drinks being poured over kids, coaches, parents, and even the Great Conall Kelly. I stand back and watch the celebration from a safe distance. I must be back at the inn by five o'clock so there's no way I'll allow myself to be a sticky mess when I get there.

Mick and Alannah approach. "Quite a match, wasn't it?" I say as they get to where I'm safely standing to avoid the revelry.

"Aye, indeed. Brilliant." Mick grins, but I note a slight discomfort.

"I've never watched a match before," Alannah speaks up. "Mick did an excellent job teaching me, but I've still got a lot to learn. Don't I?" She turns an adoring smile towards Mick. He lifts her hand, pats it and says, "Aye, but you're a quick learner, aren't ye?"

Alannah rises on her toes and gives him a tiny peck on the cheek, "You're so sweet, Mick."

She smiles at me. "I'm sure I was positively annoying with all my questions, but he'd never let on if I bother him, would he?"

Nodding in agreement, I add, "Nope. He'd just patiently answer all your questions. That's how he rolls." I smile up at Mick.

240

He smiles back before breaking the moment of mutual admiration, "Well, we're off now."

"It was nice meeting you, Nora," Alannah calls out as they turn towards the carpark.

I reply, "Nice meeting you too, Alannah."

Mick gives a small wave as he leads her to the car. I turn to fold my chair, sling it over my shoulder, and wave to Jeanne who's now covered in ginger ale. I pantomime a phone to my ear with thumb and little finger extended in the universal gesture for *call me*. I see Conall is in the middle of a group of kids and their parents signing footballs and jerseys. I can't get his attention to bid farewell, so I depart and tell myself I'll give him a ring later.

I fling the chair into the boot, slam it shut, and walk to the driver's side to get in. Just as I'm fumbling with my keys Mrs. Roach and Ava appear. They've parked beside me, so I can't act as if I don't see them. "Brilliant match wasn't it?" I exclaim.

Mrs. Roach, is busying herself with her own chairs, placing them in the boot, slamming it closed, but answers me, "Oh, yes it was a brilliant match! Did you see my grandson save that goal? He's really a fantastic goalie. Some say he could go pro."

Ava sighs. "Mum. He's still young. Who knows if he'll even like the game when he's older let alone be a star?"

Mrs. Roach scowls, but adds, "Well, can't a gran brag on her grandson? No harm in that, is there?"

I smile and answer, "None at all. It would be unheard of if ye didn't."

She gives a firm nod and climbs in the car shutting the door behind her.

"Guess she's ready to go." Ava looks at the car and back at me.

I give a soft chuckle, but curiosity has the best of me, so I continue, "How's your family, Ava? You've got how many now?"

Ava gives me a wistful smile before answering, "They're fine. I've two. Mary and Paul. They're still in Westport with their father. I just made the short trip today to watch my nephew."

I nod in acknowledgement though I've got a thousand more questions burning inside, but since her mum is in the passenger seat giving me the evil eye, I finish, "Right, so. Guess ye better get your mum home."

"Mick's well? His girl is attractive. Is she good to him?" She blurts in a soft whisper, so I know she doesn't want her mum to hear.

I follow her lead and softly say, "He's grand. Same old Mick, right as rain. Though Alannah, the girl, she's new. Seems lovely."

The somber veil lifts from her face and she whispers more to herself than me, "Good." She's playing with the keychain in her hand, rubbing her thumb back and forth over the largest key. "It was nice seeing you again, Nora."

There's more in her eyes she's not expressing but she stops her fidgeting and opens the car door. "Bye, now."

I look at that older woman seated beside her and wonder what Ava would have asked me had her biddy of a mother not been in earshot. Ava's not a happy woman, not as far as I can tell from a momentary encounter, but I also don't feel the seething dislike I once had for her. The mean girl from school cuts a rather sad figure in adulthood. I never understood why Mick dated her, but maybe she was a damsel in distress. He's always been a softie for the damsel in distress. Perhaps he pitied her because of that sour mother of hers.

I shrug and climb into the car to return to Cara Maith.

Chapter 15

June 12th – Meeting today with Cyril Hanley to discuss adding veranda for next season. Thinking of adding wine evenings with live music. Jeanne informs me that we are booked solid once again, thank goodness.

I'm in the garden cutting some of the lilies to bring into the house. I snip a tall one, look it over, then place it in the basket beside me. I reach to grab another when I hear the soft panting of Debby. "Good Day, Debby. Hello Mick."

Mick laughs. "'Tis hard to sneak up with that one. How are ye, Nora? Haven't seen ye much lately."

I snip a lily, put it in the basket, brush the dirt from my garden gloves, and stand. My knees make a loud popping sound and Mick winces in response. "Geez, did that hurt?"

Removing my gloves, I playfully swat them at him. "No, and you know it."

He looks at his watch then at me. "Are ye busy?"

It's summer, when am I not busy, these days? He looks like a man with a lot on his mind, so I say, "It's just half-nine and all the guests from last night have departed. We won't have more till after four o'clock, so I suppose I can take a break. Mrs. Flood and Imelda can handle things a while. Why?"

"I'd like to take ye for a cuppa tea."

This is highly irregular. "Is everything okay, Mick?"

He doesn't speak immediately, so I reach down and pat Debby on the head and add, "Just as long as I'm back by one o'clock. I'm meeting a contractor to discuss a veranda for next season."

Mick smiles and nods. "Oh, that will be brilliant. I was thinking a small pergola would be a nice touch too." He looks down at Debby who's relishing my attention. "I'll run get the car. Be right back."

"Sounds good. I'll go in and clean up a bit, see ya in what, ten minutes?"

He's already striding away. Debby sneezes. I interpret it as *thank you* while she turns to follow Mick and tips my basket of flowers over with her tail. I watch the pair go through the gate into the back field towards St. Coman's Farm.

When Mick returns in the car, I meet him outside and climb in the passenger side. "So, this feels rather mysterious. What's up?"

As we reach the end of the drive, he turns the signal on indicating a right-hand turn instead of the left I'd anticipated. "We're not going into Boyle?"

He sighs and says, "Na, we're going to Carrick."

Carrick-on-Shannon is slightly farther in the opposite direction but it's not unusual for him to go there so I shrug. "Oh."

It takes two trips around the block before he finds a parking space in front of *Lena's Tea Room*. I'm still puzzled by this mysterious outing, but I've heard great things about Lena's so I'm more focused on the tearoom.

Small bells jingle against the glass door as we enter. There's a large overstuffed leather sofa and on the other side of a wood crate sits a matching one. I look at Mick and exclaim, "I'm grabbing that spot, you order."

He nods in acknowledgement. "Tea and a scone okay?"

I'm busy taking in the cozy arrangement of the furniture and the quirky decorations but manage to answer. "Aye. Brilliant."

He returns with a stick and a number at the top, 12. There's only one other person in the shop so I suppose it was the first number handy. He places the number down on the crate which serves as a coffee table between the two sofas and flops down next to me. I'd thought he'd sit across from me but instead we're shoulder-to-shoulder, so I twist awkwardly and ask, "What's up, Mick? You're acting mysterious...more than usual."

Before he's able to reply, the girl from behind the counter appears with a tray of tea and scones. She gently places them on the coffee table then pulls a couple napkins from her apron pocket and adds them to the arrangement before us. "Can I get ye anything else?"

I read the name badge on her apron and answer, "No. Thank you, Bridget. This looks grand."

Bridget leaves us, and I turn to Mick. "Well?"

"I've never been to Lena's before, have you?" He looks around the tearoom and continues, "I hear they have a knitting group and a book club that meets here. I'd imagine you'd enjoy the book club. I mean, I'm not telling you what to do, or anything like that. Though at times I think you should really investigate a social life. You could use some outside interests besides the inn."

I sit up straight, but rather than answer his sudden concern about my social calendar, I lift the metal creamer and pour a drop into each cup before grabbing the tea pot and pouring us each a cup of tea. I place the pot back on the tray and begin buttering a scone. It's warm, so the butter melts the moment it touches the flakey treat. My mouth waters as I lift a small bite and devour it. "You know Mick, whatever it is you're trying to get off your chest, do it now. You're starting to freak me out."

He breaks a piece off his scone, tosses it in his mouth, chews, and finally asks, "Do you think Alannah looks like Ava?"

I could play coy and say, *Whatever, do you mean?* But I don't like to lie, especially to Mick. I take the pulling off a plaster approach. "Um, yeah. She does. Very much."

Okay, that was a little blunter than I had intended, but he's nodding in agreement, so I don't think I've done any harm. Mick takes another bite from his scone and washes it down with a full gulp of tea. "I was afraid she's too young, but the longer I've been seeing her the more I noticed…" He runs his thumb around the rim of the cup as he adds, "and the other day when we ran into Ava, well…"

We're both silent for a moment. I butter another bite of scone and enjoy it fully before continuing with the question I've wanted to ask Mick that's been burning inside me since I returned to Ireland. "What did she do to you? What did Ava do that hurt you so badly you've spent the past decade and a half alone?"

My heart's racing with nervousness and I feel uneasy, but there. I asked stoic Mick Reynolds the question I and probably half of Boyle have wanted to ask the tall quiet farmer for years.

He tops off his tea, places the pot back on the tray, and stares into the cup. His pensiveness and forlorn expression are dramatic emphasis for what's about to come. "That's why I've brought you here, Nora. I've kept it inside for so long, I needed to tell someone I trust. Someone I know won't go blabbering all around the county."

He pulls his attention away from the teacup and is now looking directly at me. His somber eyes reveal his angst-filled desire to remove this burden. "Ava and I were engaged."

I already know this, but clearly, he's struggling to get it out.

"She went to Westport for a week to visit a friend from university... there was a group of em." He turns and looks away, searching for the next part, before continuing. "A hen party, she said. One of em was to be married in a couple of weeks, so they were out on the town – a gaggle of girls."

I nod in understanding but don't dare interrupt him now that he's spilling his darkest sorrow.

"Well, ya see, apparently they were into their pints pretty hard that night and there was this lad. A banker's son, from what I'm told. At any rate, she and this banker bloke..."

He hangs his head and glares down at his shoes.

"Oh, Mick. I'm so sorry. So, so, sorry…" Reaching over I place my hand on his knee. "Is he the one she's married to now? The rich banker Mrs. Roach is always prattling on about?"

He clears his throat and looks at me. "Aye. But Nora, there's more to it."

I swallow hard, stunned by his dark expression. "What, Mick? *What*?"

He lowers his voice to a whisper so neither Bridget behind the counter nor the lady reading a paperback book across the room can hear. "A few weeks after the trip to Westport, Ava and I were at her mum's kitchen table making plans for our wedding, when she bolts upright and runs to the loo. Well, she'd gotten sick, so we all thought maybe she had a stomach bug."

I breathe in deeply at the realization of what's to follow and begin stroking his knee with my hand. "Oh, Mick."

"Right, so. She didn't have a stomach bug after all. Turns out it was a baby. The only thing, I knew I wasn't about to be a daddy because we, Ava and I, we were waiting till we were proper married before…"

I'm shocked. Mick's grief-stricken expression tugs at my heart. My mind flashes to Dylan. I wonder if Dylan looked this brokenhearted when he discovered I'd left him? I pull my hand back from his knee. "I had no idea, Mick."

"No, ye wouldn't. You'd moved to London by then." He puts his teacup down and takes my hand in his. "Once that old cow of a mother of Ava's figured out what was wrong with her daughter, she was determined to push me out of the picture."

I look down at his large hand enveloping mine then back at his sorrowful eyes as he adds, "Ava came clean with me about the lad in Westport and I thought I'd offer to marry her anyway, ya know, raise the babby as mine, but she'd already told her mum..."

"You loved her that much? Enough to raise another man's baby. *Oh,* Mick..."

He doesn't answer. He just nods and bites his lower lip. My heart is breaking for him and I assume he's finished, but instead he squeezes my hand and goes on, "The old cow saw the banker's son as a better prospect for her beautiful daughter, so she drove to Westport and gave his father what for. Next thing I know, Ava's moved to Westport, taken a job in a bank there, and married a handsome young banker. Seven months later, there's a 'honeymoon baby' who miraculously was born early. *Huh!*"

"Oh, shit."

Mick pops his head up at my uncharacteristic foul-mouthed reply and smiles. "I knew you'd find a way to sum it up brilliantly, Nora. I think that's why I wanted to tell you."

My face warms at my sudden lack of decorum. "Sorry. Does your dad know?"

"We've never spoken about it, but he's smart. He's done the math. Not sure if he wonders who the baby belongs to, but he's wise. I'm sure he's figured it out."

I'm moved by everything Mick's shared with me. His concern for Ava's honor, the fact he'd offer to raise another man's child to protect her reputation, the simple fact he thought so much of her he wanted to wait until they were married. He's calm and cool in every situation, yet he's been long-suffering over the love of a woman.

"Do you hate her?"

"No. I don't. I've moved on. The love I felt has turned to pity… I don't think she's ever been happy."

I recall the wistful expression Ava had in the carpark after the football match and nod. "You're probably right."

He lifts his teacup and takes a sip before finishing. "It was that old biddy of a mother forced her into a marriage she didn't necessarily want. The sad cow saw earning potential in Westport and thought it far better than Ava becoming a farmer's wife in County Roscommon. She forced it upon Ava and then swanned around town telling anybody in earshot that Ava dumped me for a rich banker's son."

I sigh in exasperation. "That's awful, Mick. I wondered what happened but had no idea. It's heartbreaking, truly heartbreaking."

He gives my hand another squeeze. "I saw your face when we were leaving the football match, and I knew you'd recognized Alannah looks like Ava. I've dated on and off since Ava, but never long-term relationships, and coincidentally most of em have been the spitting image of Ava Roach."

There's relief in his eyes as he's unburdened himself of the anguish he's been carrying for years. I place my free hand on top of his hand that's holding mine. "What made you want to tell me this, now? Was it seeing Ava again?"

"No and yes. Seeing Ava made me look at myself. Alannah is sweet, not too bright, but sweet and looks a lot like Ava. I knew it. I stood there in McGarry's, dripping wet from the ocean and thought I'd seen a ghost. She's not for me, it's not going anywhere, I know that. I think she knows that. No, it was seeing you that day at the football match."

"Seeing *me*?"

"Yes. I saw you and Ava together and the lightbulb turned on in my head. I've spent years, correction, *wasted* years, agonizing over a woman I thought was the love of my life. I've brooded, dated look-alikes, and been sullen all because of Ava Roach. Then I looked at sweet, beautiful Nora Fallon and saw myself. I don't know who this bloke in London is or was, but you're doing the exact same thing and I can't stand to watch."

His words score a direct hit; a forceful blow. I pull my hands away, lean back against the over-stuffed couch, and look up at the ceiling. I study the details of the pressed tin that's been painted a pale pink. For a split second I admire the color choice and think of the ceiling in my own kitchen before taking a deep breath and looking at Mick. His somber eyes fixed on me betray his genuine concern so rather than lashing out, which is my instinct, I pause to collect my thoughts. The only problem is I don't have any thoughts. I've been called out. He's right. Regardless of what I say about always wanting to own my own business, and my love for the old home that's now the Cara Maith, and the beautiful land etc. etc., I'm still focusing most of my energy towards pushing Dylan out of my mind.

After a prolonged silence I pick up his hand and hold it in mine. "Mick, you're right. Dylan is a man I want to be with, and had we met under different circumstances, I have no doubt we would have had a beautiful happy life together. But we didn't meet under different circumstances. We met under all the wrong circumstances and because of that I finally understood that however much we adore each other, however much we want to be with each other, we aren't. And the only way we can be together would hurt too many people and neither one of us could live with that, because that would be pure selfishness. It would also be destructive, which coming from my own broken home, I could never do to another family.

Mick nods in agreement but doesn't speak. "So, yes, Mick. I guess we're very alike in that regard, but you know what? I really mean this, I appreciate you telling me this and recognizing in me the same things you've done, and I want to make a deal with you."

"A *deal*? What sort of deal?" His face is softer now and there's warmth in his eyes.

"Keeping myself busy is my way of keeping my mind from straying towards those destructive thoughts and feelings, and I'm pretty certain that's why you work so hard as well."

The corners of his mouth curl upward in a knowing grin. "Aye."

"Let's promise to remind each other if we think the other is overcompensating and needs to lighten up a bit."

"How?"

"I don't know, maybe by just doing something like we're doing right now. Maybe once a week have a cup of tea away from your farm, away from the inn. You know, up until the point where you put on your superhero cape and rescued the child from the sea, the trip to Strandhill was good craic."

He gives a soft chuckle. "Aye, and until I put on my therapist's cap, this little excursion was fun too." He looks around the tearoom and I follow his gaze. The unconventional furnishings, unique wall decorations and the soft fairy lights strung around the counter give it a welcoming ambiance. Turning back to me he adds, "You know, Nora, having you back is grand. I know I find a million reasons to pop up at your door, but it's the god's truth it's because I enjoy ya. I think you're smart, funny, and I've not had a friend like that in ages."

I tuck my lower lip in, sigh, and reply, "Neither have I… so, do we have a deal? We agree to do something each week to interrupt our morose tendencies to prevent us from becoming sad cows like Mrs. Roach?"

"Oh, God, when ye put it like that… *Yes*, agreed!"

He catches me looking down at my watch and laughs. "As long as we keep it short, am I right?"

"You caught me. It's just there are guests scheduled to arrive…"

He waves his hand to interrupt. "I know, I know. But you've time for one more question, don't you?"

I shrug. "Sure, as long as it's nothing too challenging."

Without hesitation he asks, "Right, so, what's the deal with Conall Kelly?"

I laugh. "Oh, that's a question for another day, I'm afraid - but I have no idea, if you want a true answer."

He stands and lifts me from the soft leather sofa. "Well, he sure admires you, and he keeps turning up like a bad penny."

As he leads me to the door, I say, "He's growing on me. Is that silly?"

He stops to look at me and there's tenderness in his smile. "Not at all. I've noticed how you brighten up whenever he's around. He brings ye joy. That's never a bad thing, is it?"

He pushes the door open and holds it for me. The tiny bells tinkle against the glass and Bridget calls from behind the counter, "Thanks a million, come again!"

❈

When we pull up in front of Cara Maith, there's a white work van parked in front of the red Georgian door. Mick parks beside it and climbs out rather than just leaving me to my meeting.

"Don't you have to get back to the farm?"

We walk toward the house. "Yes, but if you don't mind, I'd like to listen in on the meeting." He's opening the front door before I'm able to protest so I walk in behind him to find Cyril Hanley standing in the lounge, eyes upward, studying the crown molding job his team did last summer.

"Ah! Nora, great seeing you again." He nods to the ceiling, adding, "Just admiring our work." He reaches out to shake my hand then turns and does the same to Mick.

"Have a seat, Cyril, so we can discuss what I'm thinking of adding." He takes a seat in the wing chair beside the fireplace with his long lanky legs spread and his hands folded. He leans forward, "'Tis a wine patio ye want?"

"It is. I've done some very rudimentary sketches. If you'll give me a moment, they're in my office." I look at Mick who is still standing, hands in pockets, leaning against the doorway. "Mick, perhaps you can fill Cyril in on some of the details we discussed while I get my sketches." *If he insists on being present, I may as well put him to work.*

When I return, the front door is open, and the lounge is empty, so I go outside. Mick is standing pointing up and Cyril is a step behind him, nodding in understanding. I interpret this to mean they're discussing the pergola.

I clear my throat and they turn in unison. Cyril lifts his eyebrows. "Aye, Nora, Mick is describing your ideas. Can't wait to see the sketches you've got there."

Mick must see anger in my eyes or sense that I'm upset because he's infringing upon my territory. He grins. "Hope you don't mind, Nora. I was just so excited about your idea, I brought Cyril out to see where you're thinking of adding the wine patio."

I brush past Mick and hand Cyril the sketches while throwing Mick a look that's somewhere between *I'm angry with you* and *You know I can't be angry with you.*

Cyril takes the drawings and holds them in front of him with both hands as he studies them. The longer he looks at the drawings, the more insecure I feel about their quality. I'd done them in pencil late one night when I couldn't sleep. Looking at them in the daylight in a professional's hands, I'm aware of their inexpert appearance. In my early days as an editor at Barrett &

Cuthbert, I edited a book on architectural drawing, so I'd at least put these on quality paper and used some of the techniques I'd read about.

Cyril turns the paper and walks around taking long strides as if walking off the perimeter of the patio. Looking up, he moves his hand from his chin and runs it through his thick salt and pepper hair, then looks at me. "Did you draw these sketches, Nora?"

Mick jumps in with a reply before I'm able to. "Aye. She did."

Cyril looks at the sketch and back at me. "This is brilliant. You do nice work. You'd be amazed at some of the drawings I see. I've built entire additions based off a drawing on a pub coaster." He gives a friendly smile. "I especially like your idea for the stone pavers instead of cement."

Suddenly feeling like the most brilliant woman in Ireland, I beam proudly. "I want it to keep its Irish charm but maybe add a flavor of Tuscany since it's meant to be a wine patio."

Cyril returns to where Mick and I are standing and holds the sketches in front of me. "May I keep these? I'll return 'em, but I'd like to photocopy 'em."

"There's a copier in my office, but before I hand over my plans, I'll need an estimate and a contract. We'll also need to discuss the time frame for construction. It can begin in early October. I'll still be booking guests, but naturally there are fewer visitors in October."

Cyril turns to Mick, "I keep forgetting Nora Fallon came back from London a shrewd businesswoman. I'm more accustomed to deals sealed with a handshake and a pint." He lets out a roar of laughter and Mick gives a smile. I, on the other hand, am not sure if I've been complimented or insulted.

I decide to accept Cyril's remark as a compliment and we adjourn back to the lounge where we discuss permits, work crews, and logistics. Cyril assures me he'll email an estimate along with a contract by the end of the week, and he departs as a car finds its way up the drive. Our guests for the evening have arrived.

Seeing the blue Skoda driving towards us, Mick says, "Guess I'd better go. Looks like you've got guests coming."

He starts towards his car, but I grab his hand before he leaves my side. "Mick." I look at his strong hand in mine, then back at his deep brown eyes and the golden flecks. "Mick, thanks. I know it wasn't easy telling me about Ava. Thanks for trusting me enough and..." I struggle to find the next words, "thanks for believing in me. It means the world to me, so, thank you."

Mick glances at his hand in mine and draws closer to me before whispering, "I've always believed in you, Nora. Even when you didn't." He lifts my hand and gently presses his lips to it then lets it go and walks to his car.

I'm frozen as he leaves and the new guests approach to greet me. I've got a million thoughts running through my head but turn my attention to the couple instead. "Welcome to Cara Maith. Come inside and let's get you all checked in, shall we?"

I hear Mick motor down the driveway as we enter the house. There's so much more I need to say to him, but the newlywed couple from Chicago are the focus of my attention for now, so I push thoughts of my conversation with Mick away for later and put on my game face. "So, you've come all the way to Ireland from Chicago for your honeymoon, is that right?"

The cute twenty-something bride with the sandy brown hair and cinnamon freckles sprinkled across her nose beams. "That's right. Jared and I just got married *Saturday!*" She reaches and takes his hand giving it a squeeze.

They're both smiling brightly. I can't help joining in their happiness and ponder what it's like to feel so elated over a relationship. For a split second I think of Dylan and how unfair it felt I never got to glow about the man I loved. Quite the opposite. I had to hide my feelings. Instead of exclaiming my affections from the top of the London Eye, I learned to perfect my poker face. I became secretive, and rather than risk slipping and exposing the secret, I withdrew. If I wasn't conniving to be with Dylan, I was at home or working at the office. I avoided people and friendships for fear of accidentally unmasking the conspiracy which was my love life. I'm not certain Dylan ever understood how much I sacrificed for him. Maybe he did.

I smile at the sweet young Americans and push all thoughts of Dylan from my head. "Now, let's get you settled in the *Castle Island* room, and you're welcome to come down for tea at half-four if you wish to join us in the lounge."

Chapter 16

June 23rd – Imelda and Robby have convinced me it would be great fun to have a St. John's Eve celebration of sorts. I know this tradition is bigger in the west, but if it brings good PR to the inn and provides my guests with a little extra Irish flavor to their visit, I'll give it a try.

Robby is seated at the kitchen table reading an article on his smart phone out loud. "Says here, the tradition could be from ancient times and it's probably not coincidence it's celebrated so near the Summer Solstice… communal fires built at sunset, yada yada, folks dance and sing…lads show their bravery by running through the flames…"

I interrupt, "Don't get any ideas, Robby. There'll be none of that…"

He cuts me off and smiles. "That's all ye need. Geez, you've already had a choking and a death; a man running around on fire would be the end of ye."

Imelda swats him with the dish towel in her hand. "Shut it, Robby. That's not funny." She turns back, I hand her a clean dish I've just rinsed, and she begins wiping it dry.

Looking like a schoolboy who's been reprimanded, Robby returns to his smart phone. "Ooo, says here it's also got to do with fertility."

"*What?* You never mentioned that two months ago when you convinced me to host this event, Robby. I can't have the town thinking I'm out here conjuring ancient rituals to assure population growth." I picture Mrs. Roach, blathering around town, "Ye hear Nora's having some kind of ancient fertility ritual at her place, tonight. Gawd only knows the sort of filth that will involve."

Robby laughs. "No, not people fertility, at least I don't think...nah, it's crops. Says they'd say prayers for a bountiful harvest and that the fire had magical powers that would keep fields from becoming overgrown...they'd light branches and march through the fields, which was supposed to protect the field from bugs and disease... Oh, and they'd take some of the ashes home to light the home fire with - supposed to be lucky."

I'm furiously scouring a large pot that held porridge from the morning meal. Pausing, I place the steel wool in the pot and look at Robby who's moved on to his social media site and ask, "Are you sure this is a good idea? I thought this was more about St. John, but from everything you've just read it's nothing more than pagan superstition."

He looks startled at my sudden disapproving tone and flips back to the story on his phone. "Nah, you're worried over nothing, Nora. T'was also a time of blessing." He points to his phone. "See here, the fire was often used to burn old scapulars and rosary beads that were broken, and it was all okay because it was blessed." He scrolls further. "Here's a prayer: *'In the honor of God and St. John, to the fruitfulness and profit of our planting and our work, in the name of the Father and of the Son and of the Holy Spirit. Amen.'* See, nothing sinister at all."

I return to the porridge pot and acquiesce. "Well, okay. I guess it will be okay. And fun, though I'm beginning to think you just like building bonfires. I mean we had one at Halloween, too. Maybe we should call the place the Bonfire Inn."

Robby looks at me with a quizzical expression, as if he believes I'm serious. "Nah, I like the name you've got now. Besides, it's only two bonfires. If you rename the inn, people might expect a bonfire every night."

I throw a look over my shoulder and he winks at me. "Thank goodness you're kidding, Robby. I was worried for a minute, there."

Robby stands, tucks the phone in his shirt pocket, and says to Imelda, "You done with the dishes? I'd like to go down to the field and start laying the wood for the bonfire."

Imelda folds the dishtowel and drapes it across the oven door handle. "Yep, all good." She turns to me and asks, "Do you need me for anything else, Nora?"

I look around the kitchen searching for anything that still needs tending to but find nothing. "Nope, your grandmother is upstairs finishing the last of the beds so why don't you go with Robby and start building."

"Call me on Robby's mobile if you need me again. Otherwise you know where we'll be." She flashes a big smile and joins Robby by the kitchen door. He adds, "Don't worry, Nora. I'll build a tasteful non-pagan St. John's Eve fire…not too big." He's read my mind.

Robby pulls the door open and he and Imelda are gone in a flash. I return to my porridge pot. The sticky oatmeal isn't letting go of the bottom of the pot, so I rub savagely with the steel wool until finally the last bit of oatmeal lifts allowing me to rinse it away.

The kitchen door opens but I'm too focused on the porridge pot to turn. "Did you forget something?"

"I don't think so."

I drop the pot and it crashes to the bottom of the sink. It's not Robby nor Imelda, but I know the voice.

He's taller than I remember, but then again, I was only a young girl when he left. His nut-brown hair is still thick, but he keeps it close cropped and there are strands of gray at his temples. His eyes are my eyes, hazel with more green than brown in them. It's been so long since I last saw him, I'm frozen; not knowing if I should be angry or run into his arms and hug my long-lost brother.

Picking up on my uncertainty and shock, Jack Jr. approaches, places his hand on my arm and leans in to give me a small kiss on the cheek. "Nora, my God, it's good to see you."

I don't respond. I can't speak. There are dozens of questions in my head, but no words will leave my mouth.

"I can see my being here is a bit of a shock."

A bit of a shock? Other than the occasional letter or Christmas cards that quit coming years ago, he's been only a memory for a couple of decades.

"I'm here on holiday from America. I heard about the inn and, well, I thought I'd come over and see how you are." He looks around the kitchen and then glances down at the floor trying to find his next words. "I've a wife and two kids, in America. They ask about their Auntie Nora in Ireland all the time."

I have a sister-in-law in America and apparently nieces or nephews or maybe one of each – a proper family. He moves a few inches closer and takes both my hands into his. My hands are still wet from washing the porridge pot, so I look down at them. He must not mind my wet hands in his because his eyes are on me. "Like I said, I know this is a shock, but I want us to be a family again, or at least be part of each other's lives."

I study his strong hands holding mine. His skin isn't quite as fair as mine and from its golden cast it looks as if he spends time outdoors in America. His fingernails are shaped similarly to my own, a characteristic I always thought I received from my mother. I look him in the eye and finally find my words. "I don't know, Jack. I don't know."

He swallows hard. "I wouldn't blame you if you never wanted to see me again, or if you hate me. I've been a terrible big brother."

"I don't hate you Jack... I've moved on." I grab my hands back from him. "I've been on my own so long now, you can understand that can't you?"

He looks wounded but nods. "I suppose so. I haven't been a big brother to you at all." He breathes in and releases a long slow breath. "After I left, I wanted to reach out to you, I wanted to be your big brother, I just didn't know how. I had so much anger."

"*Anger*? What on earth could have made you so angry you'd leave your mother and little sister never

269

looking back? *We* hadn't done anything to you. Quite honestly, even Dad hadn't been that terrible. Sure, he drank and catted around, but he never hid who he was. It's far easier to deal with what you know than with a deceiver." There are tears pooling in my eyes and a stray one escapes, rolling down my cheek. "We needed you, Jack. She needed you. I needed you."

He lowers his voice to a barely audible whisper, "I wanted to contact you… but the longer I stayed out of your lives, the harder it got to reach out to you. I wanted so badly to come to Mom's funeral, but I didn't have any money. But I've got a good job now, a family and… it's just when I got the invitation to St. John's Eve, I thought maybe *you* wanted *me* back in your life again."

My head is spinning with his last words, so I stagger towards the kitchen table, pull out a chair and flop into the seat. I grab the table and hold onto it as if trying to right myself on a rocking boat when Mrs. Flood comes into the room carrying an armload of sheets on her way to the washing machine in the back corner of the kitchen. She can barely see over the bed linens, so she plops them on top of the machine and turns back to me. "Shall I start a load of whites before I go?"

Seeing Jack Jr. for the first time since she walked in the room, her jaw drops, and she exclaims, "Jesus, Mary, and Joseph… Jack Jr.!" Mrs. Flood crosses the room and throws her arms around his neck. "Gosh if you aren't a sight for sore eyes, how are ye?"

Jack's face lights up. I suppose he thought this is the kind of reception he'd get from me. Mrs. Flood is prattling on about how handsome he is, but I'm still paralyzed in my chair. There's a tap at the back door but I don't get up to answer. I know who it is. Mick enters the kitchen and finds this strange scene playing out before him. His eyes widen with recognition and then cut to me seated at the table. He greets Jack Jr. then walks over pulls out the chair next to mine and sits down.

Mrs. Flood has put the kettle on to prepare the prodigal son a cup of tea, but I'm immobile and silent. Mick places his hand on my shoulder and whispers in my ear, "Can I get ye anything, Nora?"

I look at Mrs. Flood's joy as she fusses about making the tea for Jack. I look at Jack who appears to be a changed man, sorry for his prolonged absence, then turn back to Mick and sigh. "No, I'll be alright."

There's too much going on at the inn today to permit myself the luxury of being contemplative or withdrawn because of Jack Jr.'s sudden appearance. I don't know who invited him, nor do I know why he came, but I've got a full house tonight and an event to put on, so I stand and ask, "Where are you staying, Jack?"

Chapter 17

June 23ʳᵈ, continued… There are no words…

I set Jack up in the small bedroom next to mine in what I've designated as the family area of the house. It's one of the last rooms I've renovated so it's sparsely furnished with a full-sized bed, a nightstand, and a small chest of drawers. I'd found the night table at a junk sale and brought it home to refinish for one of the guest rooms. After hours of sanding, painting and finishing it off with a crackle medium, I decided it didn't meet the standards for any of the upstairs guest rooms and relegated it to the family area.

Jack sets his small suitcase on the floor by the night table and inspects the room. "Very cozy, indeed, Nora. This is perfect."

"You'll have to use the bath in the hall. I keep the door to the family area locked so it's private. There's clean towels in the linen closet and there's a door from the family area into the kitchen should you need anything."

"Brilliant." He walks to the window, pulls back the delicate lace curtain and peeks out. "Ah, terrific view of the fields from here. Is that where you'll be having the bonfire tonight?" Reaching into the back pocket of his blue jeans, he presents me with a small envelope.

Recognizing what it is, I open and pull out the invitation I had printed for Bonfire Night. *You're invited to Cara Maith Inn for the first annual St. John's Eve Bonfire Night!!* The small card with a flame in the background of the Celtic lettering was mailed out weeks ago. I flip the envelope over and note the printed address and extra postage for the trip to America.

"Ye didn't mail that to me, *did you?*"

I tuck the invitation inside the envelope and hand it back to Jack. I don't want to embarrass him, I don't want to fight, I don't know what I want. "No. I didn't, Jack. It looks like your name and address must have been added to the inn's mailing list somehow." I look at my older brother and see a striking resemblance to the memory I carry of my father. Although not the same color as Dad's, his eyes are fringed with the same long thick lashes. He inherited my father's skin tone too and has a slight tan from spending much of his days outdoors. He stands about six-foot tall, he's maybe an inch or two shorter than my father, but of course my father died when I was young so maybe he's the exact same height; it's all kind of foggy now in my memory. But it's his face that's tearing at my emotions. He has an expression of a man begging forgiveness but not knowing how to ask. "You're here and that's all that matters."

His eyes lift and there's a twinkle where there was none a moment ago. "Ah, 'tis true enough. I'm here, Nora, and there's so much I want to tell ya." He looks at me and then down at the floor.

"I know, Jack. There's a lot I want to tell you, but for now, I've got a big event to prepare for as well as a house full for the night so perhaps tomorrow, after everyone has cleared out for a few hours, you and I can catch up on life."

I turn to walk out of the room, but he catches me by the elbow and squeezes. "You've done well, Nora. I know I've been a terrible older brother, but for what it's worth, I'm proud of ye."

His eyes are brimming with tears eager to make their escape and stream down his cheeks. Seeing remorse written on his face, my throat catches and my voice cracks, "Thanks, Jack."

Fleeing the room, I call back to him from the hallway, "Settle yourself and if you're up to it, I 'm sure Imelda and Robby can use your hands down at the bonfire."

Our registered guests for the evening include a family of three from Berlin, a young British couple from Leeds, a family of four from Cork, and an American couple in their mid-fifties from South Carolina. They're all extremely excited to be staying at Cara Maith on such an auspicious occasion as the St. John's Eve Bonfire Night.

To spare Mrs. Flood and Imelda from being in the kitchen, I've catered in the snacks. Troy's Deli as well as Tonni's and the Roma Grill; so, people can purchase fish, chips, kabobs, sandwiches, and drinks. I couldn't tell if Mrs. Flood was disappointed or relieved when I told her my plans for outsourcing the concessions, though she did insist on making dozens and dozens of her chocolate chip cookies. I couldn't argue with that; the kids will enjoy them and I'm sure the adults will too.

Mindful of my recent track record with misfortune at my big events, I've asked the Boyle Fire Brigade to attend. It would be just my luck if the fire meant to secure prosperity and a rich harvest would end up morphing into Mrs. O'Leary's Cow all over again. Anthony Leyden, the fire chief, had at first been reluctant, but when I mentioned bringing the fire truck for the kids and insisted they pass the Wellie for donations, he came around and enthusiastically offered to bring the swift-water rescue team for a demonstration in addition to the fire brigade vehicle.

Jeanne has printed signs and had them laminated to direct visitors to the makeshift parking area. I've heard through the bush telephone the crowd could be large. I walk outside to the car park where I find Mick carrying the signs Jeanne made. He's nailed them to small wooden stakes and is hammering them into the ground. I watch as he meditatively taps the stakes into the ground with a rubber mallet. After the sign is secure, he straightens up, looks back at the other directional signs he's placed along the drive, then pulls a ball of fluorescent pink twine from his jacket pocket.

"What's the string for, Mick?"

Unwinding the twine, he begins tying it to one of the stakes, "I'm going to string it around the parking area to preserve as much of the grass as I can. When the carpark fills, people will have to park along the drive. That grass you'll recover quickly, but you don't want folks creating parking spaces on the lawn by the house."

"You're my hero, Mick. You think of everything."

He gives a shrug but keeps working. "How's your visitor from America?"

"Visitors, it's a couple from South Carolina."

He shakes his head, unwinds the twine, and walks to the next stake in the ground. "Not who I was talking about."

"Oh, you mean Jack. He's down in the field helping Robby and Imelda set up the fire."

Tapping the stake with the mallet he nods. "Aye."

"Yes, he arrived suddenly, to say the least."

Mick's busy wrapping the twine around one last stake. "Did he say what brings him here after all this time?"

Tired of calling to him from across the carpark, I move closer. "He got an invitation to the St. John's Eve Bonfire."

Mick whips his head to look at me. "He got a what?"

"He got an invitation in the mail to come here tonight. I haven't a clue how his name and address is on my mailing list, but there it was on the outside of the envelope he showed me."

Mick walks to where I'm standing and drops his voice, "Are you okay? Must have been a jolt."

Before I can open my mouth, we both notice a car crawling up the drive. Simultaneously, we recognize the gunmetal gray Jaguar. I turn back to Mick. "Conall --- the surprises keep coming, don't they?"

Mick places his hand on my elbow and timidly mutters in my ear, "I'm afraid I've prior knowledge of this surprise."

Conall parks his car, jumps out, and playfully shouts, "Oy! Is it okay to park here?"

He joins us and plants a big wet kiss on my cheek before shoving his hand at Mick, "Great to see ye!"

Deadpan, Mick says, "Ye want me to string some twine around the Jag so folks don't get too close?"

Playing along, Conall looks sincere. "Would ya? Gosh, that would be grand."

I interrupt, "Why don't you put it in the garage? There's room next to my car."

They both turn their gaze to me and start laughing. Conall wraps an arm around my shoulder. "Ah, darling, Nora, we're just playing. It will be fine."

"I'm not joking. I'd feel terrible if it got a scratch or somebody hit it with the door of their car. Put it in the garage."

Keeping his arm around my shoulder, Conall gives a squeeze. "Not to worry, love. Somebody already put a ding in the door in Dublin. It's all good. Besides, when the time comes for a new one, there's a Jaguar dealer in the city just waiting for the publicity of having Conall Kelly drive away from his showroom in the latest model."

Mick adds, "There's truth to that. Leave it."

Conall removes his arm from my shoulder and casually takes my hand. Mick raises his right eyebrow at Conall's familiarity but says nothing.

"So, let me guess, Conall, you received an invitation in the mail to the Cara Maith St. John's Eve Bonfire."

"Indeed, I did. 'Tis an honor to be here. Now, tell me, will there be cheese cubes served this evening, because I'm going to have to advise you to avoid those if ye plan on making a speech."

Mick's face lights up and I laugh. Conall tightens his grip on my hand and howls with laughter at his own joke at my expense.

"What's so funny?" Jeanne's waddling towards us with one hand placed on the small of her back supporting her bigness.

Stunned at her appearance, Conall blurts, "My God, would ye look at the size of ye?!"

Recognizing the exasperation on Jeanne's face, I tighten my grip on Conall's hand, intentionally digging my fingernails into his palm.

Getting my point, he adds, "But you're beautiful as the Blessed Mother Herself, Jeanne. Radiant with the glow of new life about to grace us." He turns to me and proudly nods his head for emphasis as if to say, *See, I fixed it.*

Jeanne reaches us and gives Conall a dirty look. "Oh, shut it. I'm two days overdue, I've cankles, unbelievable heartburn, and I can't hold my wind. You were right the first time."

Mick studies Jeanne carefully, his eyes stopping at her ankles. Jeanne sees him looking at her swollen feet and swats him on the arm. "Stop looking!"

Embarrassed at having been caught gawking at the sight of her bloated feet, he asks, "Is everything okay, Jeanne?"

She drops her hand from the small of her back, tucks a piece of hair behind her ear and as if suddenly remembering her purpose says, "Oh, yeah. Father Mark rang. He's excited about saying the prayer for St. John's Eve but wants to know if he should bring his fiddle."

Mick rolls his eyes and mumbles, "Not on yer Nelly, no!"

I think about Father Mark. Although I've heard his fiddle playing is greatly improved since Halloween, I'm delighted I can beg him off. "Tell him, thanks that would be lovely, however, Robby's brother Eamon is bringing his DJ kit and will be providing music."

"Got it." Jeanne smiles at me and starts waddling back to the house.

Unable to restrain himself, Conall adds, "Ye may want to tell him to bring some extra holy water; he may need to perform a christening before the night's over."

I yank my hand from his and swat him on the arm. "Conall!"

He's grinning proudly, and I notice a small grin on Mick's face as well. "Honestly, you two. She feels badly enough - look at her."

Conall looks at Jeanne who's made it to the house. She gives him a two-fingered salute and closes the door behind her. Conall roars with laughter at Jeanne's gesture. "Ah, see. She's not bothered, we're having good fun, good craic."

Switching to more pressing matters, I look at him and say, "Since you're here this early, I'm putting you to work."

He straightens and gives a mock salute. "Yes, mum. Conall Kelly reporting for duty, mum!"

He's full of himself, today.

I turn to Mick and back to Conall. "See those trash bins, over there? They need to be down in the field where the bonfire's going to be. Can you two get them down there? There's a large box of bin liners in the garage you can take with ye."

"Aye, aye, Mum," Conall barks.

I shake my head. "Knock it off."

Mick tucks the ball of twine back into his pocket and says, "Come on Corporal Conall, let's get to work." Turning toward the bins he looks back and adds, "Oh, and don't worry, Nora. He's staying with us at St. Coman's tonight."

There's a sinking feeling in the pit of my stomach thirty minutes before guests are scheduled to arrive. It's the same feeling I get every day when the inn is fully booked, only today it's ten times worse. I used to get a nervous stomach when I started working with clients at Barrett & Cuthbert; I'd end up running to the toilet after a meeting. Having advanced my way up from their bookshops, to copy editing, to working directly with authors, you'd think it would have been a gradual and easy transition. *No.* Not for me. With each new level of responsibility came a new level of anxiety and symptoms.

In the shop, it was just a case of shyness in speaking with customers. When I moved into the office, I'd get butterflies if I had to speak at a meeting or report to a superior. Then, the first time I was assigned an author to work, my nerves began affecting my stomach. I was given the task of working with a children's author. She was a sweet, middle-aged woman with children my age, so it couldn't have been a better fit for my first foray into interacting with authors. I'd worked myself up so badly before she even arrived at the office that my stomach was rumbling and turning the moment we sat down.

She was kind, and put me at ease immediately, but it was too late for my stomach. We were reviewing some notes and discussing images she envisioned in the story when I knew, it was over. I made an excuse about my pen running out of ink and that I needed to pop into the supply room and grab another. I darted from the room and down the hall so fast I almost knocked over poor old Mr. Cuthbert who was walking in the hallway carrying a cup of coffee.

Since then, my nervous stomach has improved, but Jack Jr.'s unexpected arrival, Conall appearing, and this evening's bonfire has me wondering if my nervous stomach is going to survive.

Rather than give my nerves the opportunity to start simmering, I decide to busy myself outside. I stop at the registration desk where Jeanne is seated behind the computer. She looks up and offers a pained semi-smile. "Everything okay, Nora?"

"I should be asking you that." I nod towards her swollen ankles propped on a foot stool under the desk. "But, yes. I'm fine. I'm going to walk down and check on Robby and Imelda. If our guests arrive, are you alright checking them in and directing them to their rooms?"

She sits back and folds her hands over her enormous baby bump. Her blouse struggles to stay buttoned. "I'll be grand. Besides, Mrs. Flood is in the kitchen if I need help getting out of my chair." She flashes a broad smile at me.

"I can't believe you're even here, today."

"I'd be climbing the walls at home. *Here*, at least I can keep me mind occupied on other things. Besides, the activity may motivate the baby to get moving."

"Well, Mrs. Flood's in the kitchen and I've got my mobile should you need me."

I leave Jeanne at the registration desk and walk to the kitchen where Mrs. Flood's arranging a tray of cookies. "I'm going down to the bonfire if you need me."

She doesn't lift her head from her work but waves a hand in the air. "Go on, now. We'll take care of things in the house for ye. But do send Imelda to get the cookies before the crowds arrive."

"Will do!"

I shut the kitchen door behind me and march towards the field. I meet Robby and Imelda who are walking in my direction. Robby shouts, "We've built ye a brilliant fire, Nora!" His eyes are bright with delight and there's a big grin illuminating his face.

"The fire lorry is coming up the drive, so Mick sent us to direct the driver where to park," Imelda adds.

"Just have them park it where the gravel is over there. Try and keep it off the grass."

"Exactly what Mick said to do." Robby taps me on the shoulder as he passes.

I call after them, "I'll be back in a moment to greet the Brigade Chief."

When I get to the fire, Mick and Jack are busy marking off a safety perimeter with wooden stakes and twine like they used for the parking areas. The food vendors are setting up tables and even though it killed me to let them drive on the field, the food trucks are better off here, set up close to the bonfire.

285

Imelda and Robby have strung paper lanterns encircling the area and run bright orange electrical wire clear up to the potting shed where it will be plugged in when the sun goes down. Although it's June 23rd so that won't happen until late.

There's a table with a blue and white check tablecloth draped over it with a framed sign that says, *Take One*, beside a large basket filled with glow sticks. I smile approvingly because the glow sticks were my idea. I'd ordered them in bulk online in an array of colors. This way if people don't remember to bring a torch, they'll have the light of a glow stick. Besides, it's going to look pretty.

Across from the food trucks, Eamon is arranging his DJ table. I see another orange power cord leading to the electrical outlet in the potting shed. Hopefully it's bright enough and away from where people will be walking so as not to be a tripping hazard. I let out a sigh and wonder, *when did I become such a nervous Nellie?*

It's not a foolish thought, it's just something business owners learn. You must think of every possibility because you just never know. I feel a small rumble in my stomach, so I crush the thoughts of insurance, liabilities, and potential lawsuits before they can take hold of my mind.

Mick sees me approach and waves. "Looks good, doesn't it?"

I reach him and Jack as they finish encircling the bonfire. "Is this a safe distance?"

Jack hands an extra wooden stake to Mick and looks at me. "It's good enough. This circle is really just here as a reminder not to get too close." He places his hands on his hips and surveys the area. "Besides, once the fire is roaring it will be too hot to get any closer."

Mick nods in agreement, looks down at Debby panting in front of him, and then adds, "If you're done with me here, Nora, I'm going to run home and get my father. He's got a group from his High Nelly club coming to this soirée, so I told him I'd bring him."

"No, we're fine here. Go on home and get him."

Mick casually grabs my hand and says, "Alannah is meeting me at the house. The three of us will be here shortly."

He releases my hand and walks away. Jack moves closer and in a hushed tone asks, "So, what's with that?"

"What's with what?" I turn to follow Jack's eyes which are riveted on Mick's back as he's walking away. "Oh, you mean Mick?" I shrug. "He's a good neighbor."

"I can see that. I mean what's going on with you two?"

"*Going on?* Nothing. He's seeing someone."

Jack tilts his head to the side and lifts his eyebrows in a gesture that says, *Really?*

"Okay, he may not be totally serious with Alannah, but I assure you, he and I are completely platonic." He doesn't change his expression, so I begin flailing. "You know the word platonic comes from Plato. I worked with an author on a piece about Plato's works."

He cuts me off, "Nice try, Nora. Don't change the subject. If you don't want to talk about how Mick Reynolds is obviously enamored."

"*Enamored!*" I laugh and turn on my heel to walk to the house. Jack walks along beside me so I continue, "I think you're misreading Mick."

"What's to misread? He dotes on ye. Ever since he showed up today, I've seen him taking charge like he's the man of the house, and you seem fine with that."

"You don't understand, Jack. That's just sort of happened naturally. He's one of those guys."

"One of *what* guys?"

"You know… the jump in and help sort of fella." I slow my pace as I think about what Jack's implying. Mick *is* always here at the ready and he *does* pitch in an awful lot. Jack notes my meditative expression.

"Why else would he withdraw his offer on this property?" He lifts his arm and dramatically gives a sweeping gesture of display like a model pointing at prizes on a quiz show.

I stop dead in my tracks. "What do you mean, withdraw his offer? What are you talking about?"

Panic sweeps across Jack's face. Seeing he's told me news I hadn't heard before, he stammers, "I think I'm mistaken. Right so, let's get up to the house so you're there when the guests arrive."

"Jack! What do you mean he withdrew his offer?" My voice is shrill and angrier than I intend it to be, but I want an answer. An honest answer.

He looks down at his shoes, then back at me. His eyes are somber as he treads lightly and answers, "He made an offer on this property. He wanted to take it over and farm the land, but you rang up Jeanne and wanted Jim to put in an offer for you." He rocks on his heels, a tactic he used as a boy when he was nervous about something but finishes. "When Mick heard you were the other offer and you were coming home to Boyle, he told Jim he didn't want it anymore. He wanted you to have it and come home."

I look at Jack and study his face. He has faint lines around his mouth and crow's feet at the corners of his eyes. The strands of gray in his hair are more visible in the outdoor light. There's a hint of a scar over his right eye where he had seven stitches after a row he and a classmate had when the offending lad called our father a rat-arsed drunk. He continues rocking on his heels with his hands in his pants pockets, waiting for me to say something.

I look beyond him and see cars coming up the drive and Conall playing traffic director in the makeshift parking lot. I recollect how helpful Mick's been and eager to assist while I was in the throes of renovating the old parochial house. *Why on earth would he step aside when the land was practically his?* I look at Jack Jr. and say, "Well, now. That's news to me." I look back at Conall wildly gesturing with his arms as he guides the motorists to the parking area. He's circling his right arm as if playing air guitar and pointing with his left.

It dawns on me, I left London to leave a man behind and I've replaced him with two new men. I turn back to Jack Jr. and complete my own thought, *make that three.*

"Come on, guests are arriving. I want to put on something a little nicer to greet them. Let's go to the house, shall we?"

The cloud lifts from Jack's face. "That's a great idea. I can see if Mrs. Flood needs me to help her carry the cookies."

"Brilliant idea!" Without thought I reach over and take his hand and we walk back to the house – hand in hand, just like when I was a small girl and loved having my older brother look after me. For a split second I'm that little girl again, beaming with pride, and he's my protective big brother - Jack.

Chapter 18

June 23rd p.m. – People are arriving so I'm making a quick change and then will host our first annual (maybe) St. John's Eve Bonfire!

I've changed into a light lavender sundress and a cream-colored pair of flats. It's a warm evening so I twist my hair into a knot and clip it neatly away from my face. I lightly brush on a touch of eyeshadow and mascara and apply a pale pink gloss over my lips. Standing in front of the full-length mirror I tilt my head and wonder; *how did Jack know there was a second offer on the property and how did he know about Mick being the other interested buyer?*

I stand staring into the mirror but not seeing myself. Instead I'm running scenarios through my head trying to figure out how Jack could know this. Outside, I hear tires on the gravel drive as guests are arriving. Shaking me from my thoughts is the sound of someone shouting a long, deep, "OY, JAYSUS!"

I dart out of my room and meet Mrs. Flood in the hallway. We look at each other and recognize it's Jeanne when a second cry of, "HOLY FECK!" comes from the direction of the registration desk.

I've never seen Mrs. Flood move so swiftly but she's behind the desk next to Jeanne before I'm able to move.

"Jeanne, love, are you okay?" Mrs. Flood is crouched beside Jeanne holding her hand when I get to the desk.

Jeanne's face is ashen and she's biting her bottom lip. There are tiny beads of perspiration on her forehead and I note a puddle below her chair and immediately understand what's happening. "Oh, Jeanne! Is the baby coming?"

Mrs. Flood looks at me and nods. She turns back to Jeanne, "Jeanne, love, let's give Jim a call and get you to hospital."

I exhale deeply. I'm relieved Mrs. Flood's taking charge and remaining calm. This is my first baby-birthing and I haven't a clue what to do. In the movies, there's always a call for boiling water and lots of towels, but this is real life. All I can think to do is pat Jeanne on the shoulder, and say, "There now, Jeanne, we'll get Jim and you'll go to hospital and have this bundle of joy."

I proudly remove my hand, convinced I've contributed something helpful and that soon enough I'll be able to carry on with my plans for the evening when Jeanne growls. I've never heard a sound like this before. It's somewhere between a howl and a guttural bellow.

Mrs. Flood throws a terror-stricken look my way as Jeanne cries in anguish. Finally, Jeanne breathlessly says, "I don't think I can make it to hospital."

Mrs. Flood brushes a strand of hair from Jeanne's face and says, "Sure ye can love, you've got time. You're only just starting the labor pains."

There are tears streaming down Jeanne's face now and she whimpers, "I've been having pain all day."

"Holy feck, Jeanne! You've known all day this might happen, and you still show up to work? What's wrong with you? *Are ye mad*?"

Jeanne and I are both shocked at Mrs. Flood's revelation of the harsher side of her personality, but snap to when she barks at Jeanne, "Well right, we'll have to deal with what we've got now, won't we?" She casts an admonishing eye at Jeanne then turns to me. "Nora, phone Jim and tell him to get here, *right now*."

Jeanne huffs and puffs. "He's on his way with the kids. They're coming to the bonfire."

"Brilliant, then we won't have to worry about your husband missing the blessed event." Mrs. Flood's sardonic tone would be comical under normal circumstances, but her words are razor sharp and only cause more tears to spill down Jeanne's cheeks. Turning to me, Mrs. Flood says, "ring Jim and tell him to come to the house, then go get someone from the fire brigade, I can't do this alone."

Without a word, I depart as Mrs. Flood says to Jeanne, "Come now, we'll go down the hall to Nora's room where ye can have this baby."

My room? ... But my beautiful linens! The lavender duvet cover! The new cream-colored rug! ... My room?!

Snapping out of selfish thoughts, I run down the hall, through the kitchen and as I open the door to exit, I trip over Debby, landing face first in the dirt.

"Oh, feck you, Debby. Feck you stupid lazy dog!"

Debby stretches as she stands and casts her deep brown eyes my way and then up at Mick who's standing with his mouth agape staring at me. His father and Alannah are with him but a few paces behind. He clears his throat and softly says, "I've never heard such profanity from your mouth, Nora."

Heat rises in my face at the embarrassment of having Mick witness my foul-mouth tirade at the poor creature. Before I can offer an explanation, Mick's outreached hand is pulling me from the ground. Alannah and Mr. Reynolds join us. "Are you alright, Nora dear?" Mr. Reynold's fatherly tone eases my anxiety.

"Aye, yes, sir. I'm in a wee panic. I was making a dart to get someone from the fire brigade for Jeanne."

Brushing a fallen strand of hair from my eyes, I add, "she's having the baby on me bed!"

Mick, still grasping my hand, lets it go, turns to his father and directs him, "Go to the truck and get Anthony, tell him Jeanne's in labor up at the house and to send someone, right now."

Mr. Reynolds trots swiftly towards the fire lorry without a word. Mick turns to me. "Is Jim inside?"

"No, I'm supposed to ring him. He's coming with the kids, but doesn't know about this... this thing..."

Surmising I'm about to lose it, Mick places his hands on my shoulders and encourages, "You can do this, Nora. Just decide to. Now, either you stay here and help Jeanne and I'll have Conall or Jack play master of ceremony or you go down there and handle the event."

Reading Mick's features, I see a calm strength he's exuding, almost willing me to remain as calm as he is. My heart's racing so I begin taking deep breaths, breathing in and exhaling hard before speaking. "I love Jeanne, but I'm afraid I'd be of no use in there. Mrs. Flood is with her." I glance at Alannah who's wearing a pair of Capri pants and a rose-colored top. I look at Mick, then back at Alannah.

Stepping back from Mick, I turn to Debby and whisper, "Sorry old girl, didn't mean to take it out on ye."

Petting Debby on the head, I look back at Mick and resolutely add, "I'd best tend to the business. I'll be down at the bonfire if anyone needs me, my mobile is in my pocket." I nervously smile at Alannah and then at Mick. "Oh, Mick, will ye call Jim? You've got his number, right?"

Mr. Reynolds is returning with two EMTs from the fire brigade. One's a tall dark-haired lad with a single eyebrow knitted across his forehead. In his right hand he's carrying a massive first aid kit that resembles a fishing tackle box. The other is a young lady with a sweet face. She's speaking into a walkie-talkie and slung over her shoulder is a canvas duffle bag with a red cross painted on the side.

"Jeanne's inside the house in my room. Go through the kitchen, turn right, it's the last door at the end of the hallway."

"Not to worry, Nora. We've got this under control." Mr. Reynolds brushes past me leading the EMTS into the house. I recognize how alike Mick and his father are in times like these. I hear Mick on his mobile with Jim as I continue towards the celebration. A million thoughts and emotions whirl around in my head. Just another fun event at Cara Maith.

Chapter 19

June 24th — Utterly exhausted! Despite all the commotion at the house, St. John's Eve was a brilliant success! Conall and Jack Jr. brilliantly entertained the guests and Father Mark's prayer was beautiful. He even had printed pocket-sized copies for all the attendees which was a lovely touch! Jeanne delivered a beautiful baby girl at half-ten last night. Mother and baby are at St. Patrick's Community Hospital in Carrick-on-Shannon and are in good health. Thank the Lord!

I pour a cup of tea, take it into my study, and plop down in the overstuffed chair by the fireplace. I've got a few hours to relax before this evening's guests arrive. Most of yesterday's guests departed except for the couple from South Carolina who are on their way to Castlerea for the day for a tour of Clonalis House and a stop at the Black Donkey brewery.

Imelda's upstairs changing linens and tidying rooms and I hear Mrs. Flood clanking dishes and plates as she puts things away in the kitchen. Her boundless energy amazes me, especially since I'm completely drained, both physically and mentally.

Leaning back, I shut my eyes and replay yesterday's events. I'm perplexed as to who sent the invitation to Jack Jr. Although, I'm happy he's here. Then there's the whole Mick rescinding his offer on the Cara Maith surprise. Was I the only one unaware of his wishes to buy this place? Surely, Jeanne must have known. I can't imagine Jim not telling her.

Then there's Alannah. Pretty, sweet, young Alannah. She just stood there gawking at me while I had my little foul-mouthed tirade after tripping over Debby. She either thinks I'm half mad or completely mad.

Finally, Conall. He's become a constant presence around here and I don't know why. The town people certainly enjoy having him visit Boyle, and he fits right in when he shows up.

I take a deep breath and out of habit my thoughts stray to Dylan. I wonder if he's in London or if he's at his soon-to-be retirement home in the Seychelles. The ugly bile of jealousy tinged with anger churns deep inside as I imagine the beautiful place he and Kimberly enjoy together.

I despise jealousy, so I shake my head, open my eyes and pick up the teacup from the side table. I sip from the beaker and look out the window. A few black-faced Roscommon sheep have their heads down ardently chewing the grass, never stopping for more than a second to look up before returning to the patch of green for more. *I bet Dylan has beautiful ocean views in the Seychelles.*

There's a tap on the study door and Jack Jr. sticks his head inside. "Care for company?"

"Please, join me. I'm just sitting here recovering."

Jack steps inside, closes the door and parks himself in the other chair. "You know, despite the behind-the-scenes chaos, it was a fantastic night."

"You're too kind, Jack. I hope the rest of the guests feel the same."

"Aye, they do!" He pulls his mobile out of his pocket and begins swiping and poking the screen before handing it to me. "Look, Cara Maith's St. John's Eve is the headline of the town's website."

I take the phone and see in large letters, *Cara Maith St. John's Eve a Blazing Success.* "That's a cracking headline."

"You really need to give yourself more credit, Nora." He drums his fingers on the arm of the chair. "I don't know why you're so hard on yourself. You're brilliant. *Really*."

"Why'd ya take off, Jack? And why are you here now?"

My questions blindside him. He leans back resting his head on the chair. "It's complicated, Nora." He leans forward, rests his elbows on his knees and looks at the floor. "I was angry when I left - and then the longer I stayed away, the more ashamed I felt. I was too ashamed to come back."

I look out the window at the sheep who have moved closer to the stone fence and are devouring a new shock of green grass. "Well, we could have used ye here, all the same."

"I know. And now that I have a wife and two kids of my own, I feel even worse about taking off." Jack brushes a piece of lint from his pantleg, leans back and looks at me, "Nora, you were still too small to understand just how hard it was being Jack Jr. when Jack Sr. was known as a hard-drinking womanizer. When he died, I was so mixed up." He runs his hand through his hair before continuing. "When he died, I was released. Released from the embarrassment. Released from the shame. I was out from under Jack Sr. and I was happy about that. Do you know how confusing that was?"

"Yes. Yes, I do. I may have been younger, but even at that age I could see despite her financial struggles, Ma was a changed woman too. She had different worries, but she didn't have the stress and shame of knowing her husband was out carousing and catting around anymore. So, yes, yes, I do know how confused you were because I was too. I loved our father, but I hated what he did to our mother. Even little kids pick up on that sort of thing."

Neither one of us speaks for a prolonged period. Jack's eyes are focused on the bookshelves behind my desk and I'm watching the sheep who are now being corralled by Mick and Debby.

"You haven't answered my second question, Jack. Why are you here, now?" I turn and face him.

"Mrs. Flood." He takes a deep breath and says, "Mrs. Flood wrote me. She's written to me over the years and she adores ye, wanted me to be here to support you for once."

"You expect me to believe after years of me and Ma pleading with ye to come back, a simple note from Mrs. Flood is all it took to get ye here?" I snort self-righteously for emphasis.

"No. It wasn't just the note from her. It was you, me, this town - Dad. Mostly it was my new life. Now that I'm married and have wee ones, I see just how wrong it was for me to take off on ye." He nervously pops his knuckles one at a time. "I want my family to have family. I'd like to be part of your life again, Nora. I know I've hurt ye and I don't expect you to just take me in like the prodigal son, but I'd like to try - try to be your big brother again."

Debby's dutifully barking at a few renegade sheep out in the field and Mick's trekking behind them holding a staff in his right hand with his other in his coat pocket. I watch the pair going about their business as I contemplate what Jack's just said. "Well, Jack, it's going to take time. I'm glad you're back and you're welcome to stay as long as ye like, but I need to think this through."

"I know. I'd expected you to feel this way. Can't say I blame you." He stands, walks towards the door, "Mick wanted me to ask if you'd like to go into Carrick to see Jeanne later. She'll be at St. Patrick's for another night before they send her and the baby home. She'd be thrilled if you come."

I pull my attention away from Mick, Debby, and the sheep outside and turn to see Jack Jr.'s wounded expression as he stands in the doorway awaiting my reply. "Absolutely. Come get me when you're ready to go."

"*EE-Fa, EE-fa, EE-Fa!*" Mary sternly enunciates as she rocks the tiny infant swaddled in a yellow blanket.

"I was hoping for a Liam or Eugene." Des pouts as he hovers over the newborn in his sister's arms.

"Well your father and I like Aoife. It's a lovely Irish name. Red Aoife was a daughter of the king of Connacht whose marriage was arranged by none other than St. Patrick himself," Jeanne says with finality.

I tap on the open door. "May we come in?"

Jim stands to greet us as Jeanne beams and says, "Jaysus, yes, come in the lot of ye."

Conall, Jack Jr. and Mick file in behind me as Mary calls, "Oh, Auntie Nora, isn't Aoife lovely?!" She tilts the tiny bundle towards me. "I wanted to call her Ava, but Mum insisted on the Irish of Ava, and ye know, it's growing on me, now." Mary taps Aoife's tiny nose then looks at me. "Come, sit and rock the baby; it's just like holding a doll."

Mary tenderly hands the baby to me as she gets out of the rocker. "There now Auntie Nora, sit. Aoife likes a gentle slow rock." I smile at Mary's instant affection for her new sister as I gingerly ease into the chair.

"That's it, Auntie Nora. You're a natural." Mary steps back and smiles with approval as I begin rocking. "I wish you'd have a baby, so we can have a cousin. Oh, wouldn't that be something?!"

Conall jumps in, "I think that's a grand idea, Mary." Turning to me he gives a wide grin. "So, how's about it, Nora? Tick-tock, tick-tock."

I throw an evil look at Conall as Mick clears his throat and interrupts, "We've brought ye a little something, Jeanne." He approaches Jeanne with a box of Cadbury Roses. Jack moves in and hands Jim a dish garden of lush green plants in a ceramic baby pram.

"Just what I always wanted, Jack."

"Very funny, Jim. Bring it here so I can see it," Jeanne says as she sets the box of chocolate on the nightstand. "You know, Mick, I still have the peace lily you gave me when Mary was born."

"That so? That's a hearty plant I'd say." Mick grins with satisfaction and looks my way before turning his attention back to Jeanne. "You gave us a fright last night."

"You'd think by the third time, she'd have known when it was time to skedaddle to hospital, wouldn't ye," Jim says as he takes a couple candies from the box and hands one each to Des and Mary.

"I'm so sorry, Mick. I really thought I'd plenty of time. I was sure I'd last till morning." Jeanne gestures towards me. "But Aoife there was in a hurry. I guess she didn't care her mum of geriatric maternal age should have been at hospital."

"Aye, well praise Jaysus, Mary, and Joseph that Nora practically had the entire Boyle fire brigade on-hand for ye," Jim adds.

Jeanne looks at me and says in a timid voice, "Can you forgive me, Nora? I hope I didn't ruin."

Anna Marie Jehorek

Jack interrupts, "Oh, no, you didn't ruin a thing, Jeanne. Nora's bonfire made the home page of the town website and the local radio. T'was a huge success." Jack spreads his arms wide to emphasize the enormity of the success.

"Well, that's wonderful, Nora." She gives a wink and adds, "I'm relieved. I'd have felt terrible if my birthing a baby at your inn caused a problem."

"Actually, you having Aoife at Nora's was brilliant strategy, Jeanne," Conall soberly adds.

"How's that Conall?"

"Considering she's already had one guest kick the bucket, I'd imagine a live birth counters any bad PR from …"

Mick interrupts, "Well, mother and child are in good health and the St. John's Eve gathering was brilliant. Plenty to be grateful for, indeed."

I snicker because it's clear, Mick's interruption was due to his own discomfort with the discussion. He catches my smile and gives a small grin and a wink. Aoife is sound asleep in my arms. I'm mesmerized studying her tiny eyelashes and fingernails. "She's beautiful, Jeanne. A true miracle." There's a tear pooling in the corner of each of my eyes, so I don't' dare look up.

306

The room's silent, and I feel all eyes on me and the baby as I slowly rock this tiny blessing in my lap. Finally, I glance up and see Jack, Jim, Jeanne, Mary, Des, Conall, and Mick all smiling at me and Aoife.

I for one am delighted they're going with the Irish version of the name. Ava is lovely but has such baggage in these parts.

"Well, we should probably be on our way before they toss the lot of us for exceeding the permitted number of visitors." I smile and ask, "Des, will you come take your lovely little Aoife?" Mary pulls a face of disappointment, but Jim slips her another candy and she perks up immediately.

I hand Des the baby and detect admiration in his eyes. It's obvious he adores his new sister even if he was hoping for a *Liam* or *Eugene*. He's going to be a protective big brother, no doubt. Des reminds me of how Jack used to be with me. "You're a wonderful big brother, Des." There's a catch in my throat and I look at Jack Jr. who's smiling back.

"Jim, care to join us for lunch at the Oarsman?" Conall pats him on the back. "We'd love to have you join us for a little celebratory luncheon and perhaps a wee tipple."

Jim looks at Jeanne then back at Conall, "Oh, I probably shouldn't." His voice and longing expression belie his words.

"Oh, go on, Jim," Jeanne blurts. "The kids are fine with me and ye could use a break. Go on, get some food and fresh air."

"Sounds like you've been told to get out of here." Conall laughs as he walks past Jim towards the door.

"Right, so. I guess it's settled," Mick declares taking the car keys from his pocket.

I hug Jeanne and as I lean in, she whispers, "Let me know if I messed up anything in the house."

I give her a wink. "Don't even think about it. It's all grand. Mrs. Flood's taken care of everything."

The table by the stone fireplace is large enough for our motley crew of five. Conall decides I need to be at the center of the table so there aren't too many lads sitting side-by-side. I don't care where I sit so long as the food arrives quickly. I haven't had a bite to eat since lunchtime yesterday. My nervous stomach compounded by the bonfire, the birth of Aoife, and preparing breakfast for a house full of guests prevented me from eating.

"Hi, I'm Rosaleen and I'll be taking care of you today. Can I start ye with drinks?" The tall slender waitress captures the attention of everyone at the table. Her deep blue eyes framed with long lashes and her milky white skin give her an angelic presence which momentarily renders the men unable to speak, so I begin, "I'll have a cup of tea."

Returning to earth, Conall counters, "Ah go way, Nora. This here's a celebration. At least order a pint or glass of wine, for Pete's sake." He shakes his head in mocking disappointment.

"Ok, I'll have a glass of Pinot Grigio then," I say to Rosaleen while staring at Conall.

Jack, Jim, and Mick all chime in, "Guinness, Guinness, Guinness," but when the poor girl gets to Conall he calls out, "I'll have a Galway Hooker."

To my left, Mick mumbles under his breath, "Of course ye will."

I giggle at Mick's sardonic tone and note the others at the table are still mesmerized by our waitress.

"Right, so, that's a Pinot Grigio, three pints, and a Galway Hooker," Rosaleen turns, tucks the pen in her apron and walks off. Conall's tongue is practically on the floor as she departs, her short black skirt shifting from side to side as her dark locks bounce atop her shoulders.

Once Rosaleen's out of sight, I clear my throat to break the testosterone-charged silence. "So, Jim, how'd ye arrive at *Aoife*?" I lift the menu and begin reading. "Last I talked to Jeanne she was leaning towards *Emer*."

He lifts the menu in front of him and looks at it as he answers, "Ah, ye know, we put it to Des and Mary, and they had their own ideas."

He peers over the top of the menu and adds, "Mary begged us to call the baby *Ava* if it was a girl." He cuts his eyes to Mick and continues, "but Jeanne would have none of that. Said she didn't like *Ava* and she wanted an *Irish* name."

I note Jim examining Mick's expression before he finishes, "So, we compromised. *Aoife*. Irish for *Ava*."

Jack chimes in, "That's a lovely name. Beautiful." He then turns to Conall. "So, Conall, how is it you've become a bit of a fixture in these parts?"

Jack's question lands like a lead balloon on the table in front of us as all menus are lowered in anticipation of Conall's answer. I'm as curious as the others. For months, now, I've been trying to understand Conall's presence and insertion into my life. I'm especially curious ever since Martin divulged it was Conall's request I work on his memoir.

I lean forward to hear his reply.

"That's a brilliant question," Conall runs his hand through his hair which I now understand is a delaying tactic he employs when he's gathering the right words. "There are several *reasons*." He uses air quotes for emphasis. "But mainly, it's closest to family, besides me own, I've had in a long time. I spent so many years on the road playing football or training for football, I'd forgotten what it was like to be part of a community." His eyes flicker as he looks at me. "Adding to the sense of community is Nora. Nora's let me be part of her world and…"

"Who had the *Galway Hooker*?" Rosaleen interrupts as she arrives at the table with a full tray of drinks.

Conall lifts his index finger in the air. "I'm the Galway Hooker."

The chatter turns to claiming our drinks and ordering food, and Conall's answer to Jack's inquiry is forgotten as we shift to other subjects of conversation. I'm left with his "and" hanging in the air as unfinished business. I may never get the answer.

The remainder of our celebratory luncheon revolves around stories of Conall on the football pitch, questions of when Jack Jr. returns to America, and Mick's latest farming software development. I quietly nibble at my burger and enjoy the first decent meal I've had in several days.

As I take the last swallow of wine, Conall playfully leans forward, looks past me towards Mick and asks, "What did ye do with Alannah? Did she take off after the bonfire or did ye turn her out of yer house early this morning?"

Mick lifts his napkin, wipes his mouth and softly answers, "She left last night."

"Ah, sorry to hear that mate. I thought, maybe, you know…"

Mick lifts his glass, takes a sip, and puts it down on the table. "No. No, Conall. She drove herself back to Strandhill. I don't think she'll be returning."

The rest of us at the table appreciate that Mick's an extremely private person and, although we're curious, we know when Mick has told us all he wants us to know. Conall, on the other hand, either hasn't been around Mick long enough to comprehend or he doesn't care, so he goes there. "Aw feck. Did ye get dumped?"

Conall pushes his chair a few inches back from the table to look past me at Mick. "That's bloody shite, mate.

Jaysus, I'm sorry. She's a beautiful girl. 'Tis a shame. What the feck happened?"

Mick inches back in his chair to face Conall directly and I pull in closer to my plate to not be caught in the crossfire. "Well, Conall, she had several observations she'd made and shared with me, but seeing as this is a celebration, I won't go into details. I will say, I'd had my own reservations about Alannah so 'tisn't the end of the world. I won't be grieving. We parted on good terms."

"Excellent!" Conall exclaims, grabs his half empty Galway Hooker, and lifts his glass. "To new life and new beginnings!"

We're all frozen so Conall nods at our glasses. "Come on, a toast!"

I look at my empty wine glass and decide to lift my water instead as the others pick up their nearly finished pints and echo, "To new life and new beginnings!"

Conall signals to Rosaleen and exclaims, "Another round for the table!"

All the guests are checked in and have gone about their evening plans, so Jack Jr. grabs a bottle of Paddy whiskey and two Waterford crystal glasses. We go outside to the small courtyard patio off the kitchen where he pours two fingers into each glass.

"I recognize these." He nods at the crystal as he pours. "Aren't these Ma's?"

"Aye, they are." He hands me the glass and I sniff the whiskey then take a tiny sip. The amber liquid slowly warms my throat as it goes down. "I think these glasses may have been one of her only happy memories of her and Da."

Jack nods in acknowledgement taking a draw from his drink.

I look at the sky which is slowly darkening to a smoky blue. A few stars are twinkling. I continue, "Waterford *Colleen* highball." I look at the glass, turning it in my hand, and watch the whiskey swish from side to side. "That's what she told me the glass is called. They went to Waterford and Wicklow on their honeymoon and visited the factory. They bought two highballs and sipped whiskey in the car park of their B&B while pretending they were royalty sitting on the balcony at the Powerscourt Hotel looking out over the garden."

"You're better than I am at keeping the stories alive, Nora." He tilts his head skyward and wistfully adds, "At least there were *some* good memories for her, God rest her soul."

314

"God rest her soul," I add reflexively.

"You need a telescope out here, Nora." He points upward. "I think that's Venus shining on us up there. Without the light noise of the city, it would be brilliant to have a telescope for your guests to really see the stars and planets."

I turn to see his face in the fading light. "That's a grand idea, Jack. I'll add it to the list."

He looks back at me. "Are you having a laugh or are ye serious?"

"I'm serious, Jack. It's a grand idea."

We sit listening to the evening sounds beginning. The distant lowing of cows and the faint bleating of sheep yield to crickets. I've always loved the June evenings. Night falls so slowly, it's nearly half eleven before it's dark. The weather's warm and the sky sparkles with stars putting on a dazzling display in the far-off heavens.

"Do you ever worry you'll be like him, Jack?"

He gives a soft snort. "Every day I wake up. It terrifies me."

"Me too. I try hard to be like Ma, but then again, I'm afraid of that too. She put up with so much. She should have sent him packing, but she kept taking him back." I lift my glass and study the whiskey. "I don't dare have more than a couple drinks. Ever. I'm so afraid it's in me."

"I know what ye mean but you'd know by now if you'd been saddled with that demon. I think it has a way of surfacing, rearing its ugly head. You'd know."

Jack pats my knee. "I don't drink at all at home, just in case - in case it's simmering deep below the surface waiting to destroy me the way it destroyed Jack Fallon, Sr."

"I thought he came to me one night, not long ago." I take another sip of whiskey and wait for the burn to fade. "When I was small, he'd sit me on his lap and tell me grand tales. I honestly believed he hung the moon."

Jack laughs. "He was a brilliant storyteller. Sure, everyone loved when he'd be spinning a yarn."

"Well, one night I'm in a deep sleep and he's there. He's standing there calling to me – not with his voice, but with his eyes. He's illuminated standing in the doorway. So, in my dream I speak to him, I ask, *'Is that you Da?'* He doesn't say anything, but there's this bright light and I feel it shining on me and he's saying something but not with words, only with his eyes. Finally, for some reason, I wake up. When I open my eyes, the moon is shining so brightly through my window, I feel like it's a spotlight shining on me."

"Do you think it was him?"

"I like to believe it was. I thought he hung the moon - I'm pretty sure he could direct it to shine on me to let me know he's still around."

The sound of tires on gravel in the car park interrupts our peaceful sibling moment. Conall exits his car and approaches. "Is that you, Nora, sitting in the dark?" He's upon us when he adds, "Oy, and Jack too. Ah, just the people I was looking for, mind if I join ye?"

Conall plunks down in a chair beside me, spying the whiskey bottle on the ground between me and Jack. "Ah, the old Paddy Flaherty. Good stuff."

"Would you care for some, Conall?" I tip my glass in his direction, but he waves it off.

"Na, I'm driving back to Dublin, tonight. Got to keep me wits about me." He strokes his hair and adds, "I've just come to say goodbye for now and finish what I started at lunch." He trails off searching for words, which is unusual for Conall Kelly.

Jack asks, "Finish what you started? What did you start?"

"I was answering your question, Jack. You know, why I'm here."

Jack nods and takes another sip of whiskey.

"I've been struggling with this one and I'm not sure how to - I don't know how to - but seeing as you're both here."

"Out with it Conall, you're being more cryptic than usual," I tease.

Conall's expression darkens in what's left of the evening light. "I've no way of doing this without changing everything."

His tormented tone makes me lean forward in my chair. I don't know why but I grab each arm bracing for what's coming. *Is he sick? Is he dying?* I feel my heart pounding so hard it's nearly in my throat. "What, Conall? What is it?"

"Promise you won't get angry."

"Angry, why will I be angry? What have you done, Conall?"

"I've done nothing, but someone else has… or *did*."

"Conall, I swear I'm going to smack you if you don't tell me."

Jack has pulled his chair closer. "Conall, don't bedevil her, out with it!"

Tugging at his hair, he proceeds, "The other reason I've been coming around Cara Maith and Nora has to do with some news I learned a while back. "

"What kind of news, Conall?" I can't read his expression anymore, so I place my hand on his knee.

Conall puts his hand over mine and continues, "I learned I have a half-brother and a half-sister I never knew."

His voice drops off, so I ask, "What do you mean? A half-brother and half-sister?" His hand is warm on top of mine and I hear crickets chirping when abruptly, Jack explodes, "Holy shite!"

"What? What? *Holy shite*, what?" I plead but they both ignore me.

"Now I get why you came to America to convince me to come here! *For Mrs. Flood. We'll keep it our secret. A surprise!*" Jack hisses as he dramatically throws his hands up in air quotes.

Wait, what? Conall and Jack have met before? In America? I can't wrap my brain around Conall's news but obviously Jack Jr. has.

"Me mum - she knew *your* Dad. I only ever heard her talk about him in hushed tones, so as not to upset my Dad - my *step-dad.*"

I stare at Conall for a moment and then look back at Jack Jr. before the thought finally lands in my mind like a feather slowly making its way to the ground. "No, not possible. It's not possible," I say out loud but mostly to myself.

Conall carries on, as if he needs to unload it all to excise the wound. "He was on a job in Donegal and they would go to the dances together. He charmed her - and well - ye know."

"*Ye know*?!" Jack spits. "*Ye know*?!" He looks at the glass of whiskey and just as he's about to toss it, I snatch it from his hand.

"Not the glass, Jack, not ma's good *Waterford*."

"Dear, God, Nora. The woman was a doormat for Jack Fallon, and you're worried about preserving her precious honeymoon glass!?"

His words bite, and tears are burning my eyes as he storms off swearing, "Jack Fallon was a fecker, a lousy drunk, womanizing, cheater. How many other little bastards has he got scattered across Ireland?"

"Jack, come back, we have to talk about this." Conall calls to the darkness, but all we hear is the slamming door.

I'm numb in my chair. I hear blood whooshing through my ears. Conall takes the glass from my hand, places it on the ground, and grasps both my hands. His eyes are fixed on mine, but I don't see him clearly. I'm in a daze. Visions of the past months flash in my mind.

Conall's kindness and concern, his tender kisses on the forehead or cheek, the way I could never figure out his angle or approach.

"Nora, I'm sorry to shock ye. I didn't know how to tell you. I can see I let it drag out too long. Forgive me."

I shake my head, snatch my hands from his, and whisper. "Are you sure?"

Conall reaches into the pocket of his jacket and presents an old photograph. "This is the only picture me mum had of her and my birth-father."

He pushes the faded picture in front of me. I don't touch it. I sit staring at it in what's left of the light. It's Jack Fallon. My father. He's wearing a sports coat over an open collar white shirt and there's a cigarette hanging from his mouth. Cocky Jack Fallon with his arm around a woman in a dress and ballet flats - a pregnant woman. A very pregnant woman who isn't my mother.

I peel my eyes from the photograph. I can't bear looking any longer. Instead I look at Conall. His distressed gaze is on me, but it's too dark to see his steely blue eyes. My eyes are hazel, a mix of mum's brown and Da's blue. Conall's eyes are just like Jack Fallon's. Conall has *my* father's eyes.

My tears flow at the realization of just how severe Jack Fallon's betrayal of my mother was. I wonder if she even knew. Maybe she knew about the woman and her babby in Donegal and turned a blind eye. How long did Jack Sr. bother to stick around for Conall's mom after Conall was born? Why is Conall telling me now? What am I supposed to do with this?

The salty tears stream down my cheeks, but I find the breath to utter, "I think you need to go, Conall. I think you need to go."

Chapter 20

June 25th – Famous footballer Conall Kelly is my half-brother, my father was an even worse scoundrel than originally thought, and I don't know what to do next. I'll pretend nothing is wrong for my guests' sake as I serve breakfast and usher them on their way. Imelda tells me there's only one room booked for tonight… thankfully.

"Are you okay, dear? You look like ye got a bad dose." Mrs. Flood's standing at the coffee maker looking over her shoulder as I enter the kitchen.

"I'm grand, Mrs. Flood. Grand."

She gives me the once over with a disbelieving eye before carrying on, "I hear Jeanne and baby Aoife are coming home today. Will ye be calling round to say hello?"

"I may, I may. But for now, I'm out to gather a few eggs." I grab the empty basket by the door, turn the knob slowly, and look down before stepping outside - I'm learning to make sure Debby isn't lying in wait, literally.

The coast is clear, so I wearily stride towards the chicken coop. The morning sky casts a velvety pink hue as the sun edges its way above the horizon. The mellow clucking of the chickens softens my harsh mood as I ponder what a simple existence these little ladies have. "Tut tut ladies, 'tis only me come to get a few of your finest eggs." I delicately reach under my best producer and speak to her like she's a prized employee, "Why thank you Mrs. Clucky, you're due for a performance review and a raise, aren't ye?"

"Do you often speak to hens in this manner?"

I'm startled to the point of almost dropping my egg basket, but Mick gets his hand under it before it hits the ground. "Oh, Mick, you scared the life out of me."

He hands me the basket. "You're awfully tense this morning, Nora. Everything *okay?*"

Puddles fill my eyes at the thought of last night and its life-changing revelations. My head spins and I lean back against Mrs. Clucky's cage. "Oh, Mick. Everything's wrong. Everything's completely and utterly banjaxed."

My emotional outburst and the onslaught of tears alarms him, so he snatches the basket from my hand. "Stay here, I'll take these to Mrs. Flood."

I slide down the chicken cages and collapse to the ground; my legs folding beneath me. Sitting cross-legged in the hay I begin sobbing. When Mick returns to find me in a heap blubbering, he squats down, lifts my chin with his index finger, and soothingly whispers, "Come, now, we'll walk." He extends his hand and I take it. Hoisting me from the ground he pulls me close and wipes the tears from my eyes with his sleeve. "You won't be able to see where you're going if you're crying. Let's save the tears for later, shall we?"

I nod obediently as he leads me by the hand down to the front field. Debby ambles ahead, ready to report for herding duty, glancing back every few paces to assure we're close behind. Debby wags her tail when she reaches the gate and patiently waits for Mick to open it allowing her entry. He pets her head. "Go on now, girl. Send em to the back corner, Debby."

Swinging the gate open the St. Bernard darts after her charges, nimbly going about her task. Mick, still firmly holding my hand, leads me inside and closes the gate behind us. Guiding me through the dewy grass, he looks at my feet then back at me and grins. "I've got the benefit of me Wellingtons, but your feet are damp with dew. Let's find a spot to sit down."

Mick leads me to the edge of the field where the old stone fence has been standing for centuries. The stones are stacked about four feet-tall, so he places his hands on my waist and lifts me, sitting me down on the cool stones. "There, we'll keep your feet dry from the dew, now.

I look out over the field and watch Debby chasing the herd. I have a new appreciation for the goofy dog. She deftly darts between the fleecy creatures, moving them and swiftly returning to chase the stray ones. She's more than a tripping hazard after all.

Mick gives a little whistle and Debby kicks into high gear and the sheep scurry to the corner of the field. "That a girl, Debby, that a girl." He calls to the dog as he reaches into his pocket producing a small stainless-steel thermos.

"Cuppa?" He asks as he unscrews the lid, turns it over and pours the steaming liquid into it. "I've only got the one cup, so we can share."

I take the tea from him warming my hands on the cup before taking a sip. The scorching liquid is sweeter than I'm used to, so I'm taken aback. I swallow the sweet tea slowly then hand the cup back to Mick. He takes a drink and gives it back. "Here, ye look like you need it more than I do."

"Yes, that's the Irish. No matter what the tragedy, tea will make it better." I smile and take another sip.

"Care to talk about it, or are we just being *Strong Silent Nora* this morning?"

"I'm hardly *Strong Silent Nora* after my pitiful display in the hen house."

"Oh, that was a momentary lapse, but if I know ye, you'll be tough as nails in no time at all."

Mick leans back against the fence, his right elbow touching my knee. I put my hand on his shoulder, he reaches his left hand and takes mine and says tenderly, "I know, Nora - Conall told me and Dad the other night."

I process this information wordlessly. I sit listening to a magpie chirping in the distance and the low baaing of the sheep Debby's corralling in the field before steeling myself to ask, "How long till the news is all over town? – *the bush telephone*?"

"It will go no further, unless you want it to." He squeezes my hand tightly to reassure me. "How did Jack Jr. take the news?

"He exploded." I study the veins in Mick's hand and note how tiny my hand looks in his. "I'd imagine he'll be off to Dublin and on a flight to America as soon as possible. He's been gone for donkey's years and when he finally comes home..." The words catch in my throat and my voice cracks, "he comes home only to have his whole world rocked again."

Mick lifts my hand to his mouth and brushes his lips in a small kiss. "And how about you, Nora? What do *you* plan to do with this new information?"

"I don't know. I honestly don't know. I sent Conall away last night, so I can think."

"Thinking is good, but don't forget to feel. How do you *feel*, Nora?"

I scan the front field. The grass is a lush green dewy carpet leading up to the foothills of the Curlew Mountains in the distance. This land is in my soul; I breathe in the clean air and let it go before answering. "Mick, I've spent so long fighting. I've fought memories, I've fought feelings of inadequacy, feelings of shame, feelings of inferiority, feelings of guilt - I don't know what to *feel* anymore."

Staring ahead, Mick quietly inquires, "Could you love him as a *brother*?"

His question drills to the point and the word *brother* hangs in the air before seeming to land in the damp grass. I've been struggling to view Conall in a new light since he dropped his news in my lap and I sent him away - or more accurately, since Jack Jr. and I chased him off.

"Should I? What would you do, Mick?"

Mick's eyes follow Debby across the field as she plods back to join us. "When he first started coming around, I had my suspicions. I didn't understand his motives. I only saw how he looked at ye. He adores you, but it wasn't in a bloke-in-love sort of way. Nah, t'was more of an admiration. Like he has ye on a pedestal." Turning to look at me over his shoulder, he adds, "He thinks you're grand, Nora."

I don't reply but consider Mick's words.

"Nora, I've watched him watch you from the start. It wasn't until he sent me the invite to the book launch that I started to wonder. "

"Wonder *what*?"

"He wanted you there, but he wanted you there with me - that's not something a fella does if he's interested in dating a lady, now *is it*?"

He lets go of my hand and turns to face me directly placing a hand on each side of me, so my knees are in his chest as he adds, "The whole time I was watching him with you, he was watching *you* with *me*."

The copper flecks in Mick's eyes dazzle in the early morning sunlight. His earnest gaze penetrates, and I'm transfixed as he continues, "I think you should let him be your brother. It's all he wants. He only wants you to be happy. That's why he came to me first."

I shake my head. "I don't understand, Mick."

"He wanted me to know so I could be here for you. Nora, Conall loves his sister and he asked me to."

Mick looks down, grasping for the right thing to say. "Nora, he knows I care about you more than anything in this world. He knows there's nothing I wouldn't do to make sure you're safe and happy."

Mick looks up, locking his eyes on mine. "He knows I'm in love with you and have been for a very long time. "

I examine his eyes, study his intense expression and then reach for his hair. Running my hand through the wavy brown locks, my fingers find their way down his cheeks. I stroke his soft skin before tracing the shape of his lips. "Mick, what have you been waiting for?"

Mick kisses the finger still tracing the form of his bottom lip then says, "Waiting for you to stop fighting the past, to quit trying to prove yourself to the world..." he reaches for my finger, pulls it away from his mouth and finishes, "waiting for you to forget whomever it is you left in London."

Chapter 21

December 26th St. Stephen's Day! – The sun is out but there's frost on the ground, expecting several people to join us for a small celebration on the wine patio, thank goodness for space heaters!

From my room, I hear the doorbell ring and Mrs. Flood excitedly greeting someone. "Ah, ye look a million bucks, the lot of ye!" The light melody of classical music playing fills my room as I finish applying my makeup and Jeanne adds a spritz of hairspray to set the updo and delicate curls cascading down each cheek.

Stepping back, she beams. "Ah, ye look beautiful, Nora. Your mum would be thrilled." There's a tear pooling in the corner of her eye so I playfully swat her hand. "Now, cut that out, you'll have me spoiling my mascara if ye go getting weepy."

Jeanne places the comb on the dressing table, and I stand up, looking at myself for the first time in the full-length mirror. The soft candlelight ivory crepe flows to the floor. The princess neckline accentuates the length of my neck, the pearl drop earrings frame my face, and the long delicate lace sleeves taper at my wrists giving an overall ethereal look to the ensemble.

Although I see the reflection of 38-year-old Nora - I still see the little girl inside, unsure, frightened, poor Nora. I shake my head to dislodge all thoughts of unhappy times. I intend to live in *this* moment, never looking back – not *today* anyway.

There's a gentle tap at the door and Jack Jr. pops his head inside. "All set?"

Jeanne turns and says, "We're on our way, aren't we, Nora?"

We move down the hallway to find the bright red Georgian door wide open and Conall waiting there for us. Jeanne turns to me and gives a gentle peck on my cheek before saying, "Let's do this" and she proceeds through the door.

Conall grins and loops his right arm through my left as Jack Jr. takes me by the right arm. I glance at the flowers in my hands and at each of my brothers locked arm in arm with me. I took Mick's words to heart and reluctantly decided to let myself become Conall Kelly's sister. Afterall, it's not his fault we're siblings. It's never the child's fault.

It wasn't easy, and I struggled moving beyond his deception. I just wish he'd have been honest from the beginning. Conall claims it wasn't a deception, but more of a time he wasn't completely forthcoming. Whatever that means.

According to him, he was afraid if I knew the truth from the start, I would have summarily dismissed him and his fraternal claims. His strategy meant we got to know each other and become friends first.

I suppose he's right. I'm certain I'd have told him to sod off and leave me alone had I known his secret or of Jack Fallon's other family. I know for fact had he not wormed his way into my life, there's no way he'd be here today, escorting me down the aisle.

However, it took a great deal of talking and diplomacy, just for Conall and Jack to become friends. Jack flew back to the states, but Conall followed him. Had Conall not been so charming and convincing in persuading Jack's wife, Stephanie, they wouldn't be here today, either. I hold onto the hope Jack will eventually learn to think of Conall as a brother, but for today, this is genuine progress for which I'm grateful. Drawing them both closer, I lift my head, set my gaze towards the wine patio and, as the music changes, we go forth.

We walk past the rows of guests, the small number we wanted with us on this day, but I don't see them or if I do, I'm not fully aware of their presence. I'm looking straight ahead. I see the beautiful canopy of Christmas flowers and white tulle, there's Father Mark holding his bible, and then I catch first sight of Mick.

He's wearing a black suit with a white rose pinned to the lapel as he nervously rocks back and forth. His father, his best man, is standing beside him glowing with pride, and when he spots me, a look of joy further brightens his cheery features.

Mick's tall figure is strong, and his expression is certain, resolute, but changes when he sees me. His adoring eyes dance as he takes my hand from my brothers. We turn to face Father Mark. Mick gives my hand a tender squeeze, then he whispers, "You're beautiful."

Mick Reynolds, the one person who always supports me in times of crisis. His cool demeanor talked me through the shock and realization my father had further disgraced my mother as well as me and Jack. He didn't take sides, not Mick. Mick stoically asked probing questions, directing my thoughts without telling me what to think, and ultimately enabling me to come to my own conclusions about what to do with my new-found sibling.

Mick wasn't trying to gain anything. His sole motivation was my happiness. I think that's what opened my eyes to the man who had been right here all along. Mick Reynolds never asked me to compromise or go against my principles. Mick Reynolds never asked me to change or become something I'm not. With Mick, I never felt the need or inclination to apologize for who I am. Mick Reynolds loves me, Nora Fallon, the way I am and despite all my shortcomings and past failings, he loves me for me. He simply stands back and allows me to be, or as he says, "I stand back and watch you shine."

As Father Mark, my trusted confessor and budding fiddle player speaks, I look beyond him at the wintry scene of the front field. I'm thankful he was able to give us a dispensation to be married here. The old parochial house and secret altar make the land sacred. I'm pleased I had the forethought to have the B&B approved as a wedding venue. It's a lovely and romantic setting. The grass is tipped with a mild frost, but the day has warmed so the blades of grass still holding onto their frost are dwindling. The sky's clear and brilliant blue as I stare at the foothills of the Curlew, looking forward – forward - no longer thinking of the past. I turn to look at Mick beside me. His confidence and devotion tell me he's in this for the long haul, he's not going anywhere. I turn back and repeat the lines Father Mark tells me to say, all the while feeling as if I'm in a dream. A dream that's ending yet still only beginning.

It was my dream to make something of myself and return home a success. I did just that. It was a dream to have a family. I have that, too. No, my mother isn't here, and I still struggle with the legacy of Jack Fallon, but Jack

Jr. is here today with his family and I've got Conall, too, and his date, Rosaleen. Rosaleen, our waitress from The Oarsman, the day we went to see Jeanne and Aoife in hospital - the fateful day he revealed he's my brother. The day Conall Kelly turned my world upside down.

And then there's Mick. Strong, silent, soulful, brilliant Mick Reynolds. I never knew he was my dream, but he informs me I was his. From the moment he heard I was returning home to open the Cara Maith, he knew exactly what he wanted and dreamed of; he just had to be patient.

Sure, I think of Dylan Cooney occasionally and from time to time a guest comes to Cara Maith on his referral, but he was never mine. I'm not proud of my relationship with him, but I've become philosophical about our time together. Had it not been for Dylan Cooney, I may never have found my way home. Home to Boyle, home to open the Cara Maith, and home to find Mick Reynolds - again.

"You may kiss the bride." Father Mark's words interrupt my thoughts. Mick grasps both my hands, pulling me into his chest, he kisses me like I've never been kissed before. It's a kiss, not of ownership, but of complete and unconditional love and commitment. His tender lips pressing against mine warm me, so I kiss him back as earnestly, lovingly, and passionately, sealing our sacred vow, letting him know we're man and wife, soul mates, and friends. He's forever my *Cara Maith.*

Author's Note

I've traveled frequently to Ireland and the town of Boyle. I love this part of County Roscommon because it's where my grandfather was born and raised. I went there often when I was in my 20s to visit his brother (my grand uncle) and friends I made in the area. While there, I'd stay at a nearby bed and breakfast. That bed and breakfast is the inspiration for the setting of The House with The Georgian Door.

Glencarne House was owned by Pat and Agnes Harrington. Each time I visited, the Harringtons treated me as family and Glencarne House became my home in Ireland. Or as I like to say, my favorite place in the world!

I knew one day it had to be the setting for a story. As with my previous book, *The Cottage on Lough Key*, the beauty of this region is impossible to put into words, but I hope I've managed to convey just a little of the magic of this special place on the Emerald Isle. It's in my soul and calls me back again and again.

Pat and Agnes Harrington circa 1989

Anna Marie Jehorek with Agnes Harrington, 2016

Notes and Acknowledgements

I'd like to thank my editor, Linda Clopton for her skilled eye and direction. I'm honored you took on the challenge of editing my second novel.

Next, a big thanks to my team of Beta-readers; Von Childs, Patrick O'Hannigan, Pamela Coleman Becker, Darlene Brady Shearer, Jen Dobridge, and Maura Wiggs. Your thoughtful insights, comments, and edits made this book possible. Thanks a million!

To Pat and Agnes Harrington. The two kindest people who welcomed me to Glencarne House with open arms and made me feel like part of their family. God Bless.

A special thank you to Thomas Mullaney, Boyle historian and friend. Tom took us on a personalized tour of the Boyle area when we were there in 2016. He showed us a stone altar and explained its purpose. I found it so fascinating, I included one in the story.

The cover art is a watercolor rendering of Glencarne House painted by Miranda Brown. I gave Miranda a photograph I took on my 2016 visit to Ireland and she performed magic.

The fonts for chapter headings and titles in the print version are by SM Publications of Dublin, Ireland. The scene breaks font is SL Celtic Style by Sharon Loya.

I extend a special thanks to the town of Boyle, Co. Roscommon. This beautiful place holds a dear spot in my heart and I'm forever grateful for the warmth and hospitality expressed each time I return.

I especially want to thank my family for their support and encouragement. I appreciate you so much! Also, a shout out to Lenny and Colonel Brandon my pugs. You are the cutest most faithful companions and your presence beside me as I type away brings me joy!

Finally, thank you to my handsome J. You're my muse and I love you.

To learn more about Anna Marie Jehorek visit her website:

AnnaMarieJehorek.com

Travel website: PullOverAndLetMeOut.com

Follow her on Twitter @AnnaMarieWrites

Find her on Facebook -Facebook.com/AnnaMarieWrites/

Follow her on Instagram - AnnaMarie_PullOverAndLetMeOut

Linked-in – linkedin.com/in/anna-marie-jehorek-2409449

More by Anna Marie:

The Cottage on Lough Key, 2016

Available on Amazon.com

Suggested Book Club Questions

1. What motivated Nora to act the way she did?
2. How does the book's setting contribute to the story?
3. How does Nora change throughout the book? Does this change your opinion of her?
4. Who is your favorite character and why?
5. What's your favorite or most memorable passage in the book? Why did it make an impression?
6. If you were to make a movie of this book, who would you cast?
7. Share a favorite quote from the book. Why does this quote stand out?
8. Which character in the book do you most identify with and why?
9. What was the turning point in the story? What was your reaction to the crucial moment?
10. What themes or ideas came across in the book?
11. What feelings did this book evoke for you?
12. Did the book end the way you expected?

Made in the USA
Columbia, SC
20 January 2020

86962842R00212